Malibu Secrets

a Malibu Sights novel

MK Meredith

Entangled Publishing, LLC
2614 South Timberline Road
Suite 109
Fort Collins, CO 80525
Visit our website at www.entangledpublishing.com.

Select Contemporary is an imprint of Entangled Publishing, LLC.

Edited by Kate Brauning
Cover design by Heather Howland
Cover art from iStock

Manufactured in the United States of America

First Edition December 2015

To all our mothers…
Those still with us, and those who mother us from the other side. Your love impacts us in such a way that we are forever changed.
To my mother, Karen Kauffman, who was taken too soon by breast cancer: if I'm half the mother you were, my babies will be the luckiest in the world.
To my momma, Kathy Krans, who is a fellow breast cancer survivor: since the day we met, your strength and passion to really live inspire me.
And to women everywhere who've been touched by breast cancer, you are strong, you are brave, and you are beautiful.

Chapter One

When A-list Hollywood actors got married, the weddings alone were enough to make a girl jealous, but the really big deal was the receptions. Addison Dekker swayed to the music, losing herself in the sultry tunes and decadent atmosphere only found with the celebrity elite. Rich Versace silk fabrics draped the space while Baccarat crystal reflected light like stars in the night sky. Maybe this was what Chris Pratt's or Stephen Amell's wedding had looked like. She'd never know. Hollywood wouldn't know her from the gum she'd scraped off her shoe on the way in. Just in case, she gave a quick check to the bottom of her heels.

Who the hell marries the hottest A-list movie actor, anyway? Oh yeah, that would be her sister, Sam. If it were anyone else getting married to one of the biggest actors in Hollywood she'd want to at least try to hate her, but her sister had been through so much over the last couple of years that she deserved this happy ending.

Addi's plan was to follow in her sister's footsteps. Not the celebrity husband, though it would hardly be something to complain about, but rather making her life one she wanted to live instead of the one she was expected to. She was on track toward publishing. Or at least she hoped so. After chasing the "yes" for years now, the yearning was exhausting.

This would be her year—it had to be, or she was sunk.

She was running out of time.

The clinking of silverware seemed to magnify the bleakness of her situation.

A slight hint of cologne warned her of company before she turned around, and she froze on her inhale. Distraction didn't even begin to describe Roque Gallagher. He was like a modern day Rock Hudson, but grittier, bigger, and with a fancier spelling to his name. He was the nephew of Martin and Raquel Gallagher—the Mother and Father of Malibu. The man was so good-looking, he could turn a straight man gay. And if memory served—and boy did it serve well—he used to model *underwear.*

Warm fingers slid against hers in a light grip. "I thought it was about time I met the infamous little Dekker sister." His deep voice skated down her spine, then a chill raced back up.

Forcing back the small shiver at the base of her hairline, she gently tugged her hand until he released her. She looked him over, taking in his broad shoulders under the light gray suit, the top few buttons opened, no tie. No creases or wrinkles, no lines out of place. His black, wavy hair brushed back with trimmed sideburns. A very short, groomed shadow of a mustache and goatee. Barely there, just enough to tease, to make you want to rub your skin against it. Elegant, but casual with an air of approachability.

Yeah, right. There was nothing approachable about the intense look of his too-blue eyes.

She crossed her arms. "No one infamous here." The rumors about her were annoying, almost as much as the squealing laughter let loose from a neighboring conversation.

If she were honest, she'd admit she was most annoyed with herself. Why she cared what other people might think was a mystery. Saying what was on her mind should not equal infamous. Nor should leaving a lucrative career in corporate America to be a writer, but apparently other people had different ideas. And she'd already heard most of them.

Now, maybe the time she'd spent in jail for streaking at the college football game supported the claims, or perhaps when she'd hitchhiked to Nevada for the Burning Man Festival only to get mugged and have to call her dad to come pick her up— but that time in her life had long passed.

"Aww, come on now. I heard you once sang on stage at a wedding you weren't invited to."

She rolled her eyes. "Of course I was invited. On stage, at least."

"Let me take you to dinner and see for myself."

Oh, she could spot his type with a blindfold on. Life came easy to this guy. The Gallagher name assured his every whim was handed to him on a platinum platter. She'd heard all about him. Enough to know he'd be nothing but trouble. By the way he dressed, he was all about being in control and put together—something she'd never quite mastered.

Usually she welcomed trouble that looked like him. But right now, she couldn't afford it. And her last relationship had proved that opposites don't actually attract.

Keeping her voice low, she said, "I appreciate the offer, but this infamous lady is going to have to pass. Thanks, though." Turning back to watch the bride and groom dance with their guests, she grabbed a glass of champagne from the tray of a passing waiter. A little help to hold on to her resolve.

Roque tilted his head with an easy smile. Any woman with a pulse would want to say yes, which made his persistence all the more difficult. She swallowed the sigh threatening to spill from her lips. "Look."

He put up his hand. "I only asked you to dinner. There's this little café I know." The small upturn of his lips was sincere.

Warning bells clanged in her head. Having dinner with him would be a mistake, and she'd made too many of those lately. Right now she needed to stay in and focus, not go out and get frisky. She looked him over, resisting an even bigger sigh. What a shame. "And I said no. But thank you."

He studied her for a beat as they stood amidst the other guests. "I can't say I'm not disappointed. I thought you were the life of the party."

And she was. Usually. But life had handed her some challenges lately, and she needed her wits about her to meet them head-on. The time had come for her to grow up and figure out a way to gather up the pieces of her latest disaster without her entire family—and their friends—finding out.

Needing to knock him off-kilter a bit, ruffle his fine feathers, she smiled, a slow uplift to the corners of her lips. Anyone who knew her would recognize the warning. "Life of the party, huh?" She stepped closer. "Are you coming on to me?"

Shocking people was so much fun. She reached out her hand and placed her fingertips at his Adam's apple, the heat of his skin burning into her sensitive pads, and then slid them down his chest and over the front of his shirt to his sternum.

She tapped twice, then boldly held his gaze as she trailed her finger lower over the solid plane of his abs. *Yum.* Surely he'd stop her any minute. Tilting her head, she bit her lip and looked up at him from beneath her lashes. He did say she was infamous. Her heart slammed in her chest. Any moment he'd stop her, shocked and affronted.

And she'd win. And he'd walk away so she could breathe again.

Without warning, he shot his hand around her waist and yanked her tight against him, the movement so abrupt her hair fell from its pins. The hard lines of his body pressed against her, and something warm and delicious spread through her limbs.

"Make no mistake, Miss Dekker. When I come on to you, you won't have to ask." He held her gaze, and the delicious scent of him wafted about, clouding her senses.

Well, that had blown up in her face. Blinking rapidly, she stepped back from his embrace, obviously having lost that little battle. She had to nip this in the bud, as much as she'd like to stay and get lost in such a distraction.

"Okay, now it's not no, but hell no." She hated being mean, hated how it felt, but hated more when people wouldn't listen when she talked. And the pull to stay, along with her already-pressing stress, left her with very little patience. Handing a passing waiter her empty glass, she spun on her heel and went in search of her friend Chase.

Chase listened to and believed in her, even if Addi could make chaos out of a straight line. She didn't cause disorder on purpose, but it sure had an easy time finding her. Sliding in next to Chase among a group of ladies, she snuck a peek back at Roque. As expected, he'd moved on without a hitch, laughing with Martin Gallagher Jr. as if he hadn't just faced rejection—and he probably couldn't recognize it when he did.

Grabbing a canapé from a passing waiter, she popped the savory morsel into her mouth and chewed while she watched Roque out of the corner of her eyes. His voice carried over the low murmur of the surrounding crowd.

He had a good laugh. She swallowed, and her own lips twitched up a bit at the deep sound. It moved through his whole body and into hers. She wondered what it would have been like to go to dinner with him. But with the mess her life was in, she couldn't afford it. Hell, she couldn't afford anything at this moment.

The canapé turned over in her stomach.

Not even her home.

Addi dropped her forehead to the table, unable to breathe as tears burned the back of her lids. "Oh my God. They're going to kill me. Damn. Damn. Damn."

After a long night tossing and turning, resisting dreams filled with blue eyes and easy smiles, she didn't know if she had it in her to face the letter on the table. Such bad news seemed so much worse the morning after a fairy-tale wedding. And it so clearly wasn't her fairy tale. She was the baby sister, the pampered, protected sister, the funny sidekick sister—not the one who got Prince Charming.

Her stomach churned. *What in the hell am I going to do? This can't happen.* With trembling hands, she shoved back from the table and stared at the document lying in front of her as if it were ready to strike, more threatening than a rattlesnake. Her independence, her life, was ruined with this one sheet of paper.

The doorbell shrieked and Addi jumped. "Fuck." The scare pushed her already frayed nerves over the edge, and she dropped her head to her hands, choking back angry tears. She'd been meaning to fix the damn doorbell since she'd moved into her late Aunt Addi's Malibu bungalow. Half deaf, her aunt had installed a doorbell as loud as a fire alarm. Now every time someone rang the bell, Addi lost a life and part of her hearing. She'd be joining her aunt on the other side soon if this kept up.

Trying to wipe away any sign of her tears, she finally made her way to the door, then wrenched it open. An audible gasp escaped her trembling lips, and she stepped back at the sight of her guest. "You."

Roque Gallagher's eyes flickered wide for a beat, but

his expression never wavered. He yanked a sheet of paper from his portfolio, then looked from it to the address numbers nailed above her door.

She shook her head and willed her heart to quit slamming in her chest. It only raced from the shock of seeing him on her doorstep, she was sure of it.

"No is no, buddy. I'm calling the police." Why did all the heart-stoppingly good-looking men always turn out to be so full of themselves? Addi stepped back to slam the door in his drop-dead gorgeous face. Such a shame, really.

Roque put his hand out. "I'm sorry. I had no idea this was your home." He lifted the sheet of paper for her to see, and she stepped out onto the porch for a closer look. "Public records list Addison Montgomery."

"Well, public records are wrong. The house is mine."

Looking her over from head to toe, he paused. "Are you okay?"

The concern on his face almost did her in. She sniffed, forcing back the tears that wanted to erupt. "I'm fine."

"Are you sure? I can call someone if you want."

A warm hand dropped to her shoulder, and she shied away before she cracked. "I said I'm fine." She didn't mean to snap, but if she had any hope of getting out of this situation with a shred of dignity, he needed to leave immediately. "Listen, Mr. I'm-Irresistible—" She tried for sarcasm, but it fell short with tears thickening her throat.

"Oh, so you do think I'm irresistible? I didn't get that impression last night." His tone was gentle, like he was trying to make her smile. He cracked the knuckles of his free hand with his thumb, one finger at a time, filling the silence.

"I have a lot going on. Sorry for being so rude. But now really isn't a good time." She pulled her eyes from his hands to his face.

He narrowed his baby blues, and her heart tripped. "I'll

get out of your hair, but I have a proposition for the owner of this house."

She didn't know what kind of proposition he could possibly have, but she knew Roque was in film production. It was in the family, in the blood. She could practically smell the drive radiating from his perfect, poreless skin as he stood, watching her warily. She didn't need his concern, she needed a miracle.

"A proposition?"

"I want to rent your place for my film."

Surprise fanned her interest, but reality snuffed it out. She had an idea of the going rental rate for films. It would help, but it wouldn't be enough to solve her problem. Besides, moving out would cost her, eating up any money she'd make from the rent. Because of the loan modification denial she'd just gotten, she only had thirty days to pay the lump sum she owed. And that was just the beginning of her problem. "I'm not interested, but thank you." She stepped back inside to close the door.

"I don't think you understand."

Addi swung around. "You know, the name Roque suits you—your head must be as hard as one. It's time for you to go." She couldn't take any more. Breaking down in front of practically a stranger wouldn't do anything but validate everyone's perception of her already.

"I don't think so. Like I said, I have a proposition. Give me two minutes, then I'll go."

Putting her hands on her hips, she pulled in a breath. She could hold it together for two more minutes. Listening to him was probably the quickest way to get rid of him. "Two minutes."

She led him inside, across the wide open room and into the kitchen. All of the natural light and the open concept of the main floor made her cozy home seem much bigger. "I need coffee."

Smiling, he made his way over to the table and sat down, tapping his finger against the plate of chocolate éclairs and tall glass of milk. "Ahhh, a good balanced breakfast."

Addi made a face, snatched her mail off the table, and moved the evidence of her meal to the counter, then turned, arms once again crossed over her chest like a warrior's shield. "I'm sorry. I'm not interested in renting my house."

"But I think you are."

She sighed. "Of all the arrogant—"

"Let's cut to the chase. Your house is perfect for our film and within budget. We want it for twelve weeks. We'll pay you monthly rent *per diem* and put you up in a local hotel of your choice to save you any unnecessary inconvenience."

Interest flared. They were offering more than rent? But it wouldn't be enough to save her, and the last thing she wanted was to be saved by Hollywood. She lifted her chin. "Like I said—"

"You need this, Miss Dekker," he stated gently.

Her jaw dropped open and worked silently for a second. "Why…what in the world would make you think that?"

"It's simple. Foreclosure."

She'd never moved so fast in her life. He wasn't staying one more second in her house. Pure panic fueled her attempts to yank him up by the arm, and thankfully, something human in him let her do it. She all but shoved him out the front door, closing it in his face just in time.

If he knew, did her parents know?

She couldn't let them find out. They already thought she was immature and rash. Losing the home left to her by Aunt Addi would only prove them right.

The dam broke. All the fears, the heartache, and the failure she'd been reining in over the last few weeks poured out in a waterfall of disappointment.

Through her snot and tears she managed to call Chase.

Like always, Chase said she'd be there in five. Making her way back to her kitchen, Addi paced the length of the room, swearing and sniffing with every step. Grabbing an éclair from the counter, she shoved the end into her mouth and took a bite twice as big as she could handle. A bit of custard dropped onto her sweatshirt.

"Really?" she mumbled with a slump of her shoulders. Closing her eyes, she drew in a calming breath through her nose. Scooping up the creamy filling from her shirt, she held it on the end of her finger while she struggled to chew and flopped down into the chair Roque had occupied minutes before.

Finally able to swallow, she licked the custard and took another bite. This time with a little more care.

She didn't like feeling this way. Angry. Stressed. She was the vivacious one, the life of the party. Always a big proponent of the "save the drama for your mama" mantra. But apparently, not today.

The doorbell screeched, sending Addi into an accompanying slew of swear words. Grabbing a napkin, she worked at the sticky chocolate on her fingers as she made her way to the door.

Chase Huntington breezed in, bringing the Caribbean with her. Addi'd swear her friend had stuffed her bra with mangoes and cocoa butter, she smelled so good. Chase stopped with cartoonlike precision upon spotting Addi, and her eyes all but popped out of her head. "What *happened* to you?"

Addi glanced down at herself. Her charcoal off-the-shoulder sweatshirt along with her calf-length yoga pants, smeared with custard and chocolate, spoke of her turmoil.

She gave Chase a once-over. Her ebony pixie shined like cut glass, reminding Addi of Halle Berry's famous style. She was impeccably dressed, as always, in a burnt orange thigh-skimming sheath dress. Addi hated her, but only for a second, and only in the way a best friend could hate one of her favorite people in the world.

She and Chase had been close ever since they joined forces to unseat their bully of a cheerleading captain in high school. The merger had proven beneficial. Better, in fact—they were soul sisters.

"Damn Hollywood, that's what."

Chase followed Addi back to the kitchen, humor in her low, raspy voice. "No, seriously. Love, you look like a toddler given a beater with chocolate icing."

Addi rolled her eyes and washed at the sink. Drying her hands with a towel, she turned and leaned back against the counter. "I need to call a vault." When they agreed to a vault, no matter what each thought, they'd never breathe a word of it to anyone.

Chase's brows shot up. "Really? This is serious." She lowered to a chair at the table and crossed her legs.

Addi sniffed and wiped her nose. "Love the shoes."

Chase stretched her legs out in front of her, turning a strappy gold-sandaled foot side to side. "Aren't they amazing? On sale, too."

Chase didn't need to worry about sales as the oldest heir to The Huntington Place legacy, a string of high-end hotels that spanned the globe. But her father had taught her to be frugal. Chase was a perfectionist and worked hard at everything she took on—always the consummate businesswoman.

Addi, on the other hand, *needed* a good sale. She wrinkled her nose. On second thought, she needed to stay away from spending any money, period.

Sliding her plate of éclairs across the table, she offered one to Chase. She lowered into the chair on the opposite side of the table, smiled at her friend's upturned nose, and grabbed another gooey delight.

"Don't judge. I've had a rough morning."

Chase frowned. "You didn't drink much at the wedding last night."

Addi shook her head. "I don't have a hangover. Remember…vaulted."

Chase made the motion of turning a lock at her lips. "Vaulted."

Addi took another bite of her éclair, on the way to making herself good and sick at this rate. Maybe she *was* just like a toddler. Exactly what she worked so hard at proving to her family she wasn't, and why she *had* to fix this mess she found herself in.

The muscles in the back of her neck tightened like a vise under the import of her dire situation. "The bungalow's in threat of foreclosure."

Chase's eyes shot wide. "What? Addi."

Addi dropped her head into her hands. "I know, I know," she groaned.

"Oh honey, how did this happen? I thought the bungalow was yours outright."

"It was, but I couldn't pay the taxes. In order to take care of that, I mortgaged the house. But then I got behind on paying that, too, and they denied a loan modification. So now, foreclosure. I have thirty days to pay the lump sum. But that's just the beginning."

"What about the money from your ghostwriting?"

"Gone."

Chase sat forward in her chair, worry creasing her brow. "How?"

Addi threw her hands up. "Malibu. It's expensive. The money from writing the book and the loan didn't last as long as I thought. Property tax is a bitch, and the other writing contracts I thought were as good as mine fell through. I was so sure of myself when I quit my job three years ago. But this industry is brutal and moves at a glacier's pace."

Shoving the empty plate away, Addi bit her lip. "But I can't go back. I've got to make this work, Chase. I have to. It's hard to explain, but I've never felt more myself than when I'm writing." She shook her head. "I have to figure this out, and I can't under any circumstances tell my family. I already owe them money, and if they hear about this they'll force me to move back in with them. They already think I can't handle being a homeowner."

Chase opened her mouth, then closed it. She grabbed Addi's hand across the table and held it. "You might have to."

"No. No way. They'd never let me live it down. I know they love me, but not one of them thought I'd made a good decision when I left corporate America. My mom told me it would only be a matter of time before I'd be moving back in."

"Love, I really think you don't give them enough credit."

"No, they don't give *me* enough. My parents, Luca and Sam, they've all coddled me since the day I was born. They never think I can handle anything on my own. When my ex said I was too immature and left, their *help* all but suffocated me. My mom made appointments for me with a life coach, for Christ's sake. Can you imagine?"

Chase reached across the table and patted her hand.

Addi continued. "'To help you figure things out, dear,' she would say. But I knew it was because she thought there was some validity to his reason for leaving me. He was a selfish, cheating asshole, but I was the immature one. I can't go through that again. If I go running to them now, it will only prove everything they've been saying all along. I need to be the one to fix this." She closed her eyes.

Standing, Addi stretched and sighed once her neck cracked, releasing some of the tension in her muscles. She walked over to the French doors that led to her backyard and opened them wide. Past noon, the sun warmed the ocean breeze and strengthened the botanical scents floating in from the garden. She breathed it in — an immediate salve.

Her bungalow didn't grace the sandy coast, but instead perched high on a hill, giving her the most glorious view of the ocean sunsets. She'd never have been able to afford her home if it hadn't been left to her by her namesake. Hell, she couldn't afford it now. But she'd truly believed she could handle the property tax and her expenses if she budgeted her funds carefully and landed a publishing contract. Finally.

But it had been three years without a sustainable paycheck. "I just need more time." Turning back to Chase, she put her hands out, palms up. "I know I can make it as a novelist once I break in. It's the initial foot in the door that's the hard part."

Chase got up from the table and busied herself making a fresh pot of coffee. "Well, love, you need to come up with a plan, then." Stopping, she turned, pressing a box of coffee filters to her chest.

"Yes, I do." Addi nodded. Noting the concern in Chase's eyes, she gave her a hug, crushing the filters between them. "Don't worry. I'll figure this out. I need to prove to everyone, myself included, that I'm okay on my own."

Chase sighed. "What about your old job?"

Addi drew her brows together. Chase never was one to overlook any option. "It took up so much of my life, I never got to write. So much overtime. Even if I wanted to, that position was filled a long time ago. But clearly, I need to do something."

"Then what are you going to do?"

Addi plopped back into a chair at the table, biting her lip. "The film company Roque is working with wants to rent the bungalow."

"Addi, that's great."

"But it's not enough, and it's Hollywood."

Chase sighed. "You're hiding behind all that 'Hollywood' stuff, love. Sam doesn't seem to be suffering now. She just married Gage Cutler. How much more Hollywood can you get than that? There isn't a woman in the world who isn't green with envy."

Rolling her eyes, Addi slouched in her chair. "Don't I know it, I'm one of them. Have you seen the man?"

Chase laughed. "In person and in my dreams." She grabbed clean coffee cups from the cupboard with a sideways glance. "I also saw too-hot-to-be-legal Roque Gallagher."

Addi's brows shot up. "Exactly. The last thing I need is a distraction of that proportion. I have to figure out my shit first."

"You're famous for inviting trouble where it's not wanted. This doesn't have to be hard. Take the opportunity that presents itself."

"Even with the rent, I don't think it would be enough. With the *per diem* maybe, but—"

She tapped her chin, thinking. "I'm going to do this on my own, or it won't mean anything."

A vision of Roque saying "foreclosure" popped into Addi's mind. She blinked back her tears.

"Okay. So what do you need?" Chase asked.

If only the rent, including the *per diem* and the hotel, totaled the sum she owed on the house, then she might just be able to swing it. Addi accepted the offered cup of coffee and stared into the dark-roasted brew.

An idea took shape in her mind so preposterous her first reaction was a resounding *no*.

I couldn't. Could I?

She sat forward and looked at Chase. As she took a sip from her mug, the idea took shape.

Pushing away from the table, she wandered back to the French doors and stared at nothing. At everything. She loved Malibu. Her home had a view of the ocean miles long, a little slice of paradise. Quaint, with shabby-chic old-world charm and tropical accents. Warm and cozy and perfect. Nothing quite as modern and upscale as Sam's condo. But it suited Addi's taste of having one foot in the past while holding a coconut.

Whatever it took to make her dream happen, she'd do it. She had no qualms about using Hollywood like they used everyone else. Living in Malibu gave her a bird's-eye view of all the back-stabbing and lying that went on. She'd seen more friends spiral out of control, more of them lose in Hollywood than win. Her sister successfully finding her way was no small miracle.

"I owe eighteen thousand for two years of taxes I mortgaged and a little extra padding I added since I was refinancing, and I need maybe another two grand for living expenses right now. Which will allow me to keep my home. Aunt Addi's home." Pressure built behind her eyes.

She bit her lip as an uncomfortable sensation wiggled its way between her shoulder blades, chasing the tail of her plan. Technically her idea was a bit on the deceitful side, but losing her aunt's home would be worse. Besides, she was stealing from Hollywood, not Roque. Tinseltown was known for being wasteful. They wouldn't miss it. And Roque would technically still get what he paid for, and so would she.

"But the property taxes will be due again soon, and when filming is over you're still going to need a way to support your-self. I hate to say it, but as much as you don't want to go back to corporate America, you need a job." Chase reminded her.

She didn't want to do anything but write, but this was reality, not the movies. The next best thing would be something fairly flexible, and she needed an excuse to still be around her home during filming in order to carry out her plan.

Tapping her chin, she stared at Chase as she mulled over all the facts.

Chase winced. "Oh, I don't like the look on your face, love. It's never brought anything but trouble."

Addi's mouth spread into a slow smile. "You said I need a job. And I'm saying I need Mr. Gallagher's number."

Chapter Two

Roque questioned his sanity like a man on the brink of matrimony as he hung up and set his phone carefully on his desk. Pulling in a breath, he slid his hands into the front pockets of his slacks and looked out his office window. He needed to figure out what the hell was going on, and yesterday. One hint that someone on his team was falling short and his backers would run. He couldn't afford silly mistakes. They cost money. And the bulk of his savings was sunk into this project.

He literally couldn't afford to fail. Especially now. After all the work he'd done to finally get to this point. After everything he missed out on by being away—his one last connection to his mother. To top it off, an investor hadn't returned his calls, and he'd been waiting on a check for the past few weeks.

With a sigh, he dropped his head back. He'd been accused of being a workaholic more than once, but he saw it more as having standards and refusing to stop until things were done right. Standards that would make him successful— without counting on the weight of the Gallagher name built by his father and uncle, two of the top directors in

Hollywood. Unfortunately, those same standards often came with a consequence. He was determined his success wouldn't happen because he was a Gallagher, but because he was a damned talented producer.

"What's going on?" his locations manager, Jimmy Callahan, asked as he placed a folder on the desk.

Roque snapped his head up. "Nothing's available. At least nothing that meets the requirements for the film. How is that possible?" He forced his jaw to relax, easing the burning ache climbing up the sides of his head.

"The place on Coral Canyon?" Jimmy's brow furrowed in question.

"Nope."

Jimmy shook his head. "But I'd already scoped it out. If we needed it, everything was good to go."

"That's what I can't understand. Every place that remotely meets the needs of the film is now unavailable."

"And the Dekker woman's bungalow?"

The mere hint of Addi, and the rhythmic clenching of his jaw took off all on its own. He didn't know how, but he was going to persuade her to rent him her place. He had to. Besides, she needed his help.

He thought back to the feisty, sassy woman at the wedding. Once his initial shock of her bold move settled, he'd joined in on the fun. He didn't like playing games, but if he was pushed into it, he played to win. He shouldn't have been surprised. Asking around had revealed a bit about the spoiled, youngest Dekker sibling. Loud and shocking were two adjectives reported to him time and again.

Never before interested in Disney, he'd found she had a striking resemblance to Tinker Bell, if Tink were a tall, lithe smart-mouth with curves. Asking her out had been a search for some fun, the thought of an entertaining, light-hearted distraction before diving into his next project. But when she unaccountably said no, he'd been rather intrigued. It would have been safer had he felt rejected. Rejection was easy to walk away from, but intrigue, on the other hand, continued to gnaw and demand until its hunger was satiated—and damn it, he'd been hungry.

But then the Addi he'd met at her bungalow had been doing everything she could to hide her fear and sadness behind a facade of attitude. He'd wanted to help her. The need was immediate upon seeing the tears in her eyes, and he'd genuinely thought she'd jump at the chance to rent to him, especially considering her predicament. She'd only have a limited time to save her home. The information on her public records had been his Hail Mary—for him and her, really. But she'd thrown him out.

He rounded his desk and, tugging his pant leg up a bit, sat on the edge. "I just need a little more time to get her to agree."

The laugh from his longtime friend grated on his nerves.

"You mean your usual Roque Gallagher charm didn't work? That's a first for you, isn't it?"

He lifted his hand and slowly raised his middle finger.

"You need a woman. The stress of this whole thing is making you grumpy."

"Fuck." He hadn't seriously dated in two years. Not since his mother's death. His workaholic ways had ruined too many relationships, and he'd vowed he was done letting it hurt other people. "The last thing I need is a relationship."

Jimmy smirked. "Who said anything about a relationship? I'm talking about getting laid." He tapped the folder that rested next to Roque's leg. "The papers you requested. I'll make some calls. See what's going on."

Roque watched him leave. He needed Addi's bungalow. It was perfect for the intimate tone of the film and met his tight budget needs, and at this point it was his only chance.

His phone rang, and he swiped at the face of it, then

stared at the caller ID.

Addison Dekker. Now wasn't that interesting?

"Ms. Dekker. How can I help you?"

"Actually, I think I'm the one helping you."

He pushed up from the desk, then made his way back around to his chair. Picking up the folder Jimmy left, he flipped it around and opened the cover, pausing a moment to admire his location manager's talent behind the camera. The photo of her bungalow was inspired. "By signing the papers?"

Her movements came through muffled from the other end. He imagined her pacing her kitchen. It was a small space, but with it opening right into the front of the house, they'd get the shots they needed. The effect would be perfect for the intimacy he aimed for. With the view through the window over the sink, nothing but blue ocean waters, it was a bungalow paradise. "Your place is great. Give me your terms."

She paused, then said, "It is, isn't it?" He could hear the smile in her voice. Why was she stalling? "My aunt lived here and made it a home. I've added a bit here and there, but we shared similar taste, so I didn't need to do much."

"She passed? I'm sorry." And he meant it. The pain from losing someone was inexplicable. He knew only too well. And worse was not having the time for a proper goodbye.

"She lived into her nineties. My grandma's sister on my mom's side." Addi sighed, the wistful note carrying over the line. "She was something. And the reason, as you know," she said with a soft voice, "I can't lose my home."

Roque preferred her sass to the sad tone in her voice; the latter just didn't fit.

He studied the contract in front of him. "I assume you received the digital copy?"

"A bit sure of yourself, sending it when I'd already told you I wasn't interested."

"I hoped seeing the opportunity in writing would help

change your mind."

"You know I'm in foreclosure. Something I'd like to keep private, by the way."

Her business was her business unless it affected his. But he respected her desire for privacy beyond that. "Of course. Everything is outlined clearly; you can have your lawyer look it over." He waited, not moving a muscle. At this point, his whole film depended on renting her place.

"I've sent it to my brother, Luca."

"Luca, of course." Sharing a last name was the only clue that Luca and Addi were related. Roque had worked with Luca a few times, and of course they'd all met at Sam and Gage's wedding. Luca was a studio attorney, sharp, intense, and Roque couldn't remember ever seeing the man crack a smile. He thought of Addi's bright eyes and the dimples that teased each cheek; she was nothing but smiles.

Unless she was on the verge of tears. Which he'd learned he couldn't stand.

Or annoyed with him. Which he could stand. He tightened his grip on the phone.

Silence followed.

"Ms. Dekker?" Unease settled in his gut. *What was she up to?*

"I have two conditions."

Of course she did. "What?" The tension in his neck fired back up.

"First, I want a job on the set. I've already emailed over my résumé."

"No." That felt good. He'd been wanting to reciprocate since the night of the wedding. A flat, resounding *no*. He hadn't thought it bothered him, but come on, *no* didn't sit well with anybody.

"Then no deal, Mr. Man."

"You can't be serious."

"As a heart attack."

Roque grimaced.

Addi laughed. "I'm guessing your silence is from the terrible cliché and not the job request. You producer types are so predictable. Hmmm...let me think."

He imagined her tapping the end of her little square chin with a manicured finger.

Having her on set, under foot, day and night, would be chaos. This project was his one chance to break out on his own merit. Fuck. He didn't have time to train, or to worry, about someone else. Opening the file she sent, he scanned over her experience. He was impressed, and that didn't happen often. She had extensive knowledge in PR and had worked as a liaison before. His eyes fell on the word organized, and he had to stifle a laugh. Now that he had to see.

Her voice teased across the line. "How about 'serious as a Roger Ebert review.' Better?"

Roque rubbed the back of his neck. She was a pain in the ass. "Why?"

"It's my house. I need the extra money."

"The condition of your house is covered."

Addi *tsked*. "Not good enough. Take it or leave it, *Mr. Gallagher.*"

Mr. Gallagher his ass. Her tone held less respect than if she'd called him Rocky—God forbid. He shuddered. He'd have to do everything in his power to keep her from hearing that nickname. She'd never let him live it down—of that he was sure.

Roque blew out a breath, extending the exhale, biding his time. If her résumé was any indication, she was brilliant, and he could use brilliant.

"Look, you want the house, I need the money. I'm a good worker."

He could count the reasons to say no on both of his

hands and hers, but he was a sucker for a good worker and for someone in need. The emotion in her voice now was earnest and a bit scared. But his budget was tight. Maybe if he modified his security expense and only had the director on set when the cast was being filmed. If he shifted a few things around, he should be able to make room for her.

He sighed.

She giggled softly. "You know you want me."

His brow shot up.

"To work for you, I mean," she blurted out.

He laughed. "Of course." Why did he get the feeling she'd somehow won?

He ignored her gibe and closed the file on his desk. No doubt he was going to regret this. "Deal. What's your second condition?" He hated asking questions he didn't want the answer to.

"You need to put me up at Huntington Place."

"Are you kidding me?" He gripped his hand into a tight fist. To put her up in the five-star hotel would cost close to twenty grand, twice as much as he'd originally planned for, and leaving him to tighten the belt on his already too-tight budget.

Her voice interrupted his panic. "Look, I need a safe place to stay. A home away from home. You can't expect me to hole up in some dive for three months. I know the Huntington. I'm comfortable there. How badly do you want my place?"

He wanted to tell her to go to hell. But the next affordable site wasn't available for months and the options available now were more than the increased hotel fee. Fuck.

He couldn't really blame her, though he wanted to. Sacrificing for his project himself was one thing; asking someone else to was unrealistic.

"Deal."

So much for keeping his distance.

"I'll be there in thirty minutes with the new contract," he said.

Exactly thirty minutes later, Roque slid out of his SUV, running through his mental list of checks and balances. Jimmy and a few of his team members followed suit, deep in a conversation about who made the better Bond. Their voices carried on like white noise against his thoughts.

They needed to take measurements, get a good scope of the space, check power resources, storage, and check out the security system, if Addi even had one in the first place. He was the producer, but with his savings footing part of the bill, he'd save what he could, where he could.

Glancing up at the bungalow, he shifted the strap of his bag higher onto his shoulder and pulled in a deep breath. He'd question the real reason his heart pounded in his chest later, but for now he'd chalk it up to stress. He just needed to do what any normal man would do.

Remove the stress.

So, first things first. Get Addi to sign the contract, then figure out how to keep her busy and out of his way.

The bungalow door swung open and a willowy Betty Boop greeted him with a steady smile and a serious stare. "Morning, love."

The grin stretched across his face without any help from him. He cocked his head and looked at the woman out of the corner of his eye, not sure who she was or what she was doing there. "Good afternoon?"

She laughed and stepped back to let him in. "It's almost noon, isn't it? I'm Chase Huntington, Addi's best friend."

Oh, that's why she was here. Women always called in reinforcements, whether to visit the ladies room or, apparently, sign contracts. He shook her outstretched hand. "Roque Gallagher."

"Oh, I know who you are."

He could only imagine the glowing report she'd received from Addi.

Speaking of Addi, she bounded in from the kitchen with the energy he'd witnessed at the wedding and a smile that filled the room, one of the reasons he'd spoken to her in the first place—her energy was infectious. It spread through a room like a physical entity, and he couldn't help but absorb it. A big change from when he'd seen her earlier that morning. He swore the smile was genuine, which either meant she was much happier about their deal than she let on, or it was something else. She hadn't yet said what had changed her mind.

He smiled at the two women.

"Oh, don't do that," Addi said.

He raised a brow. "Do what, exactly?"

"Smile like that. Chase won't be able to handle it, and we have things to do."

Chase laughed. "Very true." She turned to Roque. "Can I get you some coffee?"

"Yes, thank you."

Indicating his team following behind him, he said, "These guys are going to take some measurements. Okay with them poking about the place?"

Addi looked each over, then gave a curt nod. She turned to follow Chase and gave him a wink over her shoulder. "Come on into the kitchen; we'll go over the contract at the table."

He followed the girls. Who wouldn't? They presented a great view with two upside-down hearts swaying in unison and leading the way.

Running his gaze up the length of Addi, he took in her confident stride. Head up, back straight. She wore dress shorts and a button-up blouse, untucked. At the base of her neck, barely visible with her hair down, was a quarter-sized sunburst birthmark. He didn't know why, but he wanted a closer look.

A warning went off like a fucking siren in his head. No closer looks. He didn't have room for a distraction like that. Besides, he was great at producing films but sucked at maintaining any kind of relationship. He'd let those he cared about down too many times to count. From rescheduling date nights out to forgetting special events, staying on top of the important things took too much bandwidth. One night, he'd had to work late and his ex had made a special meal for some month anniversary. Coming home to an empty flat and a cold dinner on the table had left him alone in a way he hadn't felt before.

Loneliness didn't grab on quite so tight when he chose it before it chose him.

He shoved his thoughts as deep down as possible and took a seat at the table, then slid the contract to her.

She flipped through the pages then eyed him with a narrowed look.

"No games. It's all there," he said, shoving away the pinch of offense.

"Of course it is."

"Good. Then let's get this over with."

"Impatient, Mr. Gallagher?" she asked.

Steepling his fingers in front of his face, he focused on how perfect her place was for his film instead of her apparent joy at pushing his buttons.

With a flourish, she dotted the *I* in Addison and slid the contract back across the table. "There you go, partner."

Partner? Not in a million years. That might be the first storm he couldn't manage. "Don't you mean boss?"

That caught her for a second, and he enjoyed the quick flash of worry in her eyes.

She stuck out her tongue at him. Playful, feisty; he better get used to it now.

Glancing over the document one last time, he studied their signatures on the last page. Her name was big and bold with loops and swoops compared to the tight straight lines of his own.

He shoved away the worry digging between his brows. Everything would be fine. He simply needed to find a way to keep her reined in and out of the way for the next twelve weeks. He'd gotten what he wanted. Kind of. Now all he needed to do was keep her from being a massive distraction. He was good at managing people, and from her résumé, so was she.

Studying her from across the table, he shifted in his seat and strengthened his resolve. Managing Addi shouldn't be too hard. He had everything under control. Including his project and his libido.

He hadn't gotten this far to lose focus now. Especially over a feisty woman who he'd bet his left nut didn't like being told what to do.

Well, she was just going to have to get used to it.

He reached his hand across the table and gripped hers in a firm shake. "Welcome aboard, Ms. Dekker."

Chapter Three

"Your assistant?" Addi tried to hide the panic in her voice, but failed as she paced her kitchen. She should be grateful, after all. He didn't have to agree to give her a position in the first place, whether he realized it or not, and *technically* she wasn't being completely honest. She did her best to tuck that guilt away.

But his assistant? How in the hell was she going to handle being so close to him every flipping day? She was the farthest thing from a saint. And the last thing she needed was an entanglement with a too-hot-for-her-own-good, know-it-all man. Been there, done that, not interested in any reruns. Especially not now.

"You get a one week trial. Hiring you is one thing, but it has to work. Is there a problem?" He leaned back in his chair with a smile.

Oh, he was enjoying this.

She shifted from one foot to the other, resisting the urge to change her mind and forget the whole plan. "No, not a problem exactly, but a week trial? I can handle this job. That isn't a problem, but—"

"But what? You wanted a job. I get to pick said job. The last thing I need is an inexperienced employee running amok on set."

She snorted. "Did you just say amok? What am I, two?"

His raised eyebrow was answer enough, cutting like a knife. She was competent and capable and did damn good work, no matter what she took on. With her head held high, she looked down her nose at him, glad he was sitting. "I have plenty of experience, but not in film. Surely you need someone with a different set of skills as an assistant producer."

He stood and pushed in his chair. "Oh, I do. But I don't have the budget. I'll need you to figure it out quickly, or I'll find someone else." He held her gaze. "You'll actually be my *personal* assistant. You know, helping me with whatever needs that may arise."

Addi swallowed hard. Even if she wasn't already freaked out about having to learn the industry—and fast—the words "needs" and "arise" raised all sorts of scandalous images in her head. Pulling herself together, she stepped closer to him and tapped her finger on the zipper of his black pullover sweater, letting it linger. "Needs, huh?"

Roque laughed, shaking his head with a quick glance at the ceiling. The deep baritone reverberated inside her chest for an unbalanced moment.

He gently placed her hand back at her side. "Yes, *needs*, like…coffee." He ticked items off on his fingers, way too satisfied with his decision and in a too-casual manner for her taste. "Dry cleaning, emails, my schedule, odds and ends for the crew. You know, personal assistant stuff."

"Your dry cleaning?" She almost choked. The idea of handling his clothing was far too intimate to imagine without heating herself up, even if it was a simple drop-off and pickup. "I am not getting you coffee."

"Oh, but you will."

And she would. She'd make sure every single task he handed her was handled with more efficiency and competency than he'd ever seen. Then he could swallow his seemingly low opinion of her abilities or choke on it.

Addi had to hand it to him. She'd thrown down the gauntlet, and he'd picked it up. Roque Gallagher was no idiot. She'd have to be careful playing games with him. Funny thing was, she'd never been much of a game player, especially with men. Deep down she was a hardcore romantic. One reason she loved to write. A book was one of the safest places to put all her fantasies on paper without anyone suspecting too much. She blew out a breath, and her bangs tickled her brow. God, she was going to miss her hours of writing every day. She could already feel time slipping away from her.

She stopped pacing and faced him, hands on hips. "You're enjoying this way too much."

He looked her over from head to toe, and something sparked in his eyes, making her a tad uneasy. "Oh, I plan on it." Turning away, he dug through his portfolio, then handed her a check.

Her heart stopped for a beat. She took the paper from him, folded it, and slid it in the top band of her sweatpants. "Well, first things first."

He threw her a questioning look.

Grabbing his cup from the table, she lifted it in salute. "Fresh coffee."

Roque pressed his lips together in a slight smile, then turned toward the back door. "I'm going to explore a bit."

She watched him slip through, fascinated by how strongly his presence remained even after the soft *click* of the closing latch. He was determined and driven, but by what? Success, sure, but there seemed to be something more.

A commotion from the front room caught her attention.

"What's going on? Anything I can help with?"

A young man and woman, part of Roque's small crew, froze, and she almost laughed at the expressions of guilt on their faces — as if they'd been caught stealing her sofa instead of moving it in order to take measurements.

"Here, let me get you the specs of the house. It has all the measurements, load bearing walls, electrical, the works. My aunt saved it from the original design plans. That will save you the trouble and time of measuring." She glanced over at the guy fiddling with her alarm system. "I'll give you the codes and my password. I already informed the company about the rental. So you should have the system up and running to your satisfaction this morning."

He dropped his hands back to his sides with a nod. "Thanks."

She looked them over as the other two lowered her sofa. "I'm Addison Dekker; you can call me Addi."

The security system guy brushed his hand on his jeans then reached forward to shake. "Marty, and this is Billy and SueAnn." He indicated with an outstretched hand. "We'll have one more with us most days, Jimmy Callahan, our locations manager."

She grinned, liking them already. Whether it was the guilt on their faces or the fresh scent of ambition, she understood both. "If you have any questions, let me know. I'd love to help out in any way. But I do have one question: what's the most important thing, in your opinion, for me to take care of?"

They all answered in unison. "Food."

She laughed. "Okay. I can handle that."

SueAnn piped up. "We forget to eat otherwise, and it's a sticky situation with the union if we're not fed on time."

Addi nodded as panic laced through her spine. "I had no idea. Okay then. Thank you." There were union requirements? Shit. She pulled out her phone and brought up the web. If she wanted to keep this job, she needed to find out what those rules were — and fast.

A few minutes later, she found Roque contemplating the meaning of life in her backyard. She'd give back the check he'd handed her to know what he was thinking. Well, maybe not the check, but certainly a penny.

"Your coffee, sir." She hoped her curtsy mocked louder than any outright laughter could.

"Don't be a smart-ass."

She winked. "Can't help it. Have you met my family?"

Roque took the offered cup, warily peering at the dark brew. Glancing back at Addi, he lifted a brow.

Rolling her eyes, she placed her hands on her hips. "Really? What do you think I did, poison it? Oh, for shit's sake." Addi removed the cup from his hand and took a cautious sip. "It's hot, not poisoned. Damn good, if I do say so myself." She returned the coffee to him. "Look, we may not love the situation we find ourselves in with me as your assistant, but my work is important to me, no matter what it is. The one thing I can't stand is being thought of as a flake. I've lived my whole life fighting that stereotype."

He cleared his throat, nodded once, and took a sip. "Wow. You're right, this is great. What did you do different?"

Addi sauntered up to stand in front of him with a wicked grin, and he tilted his head, looking at her out of the corner of his eye.

Standing toe-to-toe, Addi leaned back slightly to give him a once-over. "I'm full of pleasant surprises," she all but purred.

He closed his eyes and sighed, and she did a mental fist pump.

"Just because you close your eyes doesn't mean I've disappeared. What are you, two?" To throw him off a bit further, she ran her finger down the front of his shirt again. "Definitely *not* a toddler." Her voice came out a bit too breathless as she emphasized her last word with a tap on the shirt button at his navel. She couldn't help but admire how hard he was everywhere she touched. He was so fun to tease, and the devil in her couldn't resist. But she found she liked playing with him a little too much.

His eyes snapped open. Dismissing her comment, and ignoring her roaming fingers, he pinned her with a look. He lifted his cup for a long swallow of a different kind of stimulant, and she was curious about her immediate disappointment.

His movement forced Addi to take a step back. "Speaking of shirts," he said.

"No one said—"

"My dry cleaning is in my car." He continued on without pause, ticking additional items off his fingers in quick succession. "You'll officially start tomorrow, but you'll need to get started tonight if you're going to have catering ready to go. How about the security system check? And you have things that need to be moved into storage, I'd imagine."

Addi crossed her arms and yawned, waiting for his passive aggressive diatribe to die down. She couldn't stand being told what to do, and she either had to pretend boredom or throttle him. The former seemed the safer choice as far as her job was concerned.

"What?"

She narrowed her eyes, enjoying the wary look in his. "Give me your keys, and I'll see to your dry cleaning. The security company has already been phoned, the system updated with a new password, and the company has consulted with your security supervisor. All of my remaining things will be out of the way by tomorrow morning, and if you want the catering taken care of, then you need to give me your filming schedule with who will be here what days so I know how many to feed."

He nodded once. "Well then, I guess you're right. You are full of pleasant surprises."

A smug grin turned up the corners of her mouth.

"You might just be able to handle this job after all."

Addi stared at him a moment with a heated desire — to see him dead. "You annoy me." She snapped her teeth together, turned on her heel, and marched back into the house.

His chuckle followed her through the kitchen. "No, I don't. You love it. This is a challenge for you, and you can't wait to tackle it."

She bit her lip to keep from smiling. Damn if he wasn't right.

A short time later, Roque and his band of merry men and a lady left, and Addi walked through her home in silence. Making a list as she went, she wrote down what needed to be moved to the attic or taken to her storage shed. She sent out a few prayers and positive thoughts to the universe and whoever was listening that they wouldn't have to tear down any walls or do too much damage to the place she loved, to her home. Standing in the wide open space of her main floor, she pulled the piece of paper from the band of her sweatpants and opened it.

Eighteen thousand dollars, made out to Addison Dekker.

She'd done it. On her own, based on her personal resources, without help from her family. She'd done what she had to do and saved her home.

For the moment. Now to keep this job she knew nothing about so she could cover her coming taxes for next year and keep her home. Oh yeah, and get published. Little things. No big deal. She choked on her laugh.

She clutched the little paper, the only thing that stood between her and certain proof that she still couldn't handle life on her own.

The relief was so great, Addi sunk to her knees and hung her head, trying to make sense of the past twenty-four hours. She blinked back tears and breathed to pull air back into her lungs against the giddy excitement that filled her chest. Her home was saved.

She didn't care that she had to make sure she could pay for living expenses and next year's taxes, and the year after that and again after that. This job and her plans would secure the rest of it. Her plan. Time to put it in motion. She hesitated. Once she started this charade, there was no going back. A small twinge joined the joy tightening her chest. Now was not the time to second-guess, but to be brave. She had one chance to prove she was capable of taking care of herself, by herself. This was it. No turning back.

Pulling in a steadying breath, she pushed up from the floor and found her way to the attic door in the back hallway leading to the bedrooms and bathroom. The cord to pull down the stairs was too far out of reach for her to grab, so she pushed her vanity stool from her room into place and stepped up onto it. Just right. Thank God she was tall. At five foot nine, she was an inch taller than her sister, which Sam hated and Addi loved, but then again Sam had bigger boobs, so she could bite it.

With a yank, she had the stairs to her "hotel room" pulled down. Once secured, she scrambled up the ladder to the attic space. This was a secret that couldn't get out. The hotel fee for Huntington Place was no small deceit. She clenched her hands into fists to keep them from shaking. On a sigh, she climbed the ladder.

Lucky for her, she loved the attic. Aunt Addi had stashed many treasures in the space, and Addi had visited often to carefully go through each piece: pictures, clothes, and keepsakes. It made her feel like her aunt wasn't gone.

But right now, Addi loved the space because it was the one place off-limits to everyone else, leaving her to easily store all her things.

Using the list she'd made, she carefully carried all of her

necessities up to her new hiding place. Pillows, bedroll, clothes, makeup, lamp, and last but not least, her laptop. The laptop was most important because while she was saving her home, she also had to break into publishing. All in a day's work. She laughed as the weight of it settled into reality. Laughing at this was the only way to remain sane.

Not for the first time that day, she worried about the plan she'd concocted—against Chase's strongly worded discouragement. Not just because a small amount of double-dealing was involved, but also the fact she'd be living and sleeping in an attic. Her hands shook. As much as she loved visiting the space during the day, the night was a different story altogether.

Hollywood would never miss the hotel money she pocketed. Besides, they would still get everything they paid for, and so would she.

The extra money would work toward securing her future and keeping the lights on. Which was paramount.

She was afraid of the dark.

Chapter Four

The aroma of freshly brewed coffee pulled Roque through the front door. Catching sight of Addi in the kitchen, he crossed the front room, then took the cup she offered with the gratitude of a man being thrown a lifeline. "Thank you." He took in her pressed ivory slacks and tailored button-up dark gray shirt. Her eyes were rimmed in a matching shade, setting her baby blues to sparkling. The whole effect was quite striking, but he couldn't figure out which he preferred: this clean, professional Addi, or the chaotic version with éclair cream on her shirt.

She smiled in question. "What?"

"Nothing at all." He moved over to the table and set down his portfolio, rummaging inside. "You're here bright and early." He sipped his coffee. "Damn, this is good. You never did tell me what's different about this coffee of yours." Raising the cup, he paused.

"It's a gift. And my little secret."

He glanced up at her when her voice caught on her last word, but was drawn back to his cup. Damn, it *was* good.

He'd never admired someone for their coffee making ability before, but this coffee was the best he'd ever tasted.

She winked. "Okay, boss. Whaddya got for me?" She stepped over to the table, bringing the scent of honey with her. He wasn't sure if it was her or the éclairs she ate that made her smell that way. But he couldn't stop himself from breathing her in.

"I don't expect you to know everything right away, but I do expect hard work and honesty. The one thing I can't tolerate is being lied to."

She swallowed. "Of course."

Clearing his throat, he pulled out a file and handed it to her. "Okay, here's everything you'll need. Any other questions, don't hesitate to ask. We'll start most mornings by seven, unless we have a need to come in earlier. The few times I'm certain of are in the schedule you'll find inside." He watched her flip it open and look through the papers. "You'll also find the cast and crew list with pictures and shooting schedule. Those are best to have on hand. And I'm giving you access to my calendar and contact list."

Finishing off his coffee, he set the cup in the sink, then turned and leaned back against the counter. "I'll need you to set up catering. There're a few appointments to make, and you'll find the list in the folder. Also, make a quick call to your security alarm company. They need you to verify some information. SueAnn needed you for something. Oh, and here—"

He pulled a set of keys out of his pocket. "If I'm in a jam, I'll count on you to help me out." He held up one key. "This is the key to my condo, and this is to my car." Tossing them to her, he picked up his portfolio. "You can finally get my dry cleaning taken care of."

Glancing up at her, he narrowed his eyes, suspicious she'd just stuck her tongue out at him. The innocent, wide-eyed look practically confirmed it. "Any questions?"

A slow turn of her head from side to side accompanied her grin. "Shall I breathe for you, too, sir?"

She'd punctuated the "sir" and tapped her heels together. Always the smart-ass. With a laugh, he walked toward the crew. "I'll let you know."

Confirming the team was setting up outside for the first takes, he mentally checked it off his list, then pulled out his phone to make a few calls. Reaching out to Heath Fairmont lately was like trying to get through to the president. Every time he reached an assistant he'd been told "the gentleman is unavoidably detained." Tension pulled at the base of his neck as he looked up Fairmont's number yet again. He cracked his knuckles on one hand, finding satisfaction in each loud pop. A female voice answered on the third ring.

"Ms. Delaney, you're answering Mr. Fairmont's personal cell now?" he asked.

He listened to her cluck and coo about how busy her boss was and further nonsense about not enough hours in the day. "Come now, Ms. Delaney. Help me out. You and I are a lot alike, you know. Always trying to make those around us happy. I have a whole cast and crew I'm trying to please over here. They'd like to be paid for their work. You understand."

After persuading her to set up a lunch for later in the week, he disconnected the call and dropped the phone into the pocket of his slacks. He'd been pacing the length of the front room and finally stopped, leaning against the wall and dropping his head back with a dull thud. His eyes fixed on the ornate whitewashed carving that surrounded the base of the light fixture in the middle of the room. It was old and worn and beautiful like the rest of the house. Like the soul of the protagonist in his movie. His mother would have loved it. He'd have to remember to use a shot of it.

"Come now. It can't be bad as all that. It's only the first

day."

He pulled his head from the wall with effort. Addi sauntered toward him with a cup and a smile. "Here. This will help. You have eaten today, right? Lunch will be ready soon."

"You're a godsend."

"Make sure to tell my boss. I'm hoping for a raise."

His bark of laughter widened her smile. "It's your first day, and you're already asking for a raise?"

Placing her hands on her hips, she shrugged. "I know my worth." Running her fingers through her long crop, she tucked one side behind her ear. "Gotta run. My boss is a slave driver."

Before he could respond, she was wrapping her arm around SueAnn's shoulders and guiding her toward the back hallway. She was something, all right. He knew he threw her in all at once, but he didn't have time for anything else. As it was, he needed to go check on the sequence being filmed out back.

To make sure he didn't disrupt any active filming, he went out the front door and walked quietly around back. He walked up and looked at the film screen, loving the simplicity of the shot.

His director called, "Cut."

Slapping a hand to his shoulder, Roque gave a gentle shake. "Looks good, doesn't it? I love the space here."

"I'm making it work." Doug Kemper was known for his keen eye and dry humor. Charm, however, was never uttered in the same sentence as the man's name. Unfortunately, the two of them had been looking through opposing lenses from the beginning. Roque had hoped he'd come around, but instead Doug argued with him at every turn. He was getting tired of it, but his hands were tied. He needed a director, and now wasn't the time to search for another one.

"That's your job, right?" Roque said, holding the man's

gaze. He let his hand fall back to his side. "Look, this film is everything to me. I'm a man with high expectations and a clear vision. I want to see space, a literal and figurative division between the characters. Show the void with lighting, use the shadows. That's what I'm looking for with this scene." He spread his hand out in front of them as if he'd already accomplished it.

"It's my job to have vision as well, and I think yours is too shortsighted."

Roque sighed. "Look, I told you this project was particularly important to me. I need your vision to see my vision. I know what I want."

"If you don't like my work, you have options. You're a Gallagher. Call your dad."

Roque gritted his teeth, working hard to keep from shoving the man's words back down his throat.

Just then, Addi stepped between them and placed a hand on Doug's arm. "Mr. Kemper, do you have a second for me? I'm so new to this, and I have so many questions about directing and was hoping you might humor me over some lunch."

She guided the man to a table under a large umbrella, then served him a plate and drink. Sitting herself across from him, she smiled and nodded, and Roque watched in awe as the broomstick slowly slid from the man's ass. Every time Addi declared, "I had no idea," his director fell further under her spell and, if he didn't know better, he'd worry he was falling under it, too.

She laughed with her head tilted back, waving her hand at the man as if he'd just made the funniest statement she'd ever heard. Probably gave her some line about putting her in his next film. Roque furrowed his brows. He couldn't see her ever working with a man like Doug.

She bit her lip, and he caught himself staring at her chin.

There was something damn sexy about the almost-there cleft. He pressed his lips together and went in search of his own plate of food. Somewhere separated from directors and chin dimples.

On the front porch, away from the cast and crew, he ate his lunch and calculated his options. He'd get the money from Fairmont, because he didn't have any other choice. Lunch would be the perfect chance to get the check. No more excuses. He felt like a juggler in a circus keeping a tight hold on Addi, his director, and the ever-tightening budget without losing his grip.

Addi's smiling face interrupted his thoughts, as unrelenting and distracting as he'd feared. What kind of man did she date? And why the hell did he care? The thought wouldn't die. Did she like someone who made her laugh—she had a great face for it—or the philosophical type who waxed poetic with observations about the state of mankind? He could see her admiring both.

The last woman he'd dated wouldn't know what "existential" meant. It wasn't her fault, really. She'd been raised for only two things: to marry well and live in Beverly Hills. She hadn't been uneducated, just unaware of any existence besides one spent marching the sidewalks of Rodeo Drive.

She'd been fun, but she probably wouldn't say the same about him. He'd worked—all the time. And in the end, her need to see and be seen with her man outweighed the guaranteed residential zip code she'd achieve by sticking with him.

It was all for the better. His film had been approaching inception and the closer the day came, the more demanding his schedule grew. He didn't have time for relationships. He didn't have room for error. Besides, he'd already learned the very difficult lesson of how badly he failed those he loved.

He wiped his hands on a napkin, set his empty plate aside, and pushed up from his seat. Walking across the colorful porch to the steps, he took them one at a time. The whole plan had been to keep his distance from Addi. Helluva good job he'd done at that. He'd wracked his mind to find an alternative position for her, but the project was too important to let her loose on set.

He counted off the number of steps to the driveway and then along the front of the house to get an idea of the size of the space for another shot he had in mind. Addi probably had the measurements somewhere. She was quickly inserting herself as part of the team, so the chance for that distance he'd been hoping for got smaller and smaller. As it was, in the few hours since that morning, she already had the crew wrapped snugly around her little finger, including his cantankerous director. He'd never seen anyone move so fast as when Addi asked his people to help her—even SueAnn. They'd all be best friends by the week's end, then he'd be in real trouble. He shook his head, tucking away the measurements for later. Addi had a way about her, to be sure. No one else had ever scattered his thoughts so efficiently. And that was something he'd do well to keep to himself, or he'd never hear the end of it. He worked hard to be taken seriously.

And he could see that she felt the same way concerning her ability to work for him. She'd proved his initial teasing wrong in a hurry, and he could relate. His modeling career had produced nothing but flak from his family and friends, even if he'd been able to put himself through school because of it—one of his proudest accomplishments. The ribbing was good-natured, to be sure, but it still caused an itch under his collar. The only one who'd never poked fun at him was his mom. She'd reminded him of how intelligent he was every day since he was a little boy. She'd thought of him as her "beautiful" child. He'd hated that word as a kid. No boy wants to be called beautiful. But his mom had had a way with words like no one else. Now he'd give anything just to hear her call him that one more time.

His throat tightened.

That was the exact reason he needed to succeed with this project.

All of his hard work, everything he'd missed—it had to mean something, to be for something.

He didn't think he could take it if it wasn't.

Addi waved as the last crew member walked out her front door. "I'm almost done. Go ahead and I'll lock up." She sighed as she slid from her crouched position onto her butt and leaned back against the wall.

Finally.

The crew had filmed well into the night. New takes and retakes layered upon one another until they blurred into one long take for Addi. The whole process was new to her, and the learning curve left her exhausted. She knew from the beginning her plan wasn't going to be an easy one, but too many nights like this and she'd surely expire. As it was, it would be hours before she could go to bed, and the idea of writing was a joke. She'd finally gotten her hands on the health and safety laws and procedures but still had to read through them. The quickest way to lose her job was for Roque to lose his crew.

There were only a few more minutes left before she had to turn out all the lights, and at half past eleven, the prospect did not please her. One too many practical jokes by her brother and sister left her fearful of what she couldn't see and who might be lurking behind each corner. It was a consequence of being the youngest sibling.

It hadn't been until she'd found the lockup sheet in the folder Roque had given her that she realized living in the house under his nose would be trickier than she'd expected: all equipment turned off, lights turned out, alarm set.

Stalling for a few more minutes of light, Addi walked around her bungalow, taking in the familiar and the not-so-familiar. With all the equipment, the makeup and costuming trailers outside, and all the crates for the set designers, the crew had to utilize every nook and cranny. She could see her home, but it was half-hidden under the production facade of Hollywood—and film equipment. She stared at the corner of the front room, where she wrote most of the time. It looked unrecognizable. Where her antique desk used to be sat a stack of steamer trunks. Her framed rejection letters were replaced with faux family photos. She sighed. Soon, she'd get back to her life…soon.

Grabbing a Greek yogurt, apple, and a bottled water from the fridge, Addi found a flashlight, then walking back through the house, secured all the windows and double-checked all the equipment. Before locking the back door, Addi stepped through to the stone path that meandered through her backyard to a sloping trail and eventually opened onto the beach far below. The ocean beckoned her, but she hadn't even an hour to spare for playing in the moonlight. The longer her writing waited, the longer it would take for her dreams became reality.

She did, however, have a moment to pull in the night's still-warm, damp air. Above the endless ocean of midnight silk, the moon's light rode each crested wave and bathed the evening in a glow of cool blue. The beautiful landscape and memories of her aunt called to her. This was the one place where she'd always felt like she belonged. Addi's love for her home swelled in her heart with desperate affection.

Aunt Addi had understood her better than anyone from

the moment she was born. It was her aunt who'd introduced her to romance novels and romantic movies, much to her mother's exasperation. *Aunt Addi, you don't need to fill her head with any more nonsense.*

Her mother had never meant anything by it, but it had been the "any more" that had hurt. When Aunt Addi had died, she'd left a letter, explaining she'd wanted her niece to have a home where she could create and be as fanciful as she liked. A place where she wouldn't have to worry about a mortgage and would be free to pursue her dream. Unfortunately, her aunt had had more faith in Addi than sense. At least that's what her family believed. She was sure of it.

She couldn't lose it. Wouldn't lose it. She'd prove her aunt's faith was deserved. She'd write every free moment she had, and she'd land that contract.

So she needed to prioritize, she needed to write, and she needed to face the dark of the night—afraid or not.

Determined, Addi marched back into her home and locked up. Finally satisfied all was locked down, she set the security alarm and, with a shaking hand, flicked out the last light. Immediately plunged into darkness, she pressed her back against the wall and willed her panicked heartbeat to calm down.

Her eyes slowly adjusted to the darkness, ears ringing, every sense on high alert. She picked her way from the kitchen to the back hallway, using the flashlight, careful not to knock into any of the expensive set pieces. That was a bill she'd rather not add to her list.

She used a bent hanger she'd stashed away earlier in the day to hook the pull rope and yank down the attic door. Once she'd made her way up the stairs and over to her makeshift bed, the warm glow of the lamp released a sigh of relief from her constricted lungs. Forcing her breath to slow, she demanded her mind let go of the shapes and shadows it swore lurked around each corner on the way. She'd laugh at herself another time, but not tonight. There was too much at stake. Right now, nothing was funny about her circumstances.

Addison Dekker would show everyone that she didn't need anyone to save her, coddle her, or take care of her.

Maneuvering the pillows against the wall, she settled back into them and stretched her legs out in front of her. With her laptop on her thighs, she studied the policies and procedures followed by the film industry.

What she really wanted to do was write. Writing was her gateway to planning, plotting, and dreaming about a world where she couldn't lose. Each letter, each word, drove her forward to revealing the next adventure, the next lesson, the next love.

Roque's charming smile stilled her fingers. She shook her head to rid her mind of the vision, but it persisted. Demanding excellence, he remained—studying her, challenging her with those blue eyes and sexy smirk.

He'd impressed her today, even though taking his instructions annoyed the hell out of her. Every time he told her what to do, the devil in her made her find some way to tease, but she couldn't deny the respect that grew from watching him handle his crew, his project. The man had a vision, one he was determined to reveal on film. He had passion and drive, something to prove, though she still couldn't imagine what. The drive she understood. His urgency to see a passion manifest into a living, breathing entity mirrored her own.

Leaving the lamp on, she turned on her side, catching a glimpse of herself with the attic reflected behind her in an antique mirror leaning against the far wall. This was a side of herself she didn't necessarily like the looks of, but she, too, had drive and something to prove.

If only she could do it without getting caught.

Chapter Five

Addi's alarm sounded, and she fumbled to turn it off. The pounding in her head argued that five a.m. was an abhorrent hour, and she agreed, but she couldn't risk being found in her p.j.s.

Every muscle in her body ached as she stretched against her hard, makeshift bed. She turned onto her back and draped her hand over her brow to shield the still-glowing lamplight from her sensitive eyes.

She turned off the lamp and glanced about the attic that was still bathed in the gentle light of the moon through one small round window near the apex of the vaulted roof. A large beam ran the length of the roof, like a spine, with crossbeams that ran wall to wall. The bones of the bungalow. Straight and strong, just like she needed to be.

"Ugh, if the moon's still out, I should be, too." Her voice was a haunting echo in the silence of her home. She was wont to talk to herself anyway, but it seemed very clandestine in the dark when she was kind of, maybe, breaking the law. Breach of contract at the very least. Okay, maybe more. Addi shook her head to rid the worry and the lecturing, nagging voice.

Hollywood could handle it.

Pulling the bedding up on her bed, Addi glanced at the clock, a spike of worry sharp at the base of her neck. Roque's schedule showed start time at seven but anyone could show up at any time.

She grabbed her overnight bag and hurried down to the bathroom. The irony that she had an overnight bag in her own home didn't escape her, and she shook her head with a chuckle of derision. The glow from the moon was now accompanied by the very early rays of sunrise. She yearned for a shower, but until she knew exactly what the morning schedule would be, she didn't dare.

With a quick face wash, a little makeup with extra eyeliner, and her hair slicked back into a tight high ponytail, she cleaned away any telltale signs she'd used the bathroom—Roque noticed everything.

The sun was persistent, light filtering through the blinds, and Addi gave a quick check out the front window. All clear. Skirting the set pieces in the living room, she made her way back to the attic.

Tossing yesterday's clothes in a pile, she pulled on a crisp white button-up and deep cherry slacks. Grabbing black patent wedges and a matching belt, she then made her way back down the ladder.

After everything was closed back up, heels on and belt in place, Addi heaved a sigh of relief and yawned. Damn, she was ready for bed.

An hour later, Addi walked out from the kitchen, two cups of coffee in hand, as Roque stepped through the front door. His look of surprise would have made her giggle if she hadn't been concentrating so hard on not spilling her peace offering.

A rush of awareness warmed her chest when he raised a brow in hesitant question, those damn eyes narrowing with a questioning look. He slowly set his bag at his feet, as if a sudden move might spook her. Once he straightened back to his full height, she offered him a cup.

He wrapped his long thick fingers around the porcelain, overlapping hers. His touch seemed to steal the air as she slid her fingers from beneath his, and her breath hitched. "Everything okay?" He looked at her.

Heat flushed clear to her hairline with his question. With a quick shrug, she rubbed her hand against her slacks, then tucked it behind her back. "Of course." Her breathless tone fell on her own ears, and she winced.

With a quick nod, he headed toward the kitchen.

She peeked at him from beneath her lashes. What in the hell was she doing? Without question, she admired his work ethic and the way he handled his crew. Looks were one thing—and man did he have them—but men with integrity and compassion were on the endangered species list. So it made sense that she was attracted to him.

What didn't make sense was why she felt so shy about it. That was very un-Addi-like. He threw her off her game every time she got lost in his gaze or distracted by his touch. She'd have to stay on her toes around him. Following him into the kitchen, she blamed the uncharacteristic sensation on her situation. There was a lot at stake.

Roque sipped the coffee, a look of pure joy shining from his too-blue eyes before he narrowed them again. "What's the catch?"

Addi smiled. "I want to call a truce."

"A truce?" His question was hesitant. "I didn't realize we were at war."

She raised an eyebrow. "Really? Well, to be fair, you probably didn't, but I took a little pleasure from pushing your buttons." She held up her hand with her pointer finger a small distance from her thumb to indicate just how little.

He studied her for a beat. "I give. You're right. You can be hardheaded and abrasive." His face remained serious, then crumpled with a chuckle.

"Hey, I said 'a truce,' no name calling." Secretly tickled by his assessment, she grinned. After being thought of as ditzy or flighty—at best—for so long, hardheaded and abrasive was a step in the right direction.

Roque took a seat at the table. "Okay, okay. A truce." He took another long swallow of his coffee. "Damn, this is good. I'm impressed with what you've shown me so far. Speaking of which, why are you here so early?"

Addi took the seat adjacent to his. She ran her fingertip along the edge of her cup.

Roque shifted in his seat. She glanced up to find him watching her finger's slow perusal along the ceramic's edge. Her body's immediate response annoyed her, which, unfair or not, made her want to make him pay. Again, just a little.

She bit the end of her finger, sucking the tip, and then picked up her cup for a sip.

His gaze locked on her mouth, and she struggled to keep from smiling.

Could he suffer from the same attraction? All of her little ploys to throw him off-balance had been met by a cool professionalism she had to admire. Maybe that rock wasn't as cold as the name implied.

Good. It wasn't right for her to suffer alone.

He cleared his throat, pulling his eyes from her finger, and made a show of straightening the linens on the table.

She sipped from her cup then said, "To your first statement, thank you. My work, no matter what it may be, is important to me. Second, this is my home. I prefer to be the first in and the last out when possible. It gives me reassurance. Besides, I figured it was my job to get things opened up and the coffee started." Placing her cup on the table, she tapped the ceramic once with her nail.

Roque studied her again in that unsettling way of his. She feared he could see the lies like a headline running across her forehead. It was her turn to shift in her seat in the face of his endless silence.

Without warning, his hand shot out, grabbed the edge of her chair, and pulled her toward him, the grating of wood on wood loud in the quiet hum of morning. Her breath seized in her lungs as she grabbed onto the edges of the chair to keep from falling, her hand closing over his larger one, his heat warming her palm. Roque's nose inches from her own, he narrowed his eyes to twin blue slivers.

Her gaze slipped to his lips—big mistake. Her mouth watered. *What was wrong with her?*

"What are you up to?"

She swore her heart stopped. Did he know? No, he couldn't. Studying him a beat longer, she outright laughed. "You don't trust people easily, do you? Nothing's going on." She flicked her gaze to his mouth, then back to his eyes.

He stilled, and her body tightened. God, the man was delicious. "Don't you think it'll be more fun if we get along?" She gave his hand a slight squeeze.

He held her gaze, then broke into a grin. After a pause, he slid his hand from under hers and leaned back in his chair. "You've got a point. And unfortunately for you, after introducing us to your coffee, no one else is allowed near the coffee press."

Addi struggled to hide the enormous relief his words produced. When her shoulders wanted to sag, she pulled them back. She slowly controlled her exhale. Freaking out about him finding out what she was really doing was exhausting. "I can live with that—besides, I can't stomach anyone else's coffee, anyway."

Roque pushed back from the table, then took his cup over to the sink, rinsing it and setting it on the counter before turning to face her. Thank God, that ass was a distraction. She bit her lower lip and dragged her gaze back to his face.

He raised a brow. "I've got work to do. Jimmy, the location manager, is going downtown to get permission to mark off a portion of the road out front for tomorrow's shoot."

She stood, pushing in her chair as she straightened. "Perfect, I'll go with him. Catering is set up for tomorrow, but I need to handle today, so I need to stop at the store. Good with you, boss?"

Roque stepped close, and besides the pulse throbbing in the side of his neck, she couldn't even tell he breathed for how still he stood. "I like the sound of that."

She played with the button over his sternum. "Oh, I could get used to it, too. Under the right circumstances."

His eyes widened for the briefest of seconds before wrapping his hand around hers and releasing it at her side with a chuckle. "Behave."

"But where's the fun in that?" She bit her lip with a grin.

Roque's teeth flashed white as he returned a smile more predator than prey. Yes, she'd have to remember to be careful with this one.

"One more thing, I'll need you to assist with securing clearances for a few copyright materials. The list is in the folder I gave you." He headed out to greet the crew who clamored through the front door. It always sounded like a frat house when they were all in attendance.

Addi couldn't help but watch him go.

An alarm sounded in her head, and for the second time that day she was jerked out of dreamland. A dream as vivid as any blockbuster movie.

And damn it if Roque Gallagher didn't have the starring role.

She blinked. What had he said? Secure copyright materials? How the hell was she supposed to do that? Grabbing her laptop, she typed in "secure copyright materials," then clicked enter.

Her heart stopped. If there was a film clip which also included a soundtrack, or a scene in which a notable painting could be seen hanging on the wall, or any other similar use of copyrighted materials, she'd need to gain the licenses from the music publisher, music performer, the painting's rights holder. She placed a shaking hand to her forehead. No problem. Days had twenty-four hours built into them for a reason. Who needed sleep?

A short time later Addi waited in the car, poring over the list of needed copyright materials while Jimmy took care of a few things. The courthouse and sheriff's department were a stone's throw from the Country Mart, Malibu's seaside version of a city center.

After Jimmy procured the necessary permits, they stopped at the bank.

Addi took her check inside, just to make sure it deposited with no issues. As she signed her name to the back of the check and handed it to the teller, the weight she'd been carrying lightened a bit.

She'd done it. She was saving her home. For now. The small nagging voice in the back of her head reminded her of how much more she had to do before she secured it, but she shoved it aside. She needed this victory, this moment to celebrate. It was a huge move in the right direction.

With a skip in her step, she followed Jimmy into the coffee shop, then back outside onto the patio, disappointing a few fans when she announced she was not, in fact, the actress Jaime Pressly, and took a chair across from him.

Jimmy's low chuckle followed the fallen spirits of the two young men. "That happen often?"

"More than I'd like. If I made that kind of money, I wouldn't need this gig."

He nodded. "I can see it, though. Quite striking, actually."

"Yeah? Find me her kind of work then." Addi grinned

and watched all the comings and goings around them.

She adored Malibu. She loved the hills that shot up to the east and the exhilarating expanse of the ocean to the west, as if protecting her little slice of paradise from the rest of the world. The combination of salty ocean air and fresh green earth always made her think of paradise.

Everywhere she looked, shoppers were out and about, filling their bags and emptying their wallets. A few families played in the park or took pictures with Mr. Hammer, or as she liked to call him, Mr. Tush, a huge metal sculpture of a hammer with a happy presence and a cute perky butt. Malibu was her home as much as her bungalow was, and she vowed she'd keep them both.

Jimmy took a sip of his coffee, his tattooed bicep bunching tight, then raised the mug in salute. "Delicious. Almost as good as yours."

She smiled. "Brownie points for you." Sipping from her own cup, her grin broadened with his deep chuckle. Jimmy was a big guy with dark hair that always looked as if he was a week overdue for a haircut and scruff that he kept edged and groomed. He looked more like a hot biker than a location manager. Apparently he'd always wanted to act, but as soon as the cameras started rolling, he'd discovered that he didn't. So working on films was the next best thing until he could make a living from his photography. A man of many talents.

Addi had liked him right off. Upon introduction, she'd raised up on tiptoe and swung her arm over his shoulder, pulling him close. "You got good taste, Gallagher."

Jimmy's grin had practically glowed as Roque had rolled his eyes.

They'd been immediate friends. He helped her figure out some of her responsibilities, and she made him coffee upon his every request. The better deal fell into her court as far as she was concerned, because the man had skills and knowledge.

His eyes followed a pair of well-developed, or purchased, tushes encased in yoga pants across the parking lot as he spoke. "You're coming along."

Addi watched with him. She was no hater, and a fan of yoga pants herself. Her bottom never looked so good as when propped up by spandex. "It's only been three days, but I'm learning. I need the extra cash so I don't want to screw up anything. But I need to do a bit more research on the industry. When you all start talking shop, it sounds like a different language to me." The list she had waiting for her made her shudder.

"Roque has high standards. But it isn't only all about his project. He takes care of his people. When a job's done right, he says so. I've worked for plenty of people who'd rather choke on their own arrogance than say a kind word. If he was one of 'em, I wouldn't be here."

Addi's phone chirped. Digging through odds and ends, she pulled it from her bag, fumbling to turn it right side up. "Crap, crap, crap." She stared at the email notification. Re: Blue Winged Press.

Her stomach clamped down as if spring-loaded, and she straightened in her seat against the pressure.

Jimmy tilted his head. "Everything okay?"

Addi twitched her head in a quick *no*. "Email from the publisher I submitted to."

"Open it."

Addi sighed. "If it were good news, they'd have called. Maybe."

Leaning forward, Jimmy squeezed her shoulder. "It's all part of the process: open it, get it over with…then keep writing. Right?"

She flicked her eyes to his, then opened the email. A quick scan confirmed what she already knew. They loved her voice, she had great characters—but—there was always a but.

With a heavy heart, she pulled in a breath and closed the email. She laid the phone on the table and glanced out to the hills. Maybe she could get lost in them, some place where no one could find her, some place she could lick her wounds. It didn't matter how many times it happened, every "no" was a knife in the chest. Every "no" pushed her dream further from her grasp and made her question why she thought she had a right to be successful in such a finicky industry.

Jimmy cleared his throat. "You okay?"

Addi blinked back the tears that stung behind her lids. "Yes, sucks, but I'll be fine. Like you said, all part of the process."

She had more submissions out, more chances for a "yes," but more for a "no" as well. She dreaded the potential for pain more than she relished the excitement of a "yes," probably because one seemed more likely than the other. Quitting wasn't an option, but damn if the thought didn't dance about her head with every rejection. *Welcome to the world of writing, Addi.*

He nodded. "Keep moving forward."

Addi lifted her chin and smiled. Moving forward, yes, the only thing she could do. Move forward with her writing, saving her home, and proving to her family she could take care of herself. "Absolutely." Which was why she needed to keep this job through the end of filming. How else would she have the access she needed to her house to keep living there without anyone finding out?

"Come on, we need to get back."

Jimmy paused, cup midway to his mouth. "What's the rush?"

"I need this job for quite a few reasons. I need to show him what I'm made of."

A short time later, Addi flew from the truck before Jimmy had come to a full stop, anxiety pushing her to move. There was nothing she could do at the moment about her rejection, but she could tackle lunch.

Rounding to the tailgate, she lowered it, then grabbed her grocery bags, three to each arm.

Jimmy came around to join her. "Here, let me get those."

She jerked her chin toward the open bed. "Just close the tailgate for me. Thanks."

The front door flew open, and Roque crowded the entrance. "Need a hand?"

She threw him a smile, then nudged past him. "Nope, just get out of my way, these are heavy." Her arms burned with effort, and she needed to set her load down before she dropped it all.

Once in the kitchen, she placed her assortment of fresh produce and deli goods on the counter and got to work.

"I could have helped," Roque said, stepping beside her at the counter.

"I've got my job, you've got yours. Go do it." Blowing her bangs from her forehead, she forced herself to focus. Slice, chop, dice, repeat.

He watched her work for a moment longer then left her with a nod. She could handle her work, needed to handle her work. His offer to help was kind, but he couldn't do his job if he was helping her figure out hers. If Addi did anything right in the next few months, it would be her position as his assistant. With her little plan, it was the least she could do. She placed a hand to her forehead, surprised by her own clammy touch.

Addi washed her hands, stacked sandwiches on a platter, then, balancing a tray on each hand, she headed through the French doors to the tables that were set up in the backyard for lunch.

The last thing she needed was to give the man any reason to fire her from the set, especially right after they'd become sort-of friends. It would be a hell of a lot harder to see her brilliant plan through to the end without her job, and seeing it through to the end was non-negotiable. If there'd been any question before, her rejection solidified it. No writing contract meant no money, and no money meant her plan was the only way to save her home.

Chapter Six

Roque watched Addi work throughout lunch. Efficient and precise, filling plates, producing sauces and dips at a moment's notice, even fresh-baked cookies. When the hell had she baked cookies? Not one request for help or one hesitation in her step. That was work he admired.

She was a force, one he'd felt from the beginning.

As he watched her move about, he couldn't help but admire what he saw. Her red-encased derriere called out to his hands, and just a hint of cleavage taunted him from the opening of her blouse. Her severe hairstyle had him itching to pull it, or release it and muss it up, he wasn't sure which— the hell he didn't. A vision of her leaning over him, breasts swaying, her hair a wild halo around her face, had him shifting uncomfortably in his chair. Fuck.

Oh, he'd pull it, too, but that would be from a different position.

He shook his head and furtively looked about. If only he could get past their conversation this morning. He'd been surprised to find her already on set and ready to go. Coffee for him, no less. She did have a familiarity and a stake in the project, since it was her house, so maybe he shouldn't have been so surprised.

Her teasing had been torture, the minx, but the anxiety that peeked through her defiant gaze nagged at him. He usually had a good sense for when people were hiding something from him.

Usually.

The familiar pain rolled into his chest and settled like lead in his gut. Suddenly not hungry, he pushed away the plate of remaining food.

"Are you okay?"

Addi's concerned voice broke through his memory. He flexed fingers stiff from being clenched into tight fists. Clearing his throat, he glanced up into her wary gaze. "Yeah, yeah, just thinking."

She extended a plate toward him. "Cookies help." She shifted from one foot to the other in his silence.

He glanced at her, taking in the sincerity on her face. Remembering the plate of éclairs on her kitchen counter, he had no doubt she believed every word. He grabbed one. "Thank you."

Looking away and then back to him, she pointed toward the house, then picked up his plate. "I'm going to get everything cleaned up. The crew's inside."

He nodded once and took a bite, almost sighing when the warm chocolate melted on his tongue. "Great work today."

Tilting her head, she hesitated and then beamed. "Jimmy was right."

Not a clue what she was talking about, he remained silent and soothed his raw emotions by watching her walk away. Unfortunately, it had the opposite effect.

Lowering his head to one side, then the other, in an attempt to ease his stiff neck and strained muscles, he shoved down his cynical thoughts. Maybe it was the importance of his project. If he were ever going to get out of his father's and uncle's shadows, this was it. But not everyone wanted to see him succeed. There were more than a few people in the industry who were sick of the Gallagher monopoly. It seemed if they put as much effort into trying to be successful themselves as they did in trying to see him fail, they'd already have made it.

He'd been putting out fires since day one with his casting director, who'd apparently been fed erroneous information about Roque and the family—something about his uncle misleading investors. Not even close to true, just the press trying to create a story where there was none. Little things, annoying things, but enough that Roque decided to keep a tight vigilance on the happenings with his crew. Then his investor had canceled lunch. He could only imagine it had something to do with the rumors. The phone had been stuck to his ear all morning, and he wished it would have been with good news at least one time.

But no matter, he'd find a way. Work harder, longer hours—whatever it took. As it was, he worked from sunup to sundown and sometimes well past night and into the morning, too. Hard work wasn't what scared him.

The ringing of his phone pulled him from his thoughts. Slipping it from his pocket, he glanced at the screen and stood up. "Fairmont. I've been waiting for your call." Quick strides carried him through the house to the back guest room, and then he carefully closed the door. Silence filled the line as he sat down at the small antique desk. "Hello?"

"Mr. Gallagher, I'm really sorry but—"

"Ms. Delaney?"

"Yes, sir. I—"

A heavy stone settled in Roque's gut with her stammer. "Be straight with me, Ms. Delaney."

The silence screamed in his ear before the soft tone of her voice finally reached him. "Mr. Fairmont is pulling out, sir. He's already handed the funds over to another project."

"No, we have a contract. He's legally obligated to—"

"He's made up his mind. I'm sorry."

"Motherfucker!" His phone flew out of his hand before he finished swearing, then landed on the carpet with a thud.

Roque stared at it, his ragged breaths burning through his chest. He supposed it was good his aim was off, though the smashing of his phone against the wall would have felt so much better than the dull sound of it falling to the floor.

He could take the man to court. And he would. They had a signed contract—but by the time he'd be able to wring the money out of him, the film would already have stalled out and his crew would have gone on to jobs that could actually pay them.

He bent at the waist, leaning against his knees with his head in his hands. His stomach turned, and he feared he might be sick all over the whitewashed floor. Stunned couldn't begin to cover his state of mind. He was sure he could have persuaded Fairmont to settle up if he could have only gotten in front of the man.

He sat like that for what felt like hours, running what he could have done differently through his head. What the fuck was he going to do now? Fairmont's portion was over 30 percent of his budget. There was no way he could replace it. The point of his independent film wasn't the money it would make. Most didn't turn huge profits, because they simply didn't have the reach. It was a means to step out on his own merit, make a name for himself based on his talent, not that of his family's. At least that was the plan.

Running to his family defeated the purpose of stepping out on his own, but even if he could get past that, both his dad and uncle had their funds sunk in a pet project of their own, and his Aunt Raquel had recently taken on a new jewelry boutique. For being such a wealthy bunch, hands were tied. Tight.

He'd cut costs where possible to buy more time. But some things couldn't be helped, like the cost of bringing Addi on board, the bungalow, the hotel. Which now he couldn't afford, but he also couldn't afford not to.

Running a hand through his hair, he sighed.

This couldn't be the end.

A soft knock sounded at the door, and then it cracked open. "Everything all right?"

Keeping his eyes closed, he pulled in a breath.

Addi stepped into the room. "You've been in here over an hour. The director is having one of his fits and…" She paused. Lowering in front of him, she placed a hand on his knee. "What happened? Is it your family? Everyone okay?"

Well, that was one way to put things into perspective. He cleared his throat. "Yeah. Yes. Everyone's fine. I lost a backer—"

"What? Oh no!"

He put up his hand for her to stop. "I don't want anyone to hear about this. The last thing I need is Kemper on my ass."

She quickly glanced over her shoulder. Speaking in a hushed tone, she said, "Look, I'll take care of the director and the crew. Take as much time in here as you need. "With an efficiency he'd come to recognize as her professional mode, she crossed the room and grabbed his cell from the floor. Returning it to him, she placed a hand on his shoulder. "Make a few calls. You'll get this sorted out. I'll buy you some time."

He nodded, but stopped her before she left through the door. "Addi."

"Yes?" She turned, her cherry red pants bright against the beach tones of the room.

"Thank you."

"Anything for you, boss." She winked, closing the door behind her.

He couldn't help the smile that pulled up the corners of his mouth just a bit. Leave it to Addi to lend a bit of humor when nothing felt funny. He had to admit, he liked hearing the term "boss" falling from her lips. She was the only one who could make it sound naughty and sassy at the same time. Rubbing his hands over his face, he leaned back in his chair. He needed a miracle.

Roque called his cousin, Martin Gallagher Jr., confirming the worst of it. Fairmont had indeed invested in another project, apparently bragging about a four-wheeled luxury incentive he'd gotten out of it. A friend of a friend of a friend and all that shit. Hollywood at its finest.

He sailed through his contacts, calling anyone and everyone he could think of, until his phone beeped a low battery warning and the light shining through the window began to dim.

He didn't remember moving, but now he was reclining on the daybed, on top of a white cotton eyelet duvet with his shoes kicked off and his legs crossed at the ankles. Blowing out a breath, he counted his remaining options, which didn't fill the fingers of one hand.

The door opened, and Addi breezed in with a tray full of leftover deli sandwiches and cookies from lunch. A subtle hint of honey filled the room. His stomach growled. In that moment, she'd earned the check he had written her.

"Any luck?" Her question was hesitant as she handed him a sandwich, and he sat up.

He shook his head. "Not yet. But I'll figure it out. I have to."

"Don't films end before they get started all the time? Kind of like just part of the process?" She sat down next to him and grabbed a sandwich of her own.

He stared at her, the reality of her words turning the savory bite he chewed to dust in his mouth. "Not an option. Not for me." Shaking his head, he continued. "This industry is so small it's incestuous. How I begin is the ride I can expect in this town. If I don't break out in the beginning on my own merit, I'll simply be another Gallagher in the film industry."

"Would that really be so bad?"

"Of course not. My family is amazing, but I want to be working with people who respect me for my skill and vision, and if my work is discredited because of who I am, and the quality of my work is attributed to the involvement of my father and uncle, I'll never get there."

She held his gaze, and he could see she understood by the slight nod she returned.

He needed to get his mind off this before he drove himself crazy. "You're a writer. Tell me about what you want to do with your career."

Surprise silenced her a moment. That was a first, and he wanted to laugh.

"Do you really want to know?"

"I need to think about something other than what I'm going to do about the film for a minute."

She smiled. "I can't remember when the last time was that anyone asked me about my writing. My parents always checked in, but it was out of concern for me needing help rather than true interest. At least that's how it seemed, anyway." She shrugged, but he couldn't help the feeling there was a lot more to it.

"My sister's way too busy, and Luca's never been the warm and fuzzy type to ask. I can't really complain, though. I don't ask them much about their plans, either, so I don't know why I brought it up. It's almost like we take one another's lives for granted. Ya know?"

He tilted his head. "I'm an only child."

She waved her words away. "I knew that. Never mind." Looking out of the corner of her eye, she stared at him in contemplation. "I've always loved to write, but I denied myself for the security of work in corporate America. I hated it."

"Hated denying yourself or corporate America?"

"Both. At first I thought it was just the work I was less than enamored with, then as I began to write a little here and there, I realized it was the snuffing out of my creative side I resented the most. And I did it to myself."

"I think that's very common," he said. How many jobs had he held before he'd really figured out what he wanted to do? To be.

She mulled on the thought for a bit. "It's sad, isn't it? So many people working for work's sake with no intention of creating a life around their passions."

"It is, but then, many passions don't pay the bills. At least not right away." He turned up his palms with a flick, indicating his present circumstances.

"Don't I know it."

He chuckled. "You're brave. I admire you for it. You're going after your dream, determined to make it happen, even though it is not the easiest path."

Shock widened her eyes. "You think I'm brave?" She bit her lip and looked away then back. "I'm not."

He leaned back with narrowed eyes. "Hell yes, you are, Addi. I can go after what I want with no fear. Whether I want help or not, the Gallagher name is a safety net of incredible proportions."

She held his gaze. "My parents support me, too, but a little too much. I can count on them financially to a point, but it opens me up to being told what to do with my life. I'm tired of always needing help, needing to be taken care of. It's humiliating."

"I get that, too." Shaking his head he said, "I know you've

heard of, or God help me, have seen some of the work I did while in college."

She giggled, recalling the underwear ads, no doubt. "Hell, yes. Me and every one of my girlfriends. We had your pictures taped—"

"Okay, okay. I get it."

She giggled again, and he shoved her arm gently.

"I did the work because I was determined to put myself through college."

He laughed as her eyes shot wide for the second time. "Really? Why?"

"Partly because I wanted to see if I could. I have a bit of a stubborn streak."

"But surely being provided a college education isn't a handout."

He pressed his lips together. "All my life I've been told I'd be a success either due to my good looks or the Gallagher name. You know how emasculating that is as a young man? I had to prove I could make my dreams come true all on my own. But not by using my name. So I used my looks in a way that helped instead of being a hindrance."

Her disbelief was obvious, and he scowled. "Seriously. Either people would hold it against me, or say the only reason I achieved something was because of them." He shook his head. "Look. My point is that I understand the desire, the necessity to make it on your own." He grabbed a cookie. "Enough about me."

"I like hearing about you."

"Nope. You're deflecting. You still haven't told me why writing and, more specifically, why romance?"

"I like writing romance—happy endings, stories about love and loss and the journey to happily-ever-after."

"Surrounding yourself with intent. With what makes you happy in life," he said.

She grinned. "Yes, but not always. When I first quit work, I did so because I ghostwrote the book about my friend Phillip's success. The project and my savings were the whole reason I had the courage to quit my job. Unfortunately, I underestimated how slowly this industry operates and how difficult it is to break in. Before I knew it, I'd run through my savings. And you know the rest, thanks to public records."

Roque looked up at the ceiling and whistled casually. Addi elbowed him in the side. "That wasn't fair."

"That was business." Tossing the last bite of cookie into his mouth, he chewed with smug satisfaction. Swallowing, he leaned forward. "It was also necessary. I needed the use of your home, and I could tell you needed the opportunity whether you wanted it or not."

"And here we are."

He looked around the small guest room. "Here we are."

"What are you going to do?"

"What I'm good at."

He'd find a solution, a new investor. Thinking of Fairmont tightened his chest. It would be a long time before he could think of the man or hear his name without wanting to smash his fist through something. Preferably the man's face. He didn't like games, and he didn't like being lied to. But sitting with Addi, seeing the understanding in her eyes and hearing it in her voice, was a salve. He hadn't realized how much it meant to him to be understood. His muscles relaxed. He had plenty of people in his corner.

She surrounded herself with intent. Now it was time he did the same.

The only option was to move forward with the project as if nothing had happened.

There was no success without risk.

Chapter Seven

The late afternoon sun warmed the kitchen through the open French doors as the film crew worked take after take. Addi forced herself to keep breathing calmly. In and out, in and out, a neutral look of interest plastered on her face while chaos ensued low in her belly—the "fake it till you make it" mantra running a tight loop in her head. In reality, her heart raced every time Roque stepped close for a question or bid her come to him with a crook of his finger or tilt of his head.

She wasn't even sure what to call this tension he was stirring up in her. Anxiety over keeping her job, fascination with watching him work, anticipation of the few times each hour his attention would land on her, those blue eyes stopping her where she stood. Or maybe the heart attack she almost had when she saw him eyeing the attic door in the hallway.

He'd either been walking around her home with his phone stuck to his ear like a permanent appendage, or had been gone altogether, meeting with potential investors she'd been able to get ahold of last-minute, due to that magic Gallagher name.

The stress rolling off him was palpable, but he still greeted everyone with a smile and held it all in check while they continued filming. But she couldn't be the only one to notice how the strain in his eyes deepened his crow's feet or the hard set of his jaw.

He didn't have anything to be worried about. Hollywood always recovered. Sure, they'd lost an investor. Big deal. Where there was one there were many. The industry was an ocean of sharks waiting for the next drop of Gallagher bait. She, on the other hand, had reason to worry. She needed to get paid.

She hoped the studio he worked for appreciated how impassioned he was for this project. The fact it was his big chance to make a name for himself powered a lot of that passion, she could see that, but few people showed the kind of passion and dedication she saw in him. He really had nothing to worry about. The money he needed to finish the film would come. Hollywood was swimming in it.

She smiled with a shake of her head, her eyes tracking Roque's movements through the room. It had been a couple days since he'd asked her about her writing, and she hadn't been able to look at him the same way ever since. She was aware of him before, but this was ridiculous. Like how the lower edge of his full bottom lip squared off instead of curved. Or worse, the way he remained completely present when having a conversation, as if no one else existed but the person in front of him.

The lip was tempting, but the personal focus was devastating.

How many times had she had conversations with past boyfriends where the glazed-over look in their eyes pissed her off more than the stupidity that often fell from their mouths? Too many to count.

Ever a people-watcher, she'd increasingly noticed she

was living in a world of people who only listened in order to respond, instead of listening in order to understand. Listening for themselves, not for her. But Roque was a genuine listener—he even seemed to relax when deep in conversation, as if he had all the time in the world.

Addi couldn't resist the allure. Leaning back against the living room wall, she watched him speak to SueAnn, knowing from experience she'd feel relevant, heard. It was almost a superpower, really. Roque wielded it with grace and purpose, like a natural leader.

"See something you like?"

Addi snapped upright, and before the momentum carried her too far forward and onto her face, she slapped a hand to the wall and caught herself. "Damn it, you scared me, Jimmy."

The big man simply raised a brow. "Guilty conscience? Though I can't figure out why. You're single, he's single."

She swung to face him, and with a hand to his chest, tried to push him back in the direction of the hallway. The damn man remained immovable, like a brick wall. Mortification heated her skin as he opened his mouth again to speak. Panicked, she slapped her hand over his moving lips. His eyes widened, and he stilled.

She almost giggled at the shocked look on his face. Addi doubted a man like Jimmy had people slap his mouth shut very often. "Oh my God, I didn't mean for it to be that hard, but would you please shut up," she pleaded in a fierce whisper. She peeked over her shoulder to see Roque still deep in conversation—small favors. On an exhale, she turned back to Jimmy and slowly lowered her hand, but what she really wanted to do was wipe the mirth off his face.

Jimmy pressed his mouth in a tight line holding back a chuckle. "Woman, I don't know if you're brave or stupid, but there is no question you're interested."

"No one is interested in anyone here. For Pete's sake, I

was simply watching the crew." She swung her upturned hand in a wide arc. "This whole process is new to me. I find it... intriguing."

"You find *something* intriguing, all right."

His teasing reminded her of Luca. Though she adored Jimmy, the last thing she needed was another annoying sibling. She already had two. She suspected one more would be the end of her. Throwing him a warning look, Addi squeezed her hands into tight fists. "Shut. Up."

A deep voice sounded from behind her. "Yeah, Jimmy. Shut up. But first, fill me in."

Addi closed her eyes and wished the floor would swallow her. Talk about timing. She snapped her eyes open wide, pleading with Jimmy to keep his assessments to himself.

Roque draped his arm around Addi and pulled her in tight. "I'm dying to hear this story."

The heat of his body burned along Addi's whole right side to her hip. The cologne he wore wafted under her nose, lingering and teasing with something more, something Roque alone exuded.

She blinked twice, pulling herself out of her hormones and into reality. The smirk on Jimmy's face made her wish she'd smacked him harder.

"Addi will have to fill you in on that, boss." Jimmy laughed.

"Funny, hearing you call me boss sounds so different than when Addi does it."

Jimmy threw Addi a wink. "Hear that?"

Roque raised his brows and looked from Jimmy to Addi. She'd never wanted to kick someone so much in her life.

Jimmy jutted his thumb over his shoulder. "I gotta run. I have a few more papers I need to get signed at the courthouse."

Addi jumped at the opportunity to escape Roque's inquisitive gaze. When he looked at her like that she felt a hair's breadth from confessing all her sins, and she couldn't have that. Hollywood money, that was all she needed to remind herself. Aunt Addi's home was her home, her legacy. "Need a tour guide?"

"I'm from around here. Besides, I figure you have someone to do—"

Addi inhaled so quickly she choked and fell into a fit of coughs.

"*Something* to do," Jimmy said with a wink and a sloppy salute.

Roque rubbed her back as she fought for breath. "Here, let's get you a glass of water." He grabbed her hand and led her into the kitchen. Addi could feel the calluses that ran along the upper ridge of his palm and wondered how they came to be. Roque was a working man, but by no means a man of labor, not that she'd seen, anyway. She could feel the light abrasive rub against her sensitive palm all the way to her toes.

In the kitchen, she leaned against the counter and watched as Roque took a glass from the cupboard and filled it with water. He moved so fluidly, so sure of himself. She imagined no one questioned his capability about anything. That must be a good feeling.

Her coughs slowed and she could breathe again—at least she could if Roque would keep his distance. Turning toward her, he offered her the glass and rested his hip against the counter, watching her take a few tentative sips.

"Better?"

She sighed and finished the glass. "Yes. Much."

Addi stared at him, trying to read what was going on behind those brilliant blue eyes. He looked so serious with his brows drawn together and his lips pressed in a tight line. So stressed.

She reached up and ran her thumb pad from the inside of one brow to the outer edge. An unconscious move to help soothe his tension.

He stilled, and she froze with her palm against his cheek.

How in the hell did that get there? The heat of Roque's cheek seeped into her skin, and she snatched her hand away, finding herself in need of a fan on an eighty-degree day.

Casually, she stepped away. "Here, let me get you some coffee. Or is it too late?"

He shook his head. "I'll be up for a while yet. A cup sounds great." Crossing his arms over his chest, he watched her.

Fidgety under his scrutiny—or her guilty conscience—she sighed. "What?"

"Just watching the master. So, what was it you had to tell me?"

She slowed in her process of measuring grounds into the French press, resenting the heat rushing up her neck. With a nervous laugh, she waved away his question. "Oh, nothing." She wracked her brain to come up with something he'd swallow without too much difficulty. "I just got a rejection on my manuscript the other day is all, and I didn't want to talk about it."

He reached his hand out to rub her shoulder. "I'm sorry. I know that has to be so hard."

Nodding, she poured hot water into the press. "It is. And it never gets any easier. I just need a day or two to lick my wounds, but then I'll keep moving forward." She caught him staring at her mouth. "Onward and upward, right?"

He snapped his eyes back to hers. "Absolutely. You don't quit if it's your dream."

"Any luck yet? Speaking of dreams."

Dropping his head forward on a sigh, he turned his back to the counter and palmed the edge with his hands. "Nothing yet."

She poured two cups, then handed him one. "It'll all work out."

He held her gaze, opened his mouth to say something, but never had the chance. Doug Kemper came storming in through the French doors. "Gallagher. I need a word."

The ease she'd seen in him a moment before disappeared, his jaw clenched tight, and he pushed away from the counter. "Of course."

The man eyed him, then nailed Addi with a look.

"Oh." She grabbed her cup. "Let me just—"

Roque put a hand out to stop her. "No, Addi, finish what you were doing. And I hate to ask, but I left my dry cleaning at my condo and I need my suit for a meeting tonight."

"I'll take care of it."

He dipped his chin, looked at the director, then headed toward the back hallway. "Doug and I will speak in the back room."

Addi raised her cup to her mouth for a sip. Her guest room door slammed, and she flinched. Quickly, she moved her cup out in front of her, trying to steady it before getting scalded. Apparently, the director wasn't happy. Raised voices floated from the back room, and she bit her lip. She didn't see Roque's stress easing any time soon.

As she prepared the catered dinner for the crew, she volleyed a few questions about the heated argument in the backroom. Moving the meal onto the front porch for a change of scenery and to put as much distance between the back of the house and crew helped. Everyone seemed on edge, worried about what the argument meant, whether or not their jobs were at stake.

Addi raised her hand to stop the concerns. "You guys. Come on. You all know Roque way better than I do, but I am confident he wouldn't keep any of you in a situation that would leave you hanging. Whatever's going on, let him work it out. It's what he does, isn't it?"

Nods and grunts of agreement drifted into casual banter.

They emptied their plates, shoved down a few cookies, and then headed back to work. Once the crew was in place, finishing a few last scenery snapshots, Addi grabbed her keys.

She made the trip to Roque's condo faster than she thought. The building was only a few miles north on Pacific Coast Highway—Highway 1—and boasted ocean front property. Curious about the kind of home he lived in, she skipped the elevator and took the stairs two at a time. Thank goodness he only lived on the fourth floor. Breathless by the time she reached his door, she sucked in air and let herself in.

The first thing she noticed was the scent of him. Light and lingering, she'd know this was his place even if she hadn't had his key. The lines were clean and simple, shades of gray with understated pops of orange. Neat, clean, and everything in its place. Just like the man who lived there.

Walking through the front room, she trailed her fingers along the smooth surface of his end tables and across the leather of his couch. The silence was a welcome break to her ears after days of people being in her house—and she was a people person. But even the most extroverted sorts needed some quiet now and again. No clothes hung from his living room chairs or the kitchen. Maybe in his bedroom.

She paused along the short hallway, smiling at a picture of him flanked by his aunt and uncle, Raquel and Martin Gallagher. They took it on themselves to know everything that was going on with their kids. And "kids" meant any thirty-something even remotely connected to the art community.

Hell, both of them had read the three manuscripts she had out on submission. Martin always gave great feedback on her craft, and Raquel never failed to help her flesh out content.

She studied the grin on Roque's face, a crooked little smirk, really. He had to be all of eighteen in this picture. Her eyes trailed to the next one, and she stopped short. A beautiful woman, practically Raquel's twin, smiled in the black and white glossy, crouched by a little boy with wavy black hair, his arms thrown around her neck. His mother. There was such joy in her face. He was most certainly loved.

Moving on down the hall, she entered his bedroom and spotted the suit on a bench at the foot of his bed. She draped it over her arm and turned to leave. An old black lacquered bookshelf caught her attention. Reel-to-reel films lined one side of each shelf, alternating from the top to the bottom, then laser discs and VCR tapes were stacked as if they were art opposite the reels. *Gone with the Wind, Casablanca,* and *Until We Meet Again* graced his shelves. He was a classic movie junkie. She grinned. Another reason to like the man.

Resisting the urge to go through his medicine cabinet, or check how he folded his underwear, she tightened her hold on his suit and left his condo, locking the door behind her. The practice of self-control cost her a lot. More than anything, she wanted to go back inside and snoop around. It was only fair, since he and his whole crew had been through every square inch of her home, including her bathroom. But she'd already learned more about him than was safe. He was insanely tidy, loved his family, and collected old films. She found him intriguing. She liked him. And he was admittedly the sexiest man she'd ever laid eyes on. All sorts of ideas popped into her mind, but she pushed them down, lifting her chin with pride. She could be an adult when she needed to.

Roque was on his way out when she pulled in, pausing long enough to grab his suit and tell her everyone had gone home and to be at the bungalow by eight sharp the next morning. She snorted. Eight a.m. was easy. After the hours they'd been keeping, eight a.m. would let her sleep in.

A light bubbling sensation filled her chest as she went inside and locked up. Roque's check had cleared, which meant it was time to make it official and pay the lump sum she owed now. Half her battle had been successfully waged and won. She grabbed the bottle of champagne she'd been saving for the day she was offered a contract and scrambled up the stairs like she was being chased. She had never gotten over that sensation, no matter how old she was, and clicked on the lamp in record time with a sigh of relief.

With the lamp covered by a white pillowcase to help dim the light, she opened her laptop, then popped the cork on the bottle. Getting that contract would be the perfect occasion to enjoy a little bubbly, but so was saving her home.

Settling into her customary position, she pulled her computer onto her lap and set the bottle of champagne next to her bedding. A few clicks later, her finger hovered over the submit button. She wasn't fooled into thinking this was it. She knew she still needed to save for next year's taxes—the whole reason she was sleeping on the floor of her attic in the first place—which would be coming soon, not to mention general living expenses. But, damn, it felt all sorts of good to reach this point. With a small squeal, she pushed the submit button, effectively clearing her debt.

She lifted the bottle high in a silent toast of gratitude, sniffing against the tears burning behind her lids. She took a swig and the bubbles eased the tightening of her throat. Warm feelings for Roque rushed forward as the champagne rushed down. She was thankful. She took another long swallow.

It was nothing but lust and transference. All her happy feelings about keeping her home needed a target, and apparently they were shooting for Roque. No matter; simple lust could be easily remedied. He liked her flirting with him, she could tell, even if he didn't encourage her.

No.

Addi stared at her computer screen but saw nothing except Roque's chiseled features—daring her. It wasn't as if she was a permanent employee; if she were, then the answer would be clear.

Her gig was temporary. A means to an end. But one she needed to keep until the film was finished and, in the meantime, get a writing contract. Maybe even a little freelance work to fill the gaps. Her job was temporary, so a little fling wouldn't ruin anything.

Her conscience nagged at her, but she shut it down quickly. She wasn't screwing over Roque; she was screwing over Hollywood. There was a big difference.

Which would leave her free and clear to *actually* screw Roque. A giggle drew her fingers to her lips. She drank from the bottle again, ending on a hiccup. There were a hell of a lot worse decisions than having a fling with a super-hot, driven man who had a penchant for bossing her around and watching classic movies.

Another burp escaped, and she slapped a hand over her mouth with a chuckle. She was doing damn well on her own. She no longer needed saving.

But Roque might.

She liked a challenge, and something told her he'd resist.

At first.

Chapter Eight

Roque jogged along the sandy beach, hoping some of his stress would wash out to sea with the surf, and if not the stress, then he'd gladly be taken by a maverick wave at this point.

He'd spent the past forty-eight hours on the phone in between their weekend filming, trying to find an investor to replace Fairmont. For an industry that never sleeps, a hell of a lot of people were unavailable. Apparently, some folks actually had plans and a life over the weekend. Lucky fuckers.

The last few days, Addi had been his saving grace. Managing Kemper and keeping his crew steady had helped more than she could have known. The last thing he'd wanted was her underfoot, but he'd have been knocked on his ass without her. He shook his head. How the hell her professional organizational skills didn't translate to her personal life was a mystery.

By the time he'd left the bungalow Friday night he'd been ready to strangle someone, preferably Kemper. The damn director spoke to him as if he were doing Roque a favor, which was a load of bullshit times ten. Roque might be trying to separate himself a bit from the Gallagher name, but it was exactly because he was a Gallagher that Kemper had signed on. Associating himself with Roque would only help his career. And that was the source of Kemper's irritation. He didn't like that Roque was better known in the industry than he was. Especially since Kemper didn't think Roque had earned it. But the damn arrogant man didn't need to worry. The whole purpose of this film was to launch Roque on his own. Kemper was lucky to be part of it. Roque might question his ability to find another investor in time, but he sure as shit did not question his talent, his vision, as a producer.

His lungs and muscles burned, but he dug in and ran faster. The pain was a welcome distraction from the frustrations with the film and the buzz of energy washing over him whenever he was around Addi. He smelled honey now, even when he wasn't with her. It was as if it permanently absorbed into his clothes and skin or some shit like that. And he couldn't get past how jumpy she'd been the other day when he'd walked in to find her and Jimmy deep in conversation. The idea that there might be something between the two of them sent a surge through him, propelling him forward even faster. Why the hell should he care?

By the time he approached the deck of his building, his chest seized in protest and sweat ran into his eyes, stinging as if he'd taken a plunge in the Pacific. Using the hem of his shirt, he swiped at his face and over his head. "Fuck."

The sun slowly disappeared into the horizon, casting a warm orange glow onto the white Trex decking. He sunk to the steps, dropping his head between his knees, and concentrated on filling his lungs. He welcomed the effort, the need, to focus on anything but the phone calls he had to make that no one was answering. Besides, those who did answer only offered a regretful but firm "no."

He made his way to his condo, pausing as he closed the

door behind him. It smelled of honey. He chuckled in self-derision. Losing his mind really wasn't going to fit into his schedule at this point. The scent must have been from when she stopped to pick up his clothes. Walking through his home, he imagined her there. Giggling at his photo or trailing her fingers along the back of the couch. He'd forgotten his dry cleaning had been on the bed, which meant she'd been in his room.

An image of her sprawled on his sheets in nothing but a look of sassy challenge rose unbidden in his mind, and he shook his head. What the hell was he thinking? Sex was a good stress cure, but didn't have the time for complications.

Besides, the last thing he needed was to disappoint another woman by not being there on time, forgetting a birthday party, canceling on dinners with parents. He furrowed his brow at the memories. He hadn't meant to miss any of it. And it always seemed to be the most important events he screwed up.

After making quick work in the shower, he dragged himself to bed and made a list of contacts he'd call in the morning. Somebody would say yes. Somebody had to.

After a restless night of little sleep and a lot of worry, Roque stepped through the front door of the bungalow, greeted by the enticing combination of freshly brewed coffee and honey. What the hell did she do, bathe in it?

"Morning, boss." Addi walked up in some sort of all-white jumpsuit thing, the straight edges of her hair skimming her shoulders. The crispness of it showed off the silky gold of her skin. And why the hell was he noticing her skin?

The corners of his lips pulled up on their own accord. "Morning."

Taking the cup of coffee she offered, he headed toward the back guest room. "I have calls to make. Is Kemper in?"

"Not yet."

"Let me know when he is. No other interruptions." He slowed. "Please."

With a salute, Addi grinned. "Got it."

He looked her over. She was practically glowing. "You look like you had a good weekend."

"I did. I got a lot of writing done and fleshed out the motivation for one of my protagonists."

"Good." At least somebody was making progress. With a nod, he slid into the guest room.

A few hours later, Roque pinched the bridge of his nose, trying to relieve some tension. Not one of his contacts came through, so he took a break and checked in with the film crew. The director was a no-show, so they focused on scenery shots. But they were losing light, emotions were running high, and egos were suffering a beating. Scene take after scene take, and it still wasn't right.

They called to break and released the crew for the night. Nothing more to be done until tomorrow, anyway. He sighed. How the fuck could this day go any worse?

The front door swung open, and he looked up to find Martin Gallagher sweeping into the room, half the crew swarming his uncle at once.

He sat back and observed. Martin Gallagher wasn't called the father of Malibu for nothing. He mentored and taught, supported and created opportunities.

It was a special privilege to be one of the children. Roque had experienced the phenomena since birth. Raquel and Martin cared. They nurtured with high praise and higher expectations. It made his mood lighten.

A little.

Martin finished with his fawning fans and approached Roque. A firm hug and pat on the shoulder brought both men to stand side by side as the rest of the crew filed out the front door.

Martin waved as the last straggler made an exit, then turned back to Roque. "How's it going, my boy?"

Roque sighed. "As expected. I lost a major investor. But you already know that."

Martin furrowed bushy salt-and-pepper brows over his piercing blue eyes. Martin had the look of a Nordic Sean Connery—the kind of man women of any age still swooned over. Roque had made quite the study of it as a teen, when all he wanted was to get laid.

Rubbing a hand over his face, Roque blew out a breath. The house was blessedly quiet. He'd been at the end of his creative energies and needed space, perspective. "You know how it is. Ups and downs. One day you make magic, the next…shit."

Martin grabbed his arm. "How are you, really?"

Roque stilled. The week marked two years since his mother had died. On top of everything else, he couldn't handle the reminder, much less a conversation.

He moved into the kitchen and straight to the refrigerator. "Want a beer?"

Martin took a seat at the table. "Roque."

"Not now. Please." He looked back to soften the tone. "What's in stock?"

Roque read off the list, then grabbed two of Martin's choice.

A quick twist of the wrist and it wasn't long before both men took long swallows in the comfortable quiet of twilight.

His uncle raised his bottle in salute. "Quite the collection."

"All Addison Dekker's doing. She's working as my assistant while we're filming at the bungalow. A sticking point in the contract."

"Oh, Addi. Good girl. We've known her family for years. She's a good writer."

Roque almost scoffed at the "good girl" comment. Addi was the furthest thing in his mind from being a girl. A women, yes, a hot, sexy, too smooth, too tempting woman—yes. Girl? Ha.

Just as quickly, his mind latched onto the "good writer" comment. "Of course, you know her family. And her brother and sister, too, right?"

Martin shrugged.

"You've read her stuff? She's determined to break into the industry."

Martin nodded. "I believe she will. She writes romantic novels, full of passion. She's got a knack for placing old world expectations on modern heroes and heroines. Quite good."

He wasn't surprised. She exuded confidence. Even when she wasn't feeling it. She had a compelling gift of gravitation: everyone wanted to talk with her, help her, and simply be near her.

But what about Addi? Her hopes, dreams—fears? He should know those, too.

Roque pulled up short. Fuck, the last thing he needed to be worried about was Addi's dreams. Hell, he'd barely had time to remember his own name. What he needed to do was find a fucking investor. Frustration sent a restless energy through his limbs, and he pulled another long swallow from his bottle simply as a reason to move.

"Christ."

"What's that?" Martin leaned forward, as if he hadn't heard correctly.

Roque grunted. "Nothing. How's Aunt Raquel? Her art exhibit is later this week, isn't it?"

"I hate missing it, but off on location. She's great. Energetic as ever. New ideas, new hobbies. I'm exhausted."

Roque laughed. "She's keeping you young."

"She's keeping me relevant. I need to work in order to back all of her projects."

Roque's bark of laughter bounced off the kitchen walls. His aunt had a knack for making money, a savvy business woman if he'd ever known one. Uncle Martin continued to work because he couldn't not. He loved to direct, to create, and interact with people. The man couldn't sit still any more than his wife could.

They were perfect together.

Martin emptied his bottle. "Thanks for the drink. So..." He rubbed his hands together. "What will you do, my boy?"

Well, hell. Wasn't that the question?

He remained noncommittal. "What I do."

Martin nodded. "Good. I understand why you're doing what you're doing. But I must say, I hate not getting in on it."

Roque appreciated the vote of confidence. "Even if you wanted to, you have your shit sunk into your latest project, and you know I know it."

With a few undecipherable grunts, Martin waved his hand. "Where is Addison anyway? I miss her energy. She makes a room shine."

"Yes, she does." The innuendo in Roque's reply didn't register until Martin's smile widened. Roque put out a hand. "Nothing—"

His uncle stood up. "Boy, you don't owe me any explanations, just make sure you—"

Roque stood up. "Stop, there is nothing—"

Martin raised a brow.

"Shit. Go. Go home and hassle Aunt Raquel. Tell her I love her."

His uncle's laugh mocked him until the slamming of the front door cut off the echo.

Throwing the bottles into the recycling, Roque turned out the kitchen lights and made his way into the front room. Where the hell was Addi?

He pulled up short. Fuck, it had been a long day. She must have gone back to her hotel. And why wouldn't she? It was late, and he'd sent the crew home. She was basically crew, but there was nothing basic about her.

His phone buzzed. With blurry eyes, he read through the list of his appointments for the next two days. "Shit." He had a meeting with his financial advisor first thing in the morning. If he hoped to figure out how to save his film, he needed a clear head, and that meant some actual sleep. Though he knew better than to think he'd get any.

The next morning found him sitting across from his financial advisor, Gerald, with a head no clearer than the day before. He'd hoped for better news, but the constant movement of the man's head back and forth in the universal symbol of *no* made him want to punch something.

"You can't, Mr. Gallagher. Look. You hired me for a reason. Trying to sink more money into this project will be detrimental. And honestly, there is no way to make the assets you do have available liquid within the timetable you gave me. You need to find another option."

The tightening between Roque's shoulders ground down in a biting grip, making him lose the little patience he had left. "I don't have any other options, Gerald. God damn it." He dropped his fist to the table.

Immediate regret had him lifting his hands. "I'm sorry. This had been a tough week."

What the fuck was he going to do? He felt his future slipping out of his grasp. All the sacrificing, the late nights, the missed memories, could not have been for nothing.

The following few days were more of the same. Unfortunate *no*s, but exuberant well-wishes.

If one more person wished him good luck, he was going to fucking lose his shit.

Slipping his phone into his front pocket, he slouched in the antique chair in Addi's guest room. He was running out of ideas. His chest tightened, making it hard to breathe, so he moved to the day bed and sunk into the heavily pillowed corner, stretching his legs out over the edge.

The door of the guest room swung open, and Addi bustled through, stopping short. "Oh! You're still here. I'd thought you'd left."

He flung an arm over his eyes, void of the energy to reply.

"No luck, huh?"

He slit one eye open just enough to glower.

Crossing the room, she lowered onto the bed next to him, and the heat of her soft body warmed his side although he hadn't realized he'd been cold. The silk of her palm slid over the top of his hand, and he turned it over, letting her fingers entwine with his. Human contact, her touch, was like a salve to the wounds caused by so many days of rejection in a row.

"We're friends by now, aren't we?"

He paused, surprised by her question. "Well, yeah. I think so."

She turned to face him. "Let your family help. Don't lose your dream because of some misplaced pride or stubbornness."

No one understood, and trying to explain was beginning to be more work than the film itself. He sunk lower on the bed, exhaustion making his stomach turn. "Addi, I don't think I have the energy to explain."

"It's just...I hate seeing you so stressed. You're over-worked, you don't sleep. All week you've been running from meeting to meeting. We're holding things together here as well as we can, but I know production is falling behind. I'd hate to see you lose this after you told me how much it means to you."

He studied the genuine concern on her face and squeezed her fingers before pushing up from the bed. "This film is everything to me; it's not just the film itself but how I get it made, and what *I* do with it." Sliding his hands into his pockets, he paced the room. "I've been trying to distance myself from the family reputation. Trying to be taken seriously for my own talent. Not because I'm not proud of my family or who I am, but *because* I want to know I made it on my own merit. The unique vision I know I bring to the table. Being a Gallagher, using the Gallagher name, the Gallagher money…it all muddies the water. I have to do this my way, with my skill. Independent of the legacy my father and uncle have already created."

Addi smiled. The kind of smile that lit a face from the inside out. She understood. Relief swamped him, and he leaned against the wall, needing the support.

She stood and stepped in front of him. In her usual teasing manner he was beginning to love, she walked her fingers up the buttons of his shirt and loosened his tie. "Well then, Roque Gallagher, you're just going to have to figure out how to make it happen."

He blew out a breath, enjoying the teasing light in her eyes. "I need a miracle."

She tilted her head. "You'll find one."

Pulling his tie from around his neck with a zip, she held his gaze.

He narrowed his gaze. "What are you doing?"

Addi stepped closer. Her heat washed up and over his chest, and he clenched his fists at his sides.

"All work and no play makes a producer a dull, though very attractive, boy." She ran her finger over one brow, then the next.

"Addi."

"Shhhhhhh…"

He gripped her hips, his fingers flexing at the sensation of warm muscle beneath the silk of her pants.

Smiling, she tilted her head. "You work too hard. You need a little fun."

He shook his head. "I don't have time."

She leaned closer, her honey scent wafting up around his head. Her warmth radiated into him and straight to his dick. God damn it, if she was going to kiss him, she should do it already. He was so tired of resisting her and couldn't take her teasing any more. And why should he? Wanting her was becoming a larger distraction than her presence. His fingers found their way to her waist and flexed into her flesh.

Wetting her lower lip, she brought her cheek next to his, her warm breath causing a shiver to run down his spine.

He turned his face, his mouth hovering a hair's breadth from hers, every muscle screaming for her to close the distance.

She whispered, "Your aunt's jewelry show. Come with me."

He blinked twice. "My aunt's show?"

Laughing, she placed her hands on his shoulders and gave a little shake. "Lighten up, Gallagher. You looked like I was going to bite you. You're working too hard. You need a break, some inspiration, a chance to rub elbows with the industry. Let's go to your aunt's show. It's only one night. A chance to de-stress."

That was not the kind of de-stressing he'd thought she had in mind.

And thank God, because he didn't think he had it in him tonight to make a smart decision if it had anything to do with kissing and Addi. He had a feeling one wouldn't be enough.

He let out his pent-up breath in one long exhale, the corner of his mouth curving up on one side. Damn vixen. "De-stress." Maybe if he went, his aunt wouldn't send his uncle around to check up on him. No one was fooled by that little visit. "You might be on to something."

She winked at him. "Oh. I most certainly am…boss." Tapping him on the end of his nose, she stepped through the door.

He continued to stare long after she'd disappeared down the hall. Either all the stress was making him crazy, or she had something up her sleeve.

Chapter Nine

As the Mother of Malibu, Raquel Martin nurtured with a flood of love that entitled her to be obeyed when she requested the presence of her "children." And as rebellious as Addi sometimes felt, saying no to Raquel never crossed her mind, especially since she'd missed the grand opening. But finding herself on Roque's arm, dressed in a short sheath of champagne silk — thanks to Chase's closet — turned attending the already exciting event into an adventure.

Though she hadn't been able to go a few months ago thanks to her ex — he'd been very controlling, and she'd let him be that way, until she'd finally gotten her head out of her ass — her sister had been there and hadn't stopped raving about the talent of designer Liv Karsten. Raquel was throwing a series of galas that told a story through the artist's jewelry. Quite clever, to Addi's writer brain. She loved beautiful things and had been looking forward to seeing all the pieces firsthand. Having Roque by her side posed a bit of a distraction, though. If her mind wasn't clouded by the spicy scent of his cologne or the accidental brush of his arm against hers, she was fighting the rising panic of being discovered. The exhibit followed on the heels of a late shoot, and he'd promised to drop her off at the hotel and pick her up in the morning.

No reason for her to bother with her car.

Yeah, right. No reason. Crap.

A knot twisted in her gut. Determined to enjoy the evening, Addi lifted her chin. Going together was her idea, after all.

"You okay?"

"Of course."

"You don't lie well."

She snapped her eyes back to him. "What? Why would you say that?"

He grabbed her hand. She prayed it wasn't sweaty but couldn't think of a smooth way to retrieve it.

"I had a girlfriend once who was a terrible liar. She had a habit of blowing her bangs out of her face every time she tried. Luckily for me I figured it out pretty quickly."

Addi casually studied her nails. "So, what did you do? When she lied, I mean."

He gave a dismissive wave. "We broke up. I can't stand being lied to. I just can't get past it. And if I can't trust someone, there's no reason to stay. I've been burned too many times. You know?"

Quickly pasting a smile on her face, she turned her gaze to his but found she couldn't hold it. "Absolutely." She glanced around. "Look. This is fantastic." At first she was worried about where the hell she was going to sleep tonight, but now she was freaked out that he'd be able to tell when she was lying. With a mental curse, she shook out her free hand. The one he held was surely a sweaty mess by now. Pushing her fears to the far recesses of her brain, she forced herself to focus on the night in front of her.

The gallery, a glistening and glimmering abalone shell

paradise, washed patrons in reflections of deep purples and midnight blues. The exhibit itself was a stunning masterpiece, and she hadn't even glimpsed a piece of the jewelry yet.

Roque pulled her through the crowd of hushed jewelry connoisseurs. Losing her hand in that callused palm of his made her heart race and her mind cloud as if all she could concentrate on was how his skin felt against hers. She clutched her other hand in a tight fist. Keeping her hormones at bay wasn't going to be easy, but Addi wasn't a stranger to hard work.

The film was making progress, but Roque was under an immense load of stress. She was quite surprised he hadn't found another backer by now. Hollywood always seemed to be circling for a bite of the next big thing. And anyone in their right mind could see he was it.

Walking through the tables, she whistled. Raquel had an eye for beauty and how to display it to its best potential.

While Roque studied a pair of cufflinks, Addi studied him. The man was drop-dead gorgeous to start, but suit him up in Armani with a silk tie and pocket square, and she feared she'd get pregnant by simply looking at him. His dark hair fell back in short waves from his chiseled features and, as he considered the artwork in his hand, his eyes took on an intensity that she felt to her very core.

A vision of him focusing that same intensity on her turned said core to liquid, and she stepped away, faking a casual stance with one foot crossed over the other.

Pull yourself together, woman.

"Don't you think? Addison?"

She snapped to attention at the sound of Raquel's voice, almost falling over her entwined feet. Roque dropped the cufflinks and grabbed her by the arms before she teetered past no return. Heat shot up her chest and face, stinging her ears as she finally got her feet under control once again.

Raquel gathered the cufflinks from the velvet-covered

table. "Darling, please. These are works of art."

Roque held Addi for a brief second longer before sliding his hands down her arms, running his fingers over her hands to her fingertips.

Heat rose to her hairline. Roque gave her a questioning stare. Then, turning to Raquel, he nodded. "I don't disagree, but it was the cufflinks or Addi."

Raquel looked him over, intrigued. If Addi hadn't been watching, she'd have missed the subtle switch.

Oh no.

The last thing she needed was for the Mother of Malibu to get any ideas. Controlling her own interest was challenging enough.

She should just jump the man and get it over with. No harm, no foul.

Her eyes perused the table, and her hand drifted to her chest. With sincere delight, she stepped between the two and slid her hands under a necklace of black abalone spread out like a fan. "Ohhh…"

"Exquisite choice, darling. With your height, the piece would be displayed to perfection."

The price tag hidden respectfully against the underside of the largest shell snuffed out any dream of wearing the beautiful piece, and Addi closed her mouth against the immediate disappointment climbing up her throat. Careful to keep her expression serene, she ran a fingertip one more time over the necklace and returned it to its perch of honor.

"Darling, it was made for you." Raquel's protest almost made her laugh. Even corporate America hadn't paid her enough to acquire that gem.

She shook her head and, ignoring the questioning look from Roque, she reached out to Raquel. "Is Martin here?" Nothing distracted Raquel better than the mention of her husband.

Necklace forgotten, Raquel dove into one of her favorite

topics with fervor. Martin hated to miss it, but a remote location hunt for his newest film with his location manager couldn't be put off.

"Is that the film Gage is directing and starring in?"

Raquel smiled. "It's going to be fabulous."

Martin had taken Gage Cutler under his wing. When Gage had taken an interest in directing, beyond acting, Martin was all too happy to offer up an opportunity.

Opportunity. What she wouldn't give for one. A case of wanting tightened her belly. She wanted to write, she wanted to publish, she wanted to be a sought-after author. The sensation of wanting was all too familiar.

She stared at Roque as he listened to his aunt with complete focus. *I want Roque Gallagher.*

"Oh, shut up," she said, *sotto voce*.

"What was that, darling?"

Again, Addi snapped to attention, this time keeping both feet firmly on the ground. "Oh, I said, 'shut up'…look at this ring." Hastily, she grabbed the closest ring off the display and held it out to Raquel.

She glanced at the ring, then back at Addi with a quizzical look before turning back to Roque.

Addi rolled the ring onto her opened palm and inhaled a gasp. The ring was male genitalia made of abalone wrapped in a circle to fit a size seven. Just her size.

She smothered a giggle with her hand when the title, *Wrapped Around Her Finger*, took on an all too literal meaning.

"How are you really, darling?" Raquel asked Roque.

The concern in her question yanked Addi out of her self-amusement.

Roque stilled, his face expressionless. "I'm fine."

"It'll be two years this weekend."

He remained unmoved, and Addi found herself drawn to

his side. She'd heard about his mother, Roxanne Gallagher. Another dynamo, not surprising since she was Raquel's younger sister. Breast cancer took her and everyone else by surprise. Roque's reaction took Addi by surprise, too. He stood like granite.

Raquel clasped her hands together. "Oh, she loved you." A sadness filled her eyes as she studied Roque's stoic form. "I wonder how she'd feel knowing the real reason she chose your name materialized after all."

Addi slid a surreptitious glance to Roque's face. His jaw clenched, and he stared at a point above Raquel's head. She placed her hand on his upper arm, the steely strength beneath her fingers not unlike stone itself. Her touch jerked him from his trance, and his eyes roamed her face for a beat. The pain she witnessed there made her suck in her breath, made her want to ease the tension from his brow. Her heart gave a quick thump.

Life returned to his blue gaze, and he turned back to his aunt. "I loved her, too, as I love you." He pulled in a breath. "Addi and I need to make our rounds and get going. We have an early shoot tomorrow to make up for some lost time on the film."

Addi stepped back as Raquel wrapped her arms around her nephew's giant form. She whispered something in his ear, and his brows drew together. He shot a look at Addi then quickly back to Raquel as she stepped back. "Okay, off with you." She embraced Roque one more time, then Addi.

Against Addi's ear, she whispered, "Take care of him. He's hurting."

Addi shook her head against the implication as her heart yearned to rid him of the closed facade he retreated to in times of stress.

His stillness usually amused her, but in this circumstance it made her feel a myriad of things. A twist in her gut, a squeeze to her heart—afraid.

Sticky, sweet, unwelcome things. Emotions weren't going to help her where Roque Gallagher was concerned. A horizontal romp would, but no emotions. She'd have to keep a tight lock on those bad boys, because she couldn't afford this softening toward him.

Literally.

After leaving the exhibit and picking up a couple bottles of wine, Roque drove like he was being chased by the paparazzi. Bad joke. Addi shook the morbid thought from her head.

She gripped the door's arm rest, knuckles white. "Look, I'm all for wild, crazy fun, but I'd like to still be alive after."

Roque shot a confused look her way, as if surprised to find her in the car.

His blue eyes burned right through her before he focused on the road again. Shaking the itchy sensation from the nape of her neck—she'd revisit that reaction at another time, right now her life was at stake—she turned toward him. "Can you slow down a bit?"

The car immediately slowed. "Sorry, lost in thought."

"No kidding."

He continued to drive in silence.

"Can I ask where we're going?" Her nerves played tag in her stomach waiting for his response. *Please don't say my hotel. Please don't say my hotel.*

"The beach."

Immediate relief carried with it a not-so-friendly consequence as nausea rolled in her gut, chasing after her panic. Pulling in a few deep breaths, she willed her stomach to settle down.

Chase had begrudgingly set her up with a mailbox at The Huntington Place along with documentation of her stay, but not an actual room. She didn't know how she'd explain it if he'd been heading to "her place" for a drink. *Phew.*

Roque pulled into the parking lot and cut the engine. Grabbing the wine, he got out, and she had to scramble to catch up with him.

Counting backward from ten, she followed a few steps behind him. "Do you really want me here?"

Roque swung around, his expression a naked canvas of raw emotion.

She seized on her breath, but just as quickly his face cleared, and he answered with a curt nod.

He continued a few yards closer to the water's edge. Finally, he stopped and sank to the sand. Twisting the caps off both bottles of wine, he handed one to her.

Accepting the Cabernet as she settled in beside him, she lifted it in salute. "Convenient."

Roque took a few long swallows as he stared out over the rolling waves. With gratitude, she sipped hers, letting the full-bodied nectar wash over her tongue and slide down her throat.

She loved wine. And she needed a drink.

A slight breeze danced around them, chilling the air, as they sat in the moonlight.

Addi scooted closer. She wasn't about to freeze for the man.

She nudged his arm. "Do you want to talk about it?"

"What do you think?"

"No, but then again, why'd you bring me out here?"

He tipped his head in acknowledgment, then stared at her, holding her gaze so she couldn't look away if she tried. "Is there something going on between you and Jimmy?"

She choked on her wine, almost spilling it on Chase's dress. Holding the bottle away from her as she brought her breathing back under control, she lifted her hand in question. "What the hell gave you that idea?"

He shrugged. "Just a question. You two are always laughing, and the other day you'd had some sort of inside joke between the two of you. Looked like flirting."

She sputtered, then stopped to pull herself together. Men were such idiots sometimes. How would he feel, knowing he was the inside joke? Well, not him so much as her wanting him. She tried again. "There is nothing going on between me and Jimmy."

He stared out over the cresting waves. "Ever wonder where my parents came up with Roque?"

The switch in conversation caught her by surprise, but Addi considered his question with care. Though she didn't understand why, she understood the reason held meaning. "I've always considered it unique, especially the spelling."

Roque chuckled. "Meaning R-O-C-K would be more apt?"

"You disagree?" She chuckled softly.

He shook his head and continued to drink. "No. But at one time I would have."

She waited. His attempt to pull in air seemed to take effort, like his body resisted the expansion or any movement at all. She reached out and settled her hand on his forearm.

His skin scorched hers even in the coolness of the night, and she resisted the urge to pull away. Not out of fear or the shock in sensation, but because the soft hair that tickled her palm, the heat that radiated through her fingers to her soul, made her want to sink in deeper. Now *that* was terrifying.

But he needed something, and she wasn't willing to take their small connection away.

"The way the story goes, I was an active baby in the womb. So active my mother couldn't sleep, couldn't sit, could barely stand for that matter. In hopes of getting me to calm down, she reached back into her Spanish heritage and named me Roque, which loosely translates to rest."

His voice thickened, tugging Addi along to share the emotion. It seemed his mother's wish came tenfold. She'd never met a man more stubborn and, at times, more immovable than a mountain. Why did that now seem so heartbreaking?

He shifted in the sand and continued talking. "The joke was on her, though, because I came out even more high energy, if that was possible. I'd get into everything, wanted to do…everything. And she was beside me every step of the way, dark circles under her eyes and all. My biggest cheerleader, my champion. She believed in me, for me. She always told me I could be whatever I dreamed."

Sadness filled his voice, and it seemed he spoke from deep in his chest. "And she was so determined not to get in the way that she never told me she was sick and made my dad promise not to, either. They kept it all a secret. They lied. And I'd been working so hard with my head so far up my ass, I hadn't noticed until it was the end."

Blinking back tears, her fingers caressed his forearm, the hairs tickling her pads. He'd ditched his jacket and tie when they'd gotten in the car, and now he sat with his shirt partially unbuttoned and the sleeves rolled up to his elbows.

He raised his other hand, then let it drop to his lap. "My mom loved the whole concept of this film. I talked with her about it a lot, so much, before I knew she was sick. She'd want me to finish it, and I want to dedicate it to her."

She worried for this man, was terrified of this man. His vulnerability increased her own, and the fact he'd let her see it unsettled her. Stilling her roaming fingers, she withdrew and placed her hand in her lap.

Roque glanced down as if the absence of her touch was more noticeable than the glide of her fingertips. He studied her a moment, then slid his fingers under hers and placed them on his arm. Turning toward her, he was so close she could feel his warm, wine-scented breath wash over her parted lips.

It was Addi's turn to still, to sit motionless, transfixed. The intensity she had felt from him at the exhibit was back again, only now it was focused on her. "Jimmy and I were talking about you," she said.

His eyes settled fully on her face. He knew she was there now.

She'd have bolted if she could have moved.

Trying to swallow proved impossible, her throat drier than sand. Her heart picked up a heavy, languorous beat that reverberated in her ears so loudly she could barely make out the crashing of the waves inches from her feet.

She knew what was about to happen, wanted it to happen, had dreamed of it happening.

And in that moment, all bawdy jokes aside, she wanted the feel of this man's lips on hers more than she wanted a publishing contract, more than her next breath.

"Addison."

His mouth fell upon hers, hot and demanding. Her vision went white.

Her heart forgot its lazy, heavy beat and raced in her chest. She breathed him in with every gust of available air and sank deeper, his tongue gliding against hers, diving right in instead of taking tentative steps.

She lost herself in the feel of his arms around her, his heat beside her. How long had it been since she'd been kissed like this?

In one effortless move, she was on his lap, her tush nestled atop his very apparent arousal, spiking hers to unknown, unrealized levels, and she wrapped her arms around his massive frame, one hand finding its way through his thick, silky hair. She gave a little tug, and he moaned.

A surge of power shot through her, and she both tightened her grip and deepened the kiss. Never before was she more a woman than in this moment. After racing toward her dreams for so long, it was a heady experience to actually have something she wanted in her hands.

How could a person be so hard and soft, have the ability

to take and give, the audacity to demand and beg, all at once? She didn't know, couldn't care, and fought to answer him with every angle of her head, every stroke of her tongue, every bold, possessive caress, feeling every second all the way to her toes.

Protesting moans and begging groans joined the cacophony of the ocean's persistent waves and the roaring in her head as her belly rolled in a sweet liquid heat, settling low and heavy between her legs.

She'd dreamed of how he'd taste, how he'd feel, but she never imagined how *she'd* feel. She felt powerful. This was something new. And it was as scary as it was beautiful.

Roque's caresses became more demanding. He bent her head and exposed the back of her neck, sending a shiver down her spine. He sucked her skin and followed it with his tongue. "This damn birthmark drives me crazy."

She grinned, but as his hand slipped up her bared thigh to her hip, she faced the precipice of no return, for herself and her heart. His taste full of dark berries and his scent of heat and spice seduced her senses.

Fear streaked in with a sharp and resounding slap. Addi struggled, then pushed at his formidable chest in a panic, tearing her lips from the warm, sensuous haven of his mouth. "We can't." She forced a moan back down her throat.

Having a fling, enjoying sex for sex with this man was high on her list of priorities, but this was different. This kiss was wrapped in emotion, sadness, a need for escape. Too many strings.

If they kept going like this, it wouldn't be a fling, and she couldn't afford that now.

Roque didn't respond right away, seemed dazed and confused.

She grabbed his roaming hands. "Roque."

He stilled, an immediate transformation from fluid to transfixed, from a sea of shifting sand to stone.

She was scared, but had wanted every part of what he'd just offered. A moment of heaven, a chance to be close with someone who wanted her and understood her.

Placing her palms to his cheeks, she kissed the scar that had found a home below the outer corner of his right eye. She kissed each eye, each cheek. "I'm sorry."

When he tried to capture her mouth, she resisted, and a growl of pure male frustration erupted from his mouth. It was so honest, so naked in its truth, her fear gave way to humor, and she chuckled.

"What the fuck is so damned funny?" His words were pissed, but his tone was full of self-derision, and she empathized. Intense blue eyes bore into hers, begging to get lost for just a while longer.

She couldn't risk it, right here, right now. This one was dangerous.

She tapped the end of his nose, playful and friendly. Scooting off his lap, she stood up and held out her hand. "Don't be a grumpy teenage boy; you know I'm right. If we do this now, it wraps us all up in your mom. And you don't want that."

He grimaced. "Teenage boy, my ass. What I just showed you took years of dedicated practice."

She clapped her hands together. "Exactly." Teasing Roque she could handle, but healing him required a set of skills she didn't have. Hell, she could barely fix her own problems.

He shook his head, and she caught the curve of his mouth lifting in humor.

Her stomach rolled low and slow. She wanted to feel that mouth on hers again. All of her desire screamed in protest, while all of her dreams begged for some clear thinking.

The latter was difficult to do with Roque around.

She needed to get this man in an easygoing mood so she could get him out of his clothes—and soon.

But to do that, she had to get him out of his head.

So she could get him out of hers.

Chapter Ten

Roque and Addi rode in silence on the way to Huntington Place. He wanted to pull her back onto his lap. The unfortunate consequence of kissing her once was that now he wanted to do it again.

Fuck.

She sat with her forehead pressed against the glass, watching the world speed by in a blur of darkness, worrying her lip with her teeth.

She turned him inside out. The whole night had turned him inside out. He loved Aunt Raquel, and she meant well, but talking about his mother was difficult. Pain and anger and loss still wrapped tightly in his chest with the mention of his mother's name or the slightest hint of a memory. He avoided both at all costs, but lately both imposed more often than not.

Then there was Addi, a bigger surprise than anything. So many layers to that one.

They stopped at a red light, and he slid his gaze from the silky strands of hair escaping their pins down past the golden glow of her shoulder to the swell of her breast. He gripped the steering wheel to keep from reaching out. Then he continued his perusal over her hip and along the endless length of her toned and tanned legs tucked under her bottom. The pads of her toes peeked out from under her ass. She'd slid off her shoes before walking on the beach, and he didn't blame her. He'd never wrapped his mind around how women managed so well on such a narrow base of support, but he was glad they did.

She was spectacular.

Vibrant and brash one minute, pensive and earnest the next. Something more than just the house and her career was going on with her. He could feel it. And he hated not knowing what it was, but he'd no right to ask, either.

He steeled against her confusing layers, the wanting, the unease. She was not a distraction he needed right now. He had no time or space for any kind of relationship. Too much was at stake, and he'd already proven himself inept at finding any kind of work-life balance.

But what he did have time for was a mutual burning off of some steam. Jimmy was right, he needed to get laid. And for some goddamn reason he only had eyes for Addi.

But even more, he needed to get his head back in the game.

As a Gallagher, he'd already spent his whole life with a perception of ease forced upon him. He didn't have to work hard, because his family and his own good looks would take care of everything. No worries about becoming a world-renowned producer; being the son and nephew of two well-known, sought-after directors meant he was "in" on name alone.

Well, he didn't want to be handed anything, and he abhorred the thought of finding success on his family name or his good looks. Success would be his on the grounds of his efforts and abilities, or not at all.

First thing Monday morning he'd double his efforts. There were investors out there; it was all a matter of timing. Getting through all the *no*s until he found his yes. He had a few buddies from college he'd yet to try, and with the meetings he'd set up for early in the week, something had to give.

If all else failed, he'd be back at his financial advisor's door demanding he find him more money and get laughed at all the way out of the building, too. To get the kind of money he needed he'd have to sell some of his investments, and on such short notice he'd be losing a lot.

"Are you going to be okay?"

He shot a look her way. "Of course."

She looked pointedly at his white-knuckled grip on the steering wheel. "You're going to find the money. I know you will. I've seen you work your magic getting what you want." Shifting in her seat, she said, sotto voce, "Just find it before you have to fire me."

"What was that?"

She jerked up her chin, and her eyes darted about while she bit her lip before she said, "You always get what you want."

"You're one to talk."

"I'd simply call it great minds and all." She laughed, and the sound eased down his back like a cool breeze.

"Thanks for all your help. You're doing a really great job. Organized. Great with the crew."

Genuine pleasure shone from her eyes. "Thank you. That means a lot."

"We have a lot more to pull off before this is through, so don't stop."

"You've got my word, boss." She winked.

He pulled up in front of the valet with a laugh, feeling lighter than he had in days. "Let me hand over my car, and I'll walk you to your room."

Addi shot her hand out, her eyes round with intensity. "No."

He raised a brow and stilled.

"I mean…it's late, and we have an early morning."

Distraction or not, the rejection stung. Raising his hands, he pulled back. "Yeah. You're right, it's late. But just to be clear, I was only going to walk you up. Not ravish you outside your door."

A look of regret washed over her face.

Now wasn't that interesting?

Too interesting. His body surged in protest at her retreating form.

As she slid across the seat, he called her name. "Addi."

Pausing, she leaned back toward him, her dress hanging just enough to allow the swell of her breasts to torture him with their glow of creamy skin. He swallowed past the lump in his throat.

Fuck it.

He shot his hand out and wrapped it around the back of her neck. She grabbed the center console as he pressed his mouth firmly and hotly to hers. As soon as the sensation of her lips registered, desire streaked straight to his groin in a grip so tight he groaned into her mouth. But it was only half from the sensation of her mouth beneath his, the rest was how he felt when he was with her. The energy she brought to a space was like a catalyst. Like he could actually find his way out of this mess. She believed he could. He angled his head for one swift taste of midnight Cabernet, then released her.

She blinked twice, pushed errant strands of hair from her face with a shaky hand and blew out a breath.

Good.

Using the will of the gods, he remained still. "Good night, Addison."

She slid from the car. "Good night."

Not until she disappeared into the revolving front doors of Huntington Place did Roque release his breath. Sinking back into his seat, he closed his eyes and demanded his heart to slow down.

The woman would be the end of him, if the film didn't get him first.

A tap on his window yanked him from his recovery, and he snapped his eyes open, his heart jolting in the adrenaline of fight or flight. A valet motioned for him to roll the window down.

Roque lowered the glass.

Shifting from one foot to the next, the young valet asked, "Is there a problem, sir?"

Understatement of the century. Roque wanted to laugh.

"Yes, I believe there is."

"You kissed him?"

Addi pulled out the last pin and shook her hair. With a dejected harrumph, she dropped to Chase's sofa. "He kissed me, and then I kind of kissed him back."

Chase rounded her stone coffee table and handed a glass of wine to Addi. "You bitch. He is soooooooo hot."

Addi sighed with a whimper. "He is." She sipped from her glass, then set it on the table. "Which is a problem."

Standing, she curled her arms behind her back and tugged at the zipper.

Chase stepped around the table. "For Pete's sake, I'm right here. No reason to strain a shoulder, love."

Addi dropped her arms to her side and gave the zipper over to her friend. "I paid the bank, by the way. And the money I'm saving from working and the extra I'm pocketing with the hotel will cover next year's taxes and part of my living expenses. That should give me some time to figure out what to do next."

A disapproving grunt was all she got in return.

"Can I borrow a T-shirt and sweat pants?" Addi asked as Chase finished with the zipper.

"Do you promise not to get chocolate all over them?"

Addi laughed. "Shut up. I have real problems."

"There you go." Chase stepped back and turned toward her room. "Only problems you've created."

Addi stuck out her tongue at her friend's retreating back. "Not nice."

Looking around Chase's apartment, she couldn't help the tinge of jealousy at how put-together her friend was. Chase had graduated top of her class in graduate school, held a prestigious position—especially for someone her age—with the Huntington Place chain, she was always jet-setting from one exotic location to the next, and had her own home—which happened to be one of the top floors of her family's hotel.

And thank God, or Addi would have been SOL for a place to spend the night. Roque would notice the time stamp on the security system if she took a cab back and let herself in now.

Chase strolled back into the living room with a decidedly wicked grin, tossed the clothes to Addi, and lowered into an oversized cream leather chair. "Spill it."

Addi wiggled out of her dress and donned the borrowed clothing. Laying Chase's dress over the back of the sofa, Addi sunk in and pulled a decorative pillow to her chest with one hand and her wine glass to her lips with the other.

"Don't spill wine on that."

"Shut up."

"Seriously though."

Holding her glass just right, Addi slid her middle finger up and down the bridge of her nose, and Chase laughed. The joke about who was the tidy one and who was the sloppy one—or at least accident-prone—was as old as their friendship.

"We went to Raquel Gallagher and Liv Karsten's jewelry event, which was amazing, by the way. Nothing I could afford, but wow, Liv has talent." She sipped her wine, picturing the gorgeous abalone necklace she'd fallen in love with.

"I so wanted to make the event, but my flight just got in a bit ago."

Addi shook her head in awe. "Yet you are freshly showered, and I bet all of your travel luggage is put away."

Chase turned her nose up in the air. "*I* don't procrastinate."

Rolling her eyes, Addi continued. "So anyway, Roque and Raquel had a conversation about his mom."

"She died a couple years ago, didn't she? Breast cancer or something?"

Addi nodded. "Yeah, and he's having a hard time with it. Not anything obvious, but we ended up out on the beach with two bottles of wine. Then he kissed me."

Chase inched forward to the edge of her seat, cradling her wine glass in her palms. "Like a peck on the cheek or a tongue down your throat?"

A grin stretched Addi's lips wide and heat suffused her chest with the memory. "Chase, my mind went blank. For a brief moment he wasn't my boss, and I forgot my little scheme. Stopping the kiss was the freakin' hardest thing I've done in a long time, except I didn't want us to start things that way. I don't think one kiss has ever made me lose myself like that."

Chase leaned back on a breath. "Gaaaaaaaaawd."

Placing her empty glass on the side table, Addi frowned. "And it can't happen again…not like that."

"Why not?" Incredulity colored Chase's voice.

Addi pulled in a deep breath and blew it out with the tension that kept weighing her down. She stretched her neck to the right and the left with two resounding cracks and tallied the reasons on her fingers. "Because. It was too serious, you know? Emotionally charged. I can't screw this up, I don't need a man in my life, especially one like him. He's all take charge, be responsible, make financially wise decisions—and those guys never get me. Been there, done that, don't appreciate reruns."

"And you're stealing from him."

Addi dropped her jaw. "I am not—"

Maybe a little, but not him technically. Hollywood. Which was completely different.

She'd just ignore that remark. *Oh hell.* "I'm taking what Hollywood is offering, and yes, that is another very good reason things with him can never be serious."

Addi looked around Chase's apartment, trying to find the right words to make her friend understand. "You've got all of this. Stability. Success." She confessed. "I want that... before I try my hand at love again. God knows I tried it once and nearly married someone who thought less of me than my parents do."

"Addi."

The immediate censure in Chase's voice gave her pause. "Sorry. I know they love me. But for so long I've felt like they worried if I even tried crossing the street on my own. I want to create my own stability, to be capable in people's eyes, and not be the youngest Dekker who needs to be taken care of all the time." She shook her head. "I can't do that if I screw this up. I don't want to get into a relationship if I can't offer all of myself as the very best version of me." She set the pillow beside her and stretched out her legs. "Does that make sense?"

Chase studied her, then set her own glass down. Scooting to the edge of her seat again, she put her palms up. "Love, who said anything about a relationship? I'm not asking you to marry the man, but for an all-day pass to that amusement park? I'd sell my well-educated soul."

Addi laughed. A deep, satisfying belly laugh. "Phew. I do have to say, I would enjoy a ride on his water slide."

Chase's eyebrows arched in a very clear question. The instant blush stinging Addi's cheeks totally gave away her thoughts. She grabbed the pillow and squeezed it to her midsection, laughing.

"In those situations, love, you have to take the opportunity. Never waste a gift that big."

Addi collapsed into giggles as her friend positioned herself to pop the cork of a celebratory bottle of champagne.

Sobering, she waved her hand. "No, no. I can't. Seriously, Roque is going to be here at six a.m. since my car's at my house. I've got to get to bed."

Chase's shoulders sagged, and she frowned. "Fine. Be responsible. However, my flight doesn't leave until two. I'll do the generous thing and celebrate for the both of us. You, for potentially getting laid by the most delectable man in existence, and me, for getting all the dirty details." She popped the cork.

"I didn't say I was getting laid by anyone."

Chase stopped mid-pour and shot her gaze up to meet Addi's. "I've never seen you deny yourself before. You always go after what you want." She laughed. "Remember the time you used your textbook money to fly to New York because you wanted to see the disco ball drop on New Year's Eve? That whole semester you had to borrow mine and make copies of each chapter. Pain in the ass, but you got to see your ball."

Which was exactly the problem.

She had a habit of going after what she wanted without necessarily thinking everything through. Or considering how it would affect those around her.

And look where that had gotten her.

Chapter Eleven

Roque stood in the frame of the open French doors and rolled back on his heels, trying to wait patiently for a phone call that his gut told him wasn't coming. The week was almost closing, and he was no closer to obtaining an investor than the day Fairmont pulled out. The future he was fighting so hard for was slowly slipping through his fingers, no matter how tightly he squeezed. Punching something would surely make him feel better, but it would solve nothing. Why the hell did he always have to be so damn reasonable? Just once he'd like to lose it. Just once.

This was the film that would break him out from the pack. It was both a story of sin and redemption. The kind where the consequences of saving a life was the loss of another. A lesson in clawing some sort of existence into the side of a mountain. And it all focused on a female lead. Risky and tough—especially from an indie film—and he was determined to make it happen.

The moment the script had come across his desk over two years ago, he'd recognized it as his moment. His mother had been around the business so long and had such an analytical mind that both he and his dad had run a lot of things by her. He'd shown it to his mother, and she'd seen in it what he did.

But there wouldn't be a film if he didn't find an investor soon.

The crew was taking a break, eating the meal Addi had catered in. She had them all seated around the back table, easing from the grueling day. Everyone had been on edge, yet she pulled them all together like a family. Even Kemper had a smile on his face. He should eat something himself, but the knot in his gut had grown so big he couldn't swallow anything if he'd tried.

Kemper's phone rang and he answered it. He nailed Roque with a look. Pulling his brows together, he pushed his chair back and threw his napkin on the table. Roque turned and walked into the kitchen, Kemper close on his heels. The last thing he needed was another screaming match around the crew.

"Gallagher."

Roque moved farther into the front room and then turned around. The news had obviously found its way to his director's inner circle. Fuck. He was surprised the man hadn't heard sooner. It wasn't a secret.

"What the hell do you think you're doing? My time is valuable."

"Of course it is."

"Don't play games with me. You lost your main investor."

The words clawed in his chest, and he shoved his hands in his pockets. "Temporary setback, Kemper. The film is moving forward as scheduled."

"Look, man, I know we play in the land of make-believe, but closing your eyes and clicking your heels won't change a fucking thing. I'm not going down with your sinking ship. Sorry, Roque."

Roque's jaw dropped open. "You can't quit on me."

The director walked to the front door. "That's exactly what I'm doing. This is a business first, and I'm not connecting my name to a film that's tanked before it even started. I need to be working."

Roque followed, close on his heels. "The film is just fine. Come on." He gripped Doug's arm. "This project will succeed. You'll be sorry you walked away."

Kemper looked down at Roque's hand then back to his face. "I'll take my chances."

Roque dropped his hand and watched as his director— scratch that—as Kemper pulled out of the driveway, rear lights mocking him as they disappeared down the road.

Panic welled in his chest, keeping pace with his racing heart. Fuck! No investor, no director. He was losing before he had the chance to fucking begin. Pulling in a breath, he swung around. He needed everyone to get the hell out so he could figure out what the hell he was going to do.

"Addi." His yell carried across the backyard.

She came through the French doors, and seeing his face, rushed up to him. "What happened?" Jimmy followed close behind.

"Send everyone home."

She grabbed his hand. "Why? What's going on?"

He shrugged her off and leaned back against the counter. "Kemper's out. I need to find a new director, and if I don't find an investor soon, it's all over."

"Fucking Kemper. He's always been such an asshole," Jimmy said, then throwing a hand out toward Addi, added, "Sorry."

She laughed. "For what?" Turning back to Roque, she gave him a reassuring smile. He wished he could believe it.

"I'll send the crew home. Give me a list of people I can call. I can set up appointments for first thing tomorrow," she said.

He nodded.

Everyone cleared out without having to be asked twice. Free Friday nights didn't come often during filming. The quiet left behind roared with desperation in his ears.

Jimmy walked into the kitchen and dropped into the chair across from Roque. "What's the plan?"

Shaking his head, Roque swore. "Fuck if I know. I'll step into the director position for as long as it takes to find someone, but it isn't ideal."

Jimmy shrugged. "Maybe not, but it's done all the time."

"I know. But my skill is making the film happen, getting others excited about it, and pulling the strings—which is demanding enough right now. I don't want to be bogged down with filling the director's shoes. That almost doubles my current workload, and I'm already stretched thin. But I'll do what needs to be done. It'll buy me some time."

Addi finished clearing the meal, then pulled the French doors closed behind her. "Have that list for me?"

"Sent it to your email."

"I'll get started making calls. Good thing Hollywood never sleeps." She disappeared down the hall.

Jimmy and Roque watched after her, and Jimmy whistled.

Roque pushed back from the table, too restless to sit. When Jimmy's low whistle agitated him, it was time to move. He paced the back patio, enjoying the cool breeze tailing the rhythmic crashing of the ocean waves. The sound calmed him, and the breeze helped steady him.

Letting his head fall back, absorbing the rays of the setting sun, he wished his stress and misgivings would go out with the tide. Fuck.

"You okay, boss?"

Roque snapped his head up as Jimmy approached from the kitchen, two beers in his hands. Roque eyed the bottles.

"Looks like you could use one."

Roque dipped his chin. "Shit." Accepting a bottle, he twisted off the cap and tossed it into the trash. He pulled a long swallow and turned to look out over the Pacific.

Jimmy stood at his side and took in the blue horizon as well. The two accepted the silence that went hand in hand with the first few drafts of a cold beer, relaxing in the absence of the constant chatter on a film set.

"I have a few angles I can work. Give me a few days?"

Roque took another long swallow, finishing off the bottle. "I don't have any choice, do I?" He glanced at his friend then back out across the waters below. "I have to make this work, man."

"Then make it work."

Roque dipped his chin. Fuck. Make it work. Those three words had never seemed so impossible.

Jimmy tossed his empty bottle into the trash. "As far as tonight goes, I'll secure the lot and set up for tomorrow."

"Yeah. Good."

"Anything else?"

Roque stilled. "You into Addi?" What the fuck was wrong with him? The stress of the project was screwing with his head.

His friend laughed. "*You* are into Addi."

Roque cut a look at his amused and unflinching friend. That was the problem with having friends on the payroll, they had no respect for his intimidation. "I'm not into Addi. Fuck. Ever want to do something but knew it probably wasn't good for you?"

Jimmy nodded. "Every day."

Roque looked his buddy over. Jimmy had a passion for film, wanted to act, but found out he was more comfortable on the other side of the camera, discovering an eye for photography. What a lot of people didn't know was Jimmy had faced more loss than most. Made him want to help every stray puppy that crossed his path. He'd lost his brother, and since, his sister-in-law was in and out of prison more times than Charlie Sheen. The man battled a constant war against himself with each phone call he received, begging him for help. One more time. Just one more time, he'd always say.

Jimmy took the empty bottle from Roque and tossed it into the trash. "You need to get laid." He stretched out his tattoo-sleeved arm. "As far as Addi goes, a man my size and with all the tattoos? Most women don't throw their arms around my neck like I'm a damn kitten, usually they run or pretend I'm not there. Not Addi. From the first day, she accepted me. That's a good girl right there. She *sees* people."

Roque continued to stare at the waves rushing to the shore below and released a gust of air, then swung his gaze around to find his friend grinning ear to ear.

"Night, boss."

Jimmy took the stairs that led around the side of the house to the front drive. Roque watched him until he disappeared around the corner.

He needed to be thinking about the film, not Addi. But damned if he wasn't tired of thinking. Period.

Addi made it through the entire list, setting up appointments where she could, promising callbacks to others. The industry was like the capital with all the back-patting and favors and games. How the hell did they ever get anything done?

Walking into the kitchen, she found Roque staring through the window over the sink.

"Hey, boss. I set up a few meetings. Put them on your calendar."

Sighing, he turned and leaned back against the counter.

"Thanks."

She stepped up to him and tilted her head to the side with a grin. Her fingers itched to soothe his brow and her lips wanted to ease the firm line of his own, but instead she loosened the top button of his shirt and teased. "You need to lighten up or you're never going to make it through the weekend. No one's going to want to sign on with a tight-ass producer. No matter how fine said ass might be."

His lips twitched.

She placed her hands on her hips. "It's going to work out. Something will come from these meetings, if not a direct link, then they'll know someone who knows someone." He continued to watch, making her itch under the collar. She considered jumping on him just to shake him out of his mood, but even she knew there were appropriate times to act inappropriately. "Let me ask you something."

"What?" His voice was low and skittered over her skin with the awareness that the house was empty besides the two of them.

"When have you ever failed to accomplish what you set your mind to?"

"Remember when you stopped me out on the beach?"

She nodded slowly. "You were hurting. I—"

"I was going to thank you for keeping a clear head. That you were right…about putting a stop to it all, but I changed my mind. Clear head be damned."

Confused, she opened her mouth to speak, but before a single word came out, Roque's hand palmed the back of her head and pulled her in tight with his other hand at her lower back. As soon as her chest pressed into him, his lips crashed down and took the words right out of her mouth.

The same white heat from that night blinded her. She couldn't fight the desire to get closer even if she wanted to. And she didn't want to fight it. Not anymore. Chase was right.

They were both single and adults. Maybe if she quit trying so hard to ignore her attraction to him, she could concentrate once again on getting her home back.

One hand dove into the silky waves of his hair while the other wrapped around his waist, pulling him in. The length of his insistent arousal pressed into her belly, and she pressed back.

Roque's low growl incited a thousand butterflies in her core, and she reveled in the encouragement. She swept her tongue against his possessively.

Sliding his hands down her body, he gripped her hips and set her up on the counter. She naturally opened her legs to make room for him. He didn't just step close, but also pulled her to the very edge of the counter top so the center of her heat cradled him. He moved against her as his tongue swept into her mouth again and again.

Addi's body tightened. He tasted like Malibu sunsets, pure brawn, and spice. A combination she'd never experienced before, but would rather starve than go without again.

Out of nowhere, Addi remembered where they were and, sliding her hands to either side of Roque's face, tried to still the building storm. She spoke against his mouth. "Wait. Wait a second."

With a growl of warning that Addi was coming to love, Roque pulled back slowly. "You're trying to kill me, aren't you?"

Chuckling at the pained expression on his face, she shook her head and whispered, "No, I...I just remembered we're in the kitchen."

"So what? Does it remind you of flirting with Jimmy?"

Addi snorted. "I have never flirted with Jimmy."

Roque raised a brow and in a high-pitched voice teased, "Oh, Jimmy, shut up."

With that, Addi slapped him gently on the chest. "Oh my

God, you're ridiculous." There was no way in hell she'd tell him the real conversation. The man had a big enough head as it was. Besides, she was a healthy, sexual woman who happened to find this man attractive. *That's the understatement of the century.* And if she wanted to play, she could play. No emotion to muddy the waters, no expectations, simple, consenting, safe fun.

Making a face, she stuck out her tongue at Roque.

Without warning, he grabbed her around the waist and hoisted her over his shoulder.

She slapped at his ass and laughed. "Put me down right now."

His chuckle trailed them through the living room and along the back hallway to her bedroom. He shoved the door open with a hip.

Addi tensed against the impending upending onto the bed, but when he leveraged her off, he didn't toss her but rather slid her down his body until they pressed chest to breast. She tightened her legs about his waist, fitting herself snug against his hard heat.

Roque held her gaze. She held her breath. Questions seemed to pass through his eyes, but he shuttered them and then took her mouth, this time with tender, feather-like caresses, his tongue sliding along her lower lip to the corner where he played until rounding up and over her top lip.

She needed more, wanted more.

No more words, no more teasing. The early evening sun lost its strength as it settled into the horizon, basking the room in a warm, subtle glow.

Roque stepped to the edge of the bed and, bracing himself with one knee and one hand on the mattress, lowered Addi to her back. "You are so fucking beautiful."

"No."

As he settled his body between her legs, he frowned down

at her. "No? I'm over that word."

She laughed. "I'm cute, I'm not beautiful."

"Whoever told you that was a damned moron."

Addi knew it was silly, she knew that in moments of heat like this people said things, but hearing the word beautiful slide from between Roque's lips was the strongest of aphrodisiacs.

Women were beautiful. She was a woman—not a toddler that needed to be coddled and taken care of. She was XX all the way, baby, and the thought spread a smile across her face so wide her cheeks ached.

He dipped his head and took her still smiling lips.

Enough of this—she wanted to feel his naked skin against her own and compare the experience to her unbidden but persistent dreams.

Kissing him back with every ounce of desire that pumped through her from head to toe, she trailed her fingers down his abdomen until she reached the buckle of his belt. Making quick work of the offending accessory, she reveled in the sexy-sounding *whisk* as it snapped loose of his belt loops, then let it fly.

Pulling at his dress shirt, she didn't wait for him to work the buttons, but yanked it up and over his head, frustrated when his bulk hindered the fabric's disappearance.

He sat back on his haunches with a low chuckle, soothing her like a damn filly. "Whoa, hold on a second."

She was tired of waiting. "Don't tell me what to do."

Simply staring at her, he worked the cufflinks and finished pulling his shirt free.

She didn't waste any time. The sight of all that smooth skin stretched so deliciously over broad shoulders and a well-filled-out chest turned her mouth to dust. She tried to swallow, but one couldn't squeeze a drop from the Sahara—and she was parched.

As he tossed his shirt to the side, Addi made quick work

of the button and zipper on his slacks.

"Off."

"Now who's getting bossy?" he teased, but didn't hesitate to slide off the end of the bed and drop his drawers to the ground.

Hard lines and sharp edges. Rounded masses of muscle and dense, thick flesh as smooth as the surface of a perfectly worn river rock.

Addi opened her arms.

She was answered by a grin pulled up only at one corner. Mischief and promise shone from his eyes and played tag with her senses.

Bare and open to the world, he placed one knee on the bed. Oh, and what that did for her view. His heavy balls settled into the barest of a back and forth momentum, and she wanted to feel their weight. Anticipation sent her insides to liquid, and she pulled her legs together to ease the sensation.

"Oh, I don't think so," Roque's voice broke through the haze in her mind, and she watched, transfixed, as he removed one nude strappy heel followed by the other. Both fell to the floor with a satisfying *thunk*. The heat of his fingertips on the top of one foot sent shivers up her leg. With slow circular motions, Roque slid his fingers up her ankle and traced the bones on both sides. She'd scream if he didn't get to work. Now.

As if he had all the time in the world, he repeated the action to the other foot and ankle, then ran the base of his hands with firm pressure up the insides of her calves, up the insides of her thighs until the heel of both palms massaged firmly into the apex between her thighs. Addi arched into his touch and closed her eyes. It still wasn't nearly enough.

Splaying his fingers wide, he gently slid his thumbs up and down atop her cleft over her white skinny capris. She whimpered as heat built to an inferno inside her.

Roque lowered his head and pressed his lips where his thumbs had created a storm of sensations. His hot breath penetrated the thick denim, and she arched once more, this time against his mouth. Visions of his silky lips and tongue exploring her with no barrier taunted and teased.

"Roque. Now. Please. I can't wait."

"Yes, you can. And you will."

Sliding his hands under her cream fitted tank, he massaged and kneaded until reaching the edge of the built-in elastic that supported her breasts. He slid one finger under the edge and growled in appreciation, then in one swift glide of both hands, he'd found his way under the elastic until his hands cupped her breasts. She arched into his touch, the rough scrape of his calluses over her sensitive nipples wrenching a cry from her lips.

"Damn it, Roque. This is too much." She whimpered, she begged, she didn't care.

In one fluid motion, he supported her upper body and rid her of her top then, resting her back, he dragged his hands down over her breasts, over her belly, until he reached the button of her jeans. A quick flick and zip, followed by the slide of denim over her heated, overly sensitive skin, and she thought she'd lose it then and there.

He raised a brow. "No panties?"

"Roque." Her patience had fled her days ago.

His eyes feasted on her form as he slid on a condom. There was no denying the lust and appreciation in his heated gaze. Two could play at this game. If she couldn't get what she wanted with words, she'd get it by tempting him beyond all reason. She smiled the smile of the all-knowing and pulling her knees up and open until the outside of her thighs rested against the cool sheets of her bed.

His eyes slid from her breasts to the juncture between her thighs, spread open in invitation, and stilled. So still she feared he'd quit breathing.

"Now…no more games."

Intense blue eyes held her own for a beat. "I don't play games." He slid back between her legs, rubbing his hot length between her slick folds.

Her breath seized, and she gripped the bedding between tight fists.

"I don't rush, either. I savor." He dipped his head and circled one nipple with his tongue, ending with a suckle, then a gentle nip with his teeth. Again to the other side.

Addi deserted the bedsheets and gripped his head with her hands, pressing his face into her swollen breasts and arching her lower body into his promise of release. Dragging his face up to hers she captured his lips and plunged her tongue deep into his mouth, desperate for him to repeat the action with a whole different region of his body.

"I want it, too. Fuck, I want it, too. But I want to learn you." He spoke against her mouth. "Each and every valley, each and every curve."

Sliding down her torso, he splayed her legs wide to his gaze, and then slowly lowered his head.

She couldn't take any more.

When the tip of his tongue flicked gently, lightly against her, her hips hurtled off the mattress, and she cried out. "Later, learn me later. I need you now." Her voice ripped from her, ragged and wanting.

With a growl, he lapped his tongue from bottom to top, once, twice, then just as she thought she'd surely explode from the tension building to painful heights, he slid up her body, his cock filling her and his tongue filling her mouth in one synchronized motion.

He groaned from so deep in his chest it vibrated against her breasts, and she returned it with a cry into his mouth. Wrapping her legs around his waist, she tilted her pelvis to take his length deeper, harder. Pulling him tighter with her legs, she encouraged more.

His hands found every sensitive bit of flesh, and his tongue fulfilled its promise to her mouth. As the tension in her core twisted tighter and tighter, she held on for dear life. Roque drove deeper and faster, his gasps for air wrapping around her own. Slick flesh upon slick flesh, the heated aroma of desire, all man and all woman filled her senses, clouding her brain. She shot off her precipice with a cry.

And he followed.

With one last pleasure-blinding thrust, he shouted out his release, straining, pushing, gathering her within his embrace so tightly she felt completely surrounded by him.

She held firm as both their bodies ebbed and flowed with the pulsing waves of release. He dropped his forehead to the pillow, pressing his lips into the side of her neck by her birthmark. Sensations feathered out from the velvet of his lips against her skin.

How could there be any left?

She was spent but energized. Satiated but hungry. Cleansed of every thought she'd ever had, but full of new, intriguing, and terrifying ones.

Ignore her attraction?

Who had she been kidding?

Now she feared she'd think of nothing but.

Chapter Twelve

Roque lay stunned.

Addi dozed, her head tucked under his chin, a hand on his chest, fingers splayed wide. The setting sun offered the slightest glimmer of light to the darkening room, bouncing shadows off the walls.

What the hell was that? A deep sense of contentment at having Addi in his arms settled him deeper into the mattress. Now wasn't that a surprise?

In the kitchen, he'd intended to thank her for stopping him the other night, but he'd been tired of fighting for the film, fighting the pull she had on him, and all thoughts of gentlemanly grace fled. He'd wanted nothing more than to lose himself in her and forget about the film for a while.

Damned if it didn't do the trick, too.

Fuck.

Business was business. Sex was sex. And he'd just taken Addi in a very un-businesslike fashion. He rubbed his hand over his face, and Addi scooted closer still, sliding a thigh up and over his. She wiggled a little.

Shit.

When she'd refused his "beautiful" compliment he almost laughed at the absurdity until he'd recognized the sincerity in her face. She'd been serious. How in the hell could that woman think she was cute? Cute was a damned puppy. She was all hot flesh and warm curves wrapped around a tireless work ethic and compassionate heart. For fuck's sake, even Jimmy adored her, and Jimmy didn't adore anyone.

Addi stirred and then stretched out, arms above her head, toes pointed long, her arched back pushing her breasts high and toward his face like an offering from heaven.

His mouth watered. Roque wanted nothing more than to go another round, but it was late. His dick disagreed, desperately disagreed, growing to uncomfortable proportions thanks to the silky warmth lying next to him.

What in the hell was he was going to do about Addi Dekker?

A sigh escaped his lips, already turned up in a satisfied grin. Almost as quickly, her eyes shot open and she stilled.

Intrigued, Roque watched the emotions flitting across her face. Shock, worry, and something else he couldn't put his finger on.

She sat up, grabbing the sheet to her chest, and looked at him over her shoulder, biting that damn lip again. He swore that was what did him in every time.

He reached up and ran his thumb along her lip to release it from the sharp grasp of her teeth. "Hey."

She darted her eyes around the room, then to the clock. "Wow. It's late. We really need to go."

Roque studied her a beat. No demands, no questions about a relationship. And why did her silence sting? That was a question he didn't want to answer.

Addi scooted to the edge of the bed and stood up, the sheet wrapped around her lithe form. What a shame.

She waved her finger in his direction. "You need to go. Tomorrow starts early." Grabbing her pants, she slid them on.

He could watch the sway of her breasts as she hurriedly changed all day long. She shimmied into her top, effectively hindering his view, and he scowled.

Raking her fingers through her hair, she waved her hand in a looping gesture hinting he should get up and out. "I'll make the bed and lock the house. I have a few things I need to do before I go, anyway." Throwing him a brilliant, if a bit forced, smile, she disappeared through the door and down the hallway.

He flopped back on the bed. He'd just experienced the most mind-blowing sex he'd ever had, yet Addi got right back to business as if it were just another ordinary day.

"Shit."

She called from the living room. "What was that?"

Roque threw back the sheets and stood. "Nothing."

Once he was dressed, he made his way through the house to find Addi in the kitchen.

While she stood next to the counter rummaging through her bag, he took the opportunity to study her. He was beginning to think it was his new favorite pastime. Shit, okay, second favorite pastime where she was concerned.

Her white jeans and cream top glowed against the golden tan of her skin, lips swollen and pink, hair mussed. He liked this Addi. He liked knowing if he walked over and breathed her in, he'd smell himself as well. He liked knowing he'd made her scream and beg in pleasure—he liked knowing what that sounded like.

He liked way too many things.

Clearing his throat, he grabbed his keys. "I'll walk you to your car."

Addi shot her eyes to him, that slight look of panic he couldn't quite figure out. This time it was gone as soon as it came. "No, that's all right. I have a few more things I want to do here first."

"Addi, you've done enough here today."

She rolled her eyes with a chuckle. "Seriously, this is my house. Do you know how many times I've walked around this yard at night, walked to and from my car at all hours?"

He didn't know why, but he couldn't back down. The idea of leaving Addi to close up and walk out to her car alone didn't sit well with him. "I insist."

She stared at him, then sighed. "Fine. Let me turn off the lights in here and grab my bag. I'll meet you by the front door."

Stepping out into the cool, humid air, he paused and listened to the rhythmic crashing of the waves on the beach below. He closed his eyes. He needed a hammock. How perfect would that be? The moon high in the sky cast the world in a yellow glow, the crashing waves, the salty, humid air as he floated back and forth. He could see it play out perfectly on-screen. The cares of the world wouldn't be able to intrude so easily in such a peaceful scene.

Addi stepped out to join him, and he opened his eyes. Should it bother him that in his vision she swung with him, nestled against his side as she had only moments before? Naked, the moonlight highlighted her curves and shadowed her secrets. Any hot-blooded man would want the woman naked on a hammock.

With a shake of his head, he stepped forward, set the alarm, and closed the door.

She glanced back at the door longingly.

He could relate. There was nothing he wouldn't give to go back inside, to her bed.

The husky purr of her voice broke through his musings. "Be careful going home, Gallagher."

He laughed. "Gallagher? Really?"

"I'm trying to keep this easy."

The devil made him do it. Stepping close, he wrapped his hand around the back of her head, the other snaked about her waist and hauled her up to meet his body. He took her mouth before she could utter a word. He wondered if he'd ever get enough when a punch of lust hit hard and swift in his gut. All the blood rushed from his head to another less conscientious part of his body.

She softened under his demanding mouth immediately. Diving her hands into his hair, she pressed her breasts into his chest, and he wanted to shout in victory. Tilting his head, he swept his tongue into her mouth, gliding against the silk of her. She tasted sweet with a bit of spice.

His body tightened with need, and for a split second he considered dragging her back inside. The sun had hours before it had to get back to work, and so did he. There was a lot that could be accomplished in a few hours.

Coming to his senses, he gently but firmly disengaged from Addi's tempting embrace and set her back on her feet. Dropping his forehead to hers, he stole one last kiss. "One more thing."

"As long as it isn't another kiss. I can barely stand as it is," she said with a giggle.

He grinned and cupped her cheek. "I don't want you worrying about your job. I'm going to fix this. Got it?"

"I know you'll figure it out. Hollywood always finds its way."

"Yeah, Hollywood." He shoved his hands in his pockets. If only Hollywood would be a bit more accommodating, he'd already have this situation figured out. But she was right. He would figure it out somehow.

"Night, Dekker."

Taking her keys from her hand, he unlocked her car and held the door as she got into the front seat. Once he was certain she was good to go, he slid behind the wheel of his own car and followed her out of the driveway.

Addi was a distraction he didn't have time for, but damn if he didn't want to do that again.

And soon.

Addi yawned as she headed back to her house. Unfortunately, she had to drive practically all the way to Huntington Place before Roque turned off on another road so she could turn around. This idea of hers was showing its spots.

Her fingers drifted to her swollen lips. She could still taste Roque, smell him—feel him. She'd watched movies and read books—hell, she'd written them—where sex like that was reality, but never had she imagined it to actually be true.

The memory of his skin sliding against hers had her legs pressing closed against the sensations. He was like the worst kind of drug, one taste and you'd kill for more. She wanted him again, naked, willing, and ready.

Roque Gallagher knew his way around the bedroom. He was a pretty boy, Hollywood elite, who was used to getting his way by the Gallagher name alone, even if he claimed to not want it. He chose a career immersed in society's overinflated expectations and impossible standards. His work ethic was unparalleled. He treated his crew like family and put their needs ahead of his own as long as it didn't burn the bottom line of the film.

She grinned.

And boy, was she glad, because every bit of his experience translated into fireworks in her bedroom.

Just then she passed Decker Canyon Road. She stared at the sign as she approached. She and her sister Sam always fancied the road was named for them, just misspelled of course. They could forgive that minor oversight. So many memories. Aunt Addi, the bungalow—her self-respect. That sobered her up a bit.

She had to get to a place in her life where she felt good about her accomplishments. Anything else would muddy the waters, make her question her ability. The first thing was saving her home. Thanks to the film, she was well on her way. Second, start bringing in an income beyond her temporary gig as Roque's assistant—hopefully with her writing, but she knew how slow the whole process could be. At times, she felt as if she were a mountain climber at the base of Mount Everest, or a newbie actress wishing for an Academy Award. Writing was no different. The hurdles and obstacles alone were daunting, but when you added the individual subjectivity of editors the chances became slimmer and slimmer, like finding that one grain of sand on the world's largest beach. She really wanted to be that grain of sand.

Parking down the road under a tree overhang, she locked the car and quickly made her way down the path to her bungalow. The night was cool and a little humid; she could taste the salt of the ocean in the air.

As she approached the front porch, she glanced around then pulled her flashlight out of her purse and unlocked the door. She quickly put in the code to satisfy the alarm, and then she closed and locked the door and reset the alarm. Its glowing light caught her attention, and she stared at the time stamp.

Her stomach turned on end, and she shook out her hands. "Crap, crap, crap. Maybe he won't notice." She paced in front of the door, and then stopped again to stare at the time. "Of course he'll notice."

She contemplated all the excuses she could come up with until she tasted the slightest hint of iron. Releasing her lip from its sharp enamel shackles, she swore. Damn it.

Okay, okay, it will be fine. I'll just say I forgot something and had to come back.

Blowing out a breath, she willed her heart to slow. She grabbed her bag and headed to the bathroom.

The risk was high, but she had to take a shower. Personally she'd prefer to keep Roque's scent on her throughout the night, but there was no way she could face him in the morning smelling just like he did—he'd know. Whatever her lustful thoughts were, he didn't need the ego boost.

With the flashlight pointed straight to the ground so she could see without being plunged into darkness or allowing the light to be visible from outside, Addi grabbed her bag from under her bed and jogged to the bathroom. The quicker she could shower and get back to the attic, the better.

Would you listen to yourself? This is ridiculous.

After leaning the flashlight against her towel so it offered a gentle glow, she made quick work of her clothes. She stuffed them in the bag, pulled out soap and, after securing her hair on top of her head, stepped under the hot spray. She rubbed the soap until she worked it into a thick lather. Sliding her hands down the front of her body, she stilled from the sensations that sparked to life. Her nipples were still sensitive from Roque's teeth and tongue; she slid her hands over the still swollen globes and down the plane of her stomach. Tentatively, she slowly slid her fingers between her legs. Swollen lips met the pads of her fingertips. A tightness coiled in her stomach as she experimented with a slow slide of her fingers between her folds. Every part of her was on fire. And it was damned Roque Gallagher's fault and the images of his naked body hovering over her, pressing into her.

The house alarm beeped, and she froze.

Crap! Wasting no time, she turned off the water and grabbed her towel. Standing completely still she strained to listen for any sign of who was in the house.

Her eyes fell on the glow of the flashlight. She lunged to put it out. Wet porcelain released its grip on her wet feet, and she flailed her arms to keep from falling. Her elbow connected with the shower wall in a loud thunk. Straining to hear over the blood roaring in her ears, she froze.

Quickly, she turned off the flashlight, now more scared of being caught than being in the dark. What did it matter anyway? She wasn't alone. Which was no comfort at all.

She dried off, holding her breath, afraid to make a noise. Shoving her things in her bag, including the flashlight, she prayed no one had heard her. Towel and bag in hand, she stepped into the shower with care and pulled the shower curtain. Slowly, so as not to make a sound, she dragged the shower curtain closed, praying all the while for small favors, or big ones.

Addi rubbed the walls and the sides of the tub dry. There was nothing to be done with the curtain. Just as she'd finished, the bathroom door opened.

She held her breath. *No, no, no.*

This is what her mother always told her about. Lies and tricks always caught up with a person. *Would she never learn?*

Her mind screamed for her to run, but where could she go?

The curtain flew open just as she stepped up on the edge of the tub. Squeezed against the wall, Aunt Addi's flowing eyelet curtain settled with a swirl, obscuring her view—and hopefully the view of her company.

She held her breath, her heart pounding so loud in her ears she was sure it could be heard a mile away. Her stomach twisted, her head pounded. Had she heard this story from a girlfriend she'd have laughed herself silly, but in this moment it was nothing but pure torture.

What the hell have I gotten myself into?

One second, two seconds—it felt like an eternity, the dark shadow stood still.

She knew that stillness. She knew.

Roque.

Chapter Thirteen

Roque strained to hear a sound. Any sound. He swore he'd heard something fall, a loud knock—something. The bathroom was humid and warm, as if someone had just showered, but there was no sign, no sound.

Shit, I'm losing my mind here.

He let the curtain fall and rubbed the back of his neck. If he wasn't going crazy, he would be by the time this film wrapped up. Between the house and Addi he couldn't pin down which would be the end of him first.

At least one of them would leave a smile on his face on the way out.

His body kicked at the thought of Addi, wanting more of their earlier activities.

"Shit." He padded back through the bungalow to the kitchen, picturing Addi on a Friday night, curled up on the couch with a bowl of popcorn. He chuckled. Who was he kidding? It would be a plate of éclairs, and half of it would be smeared on her face and dripping down the front of her shirt.

The better for you to lick it off, then.

Roque shook his head. Grabbing a beer out of the well-stocked fridge, he opened the French doors that led out to the backyard and leaned against the doorjamb. One swig, two. He released a sigh. Better already.

After turning off Highway 1 to go home, he hadn't been able to get Addi, the loss of his director, any of it out of his head. Time with Addi had left him revved up, energized. If he was awake, he might as well work, so he'd turned the car and headed back to the set.

There was always something more to do. Go over and approve script changes sent to him this afternoon, prepare for his next meeting with his key creative team, and Jimmy dropped off a few location proposals he needed to take a look at. There was only so much he could do out of business hours, and only so much he could do in a day. With this project being his baby, he'd assumed more responsibility to offset cost. Scrimp on help, not on quality. Besides, if he was doing it, he knew it would be done right.

He downed another long swallow of the pale ale and let the rhythm of the crashing waves below lull his racing mind as he took in the cozy details of the backyard. A large flat-stoned patio invited guests to rest in the generous lounge chairs. Lush foliage offered privacy all along the perimeter, with trees contributing shade. Off to the far right side stood two tall palms. Roque blinked. "What the hell?"

He didn't know how he didn't remember, but hanging between the two palms was a well-netted hammock.

An immediate vision of Addi lying with him, swinging a lazy sway late in the afternoon sun, came to mind.

Shit, get your head out of your ass, man.

His legs moved of their own accord. He lowered his weight onto the netting and leaned back.

"Ohhhh...fucking heaven."

The dark sky made a velvet backdrop of midnight behind

the deep green of the palm leaves. A few stars twinkled and teased. The salty ocean air and resident honeysuckle tickled his nose. Resting one hand behind his head, Roque crossed his legs at the ankle and took a long draw from his bottle.

He stared at everything and nothing. Emptying his brain of the past few weeks as it filled with every memory. What the hell was he going to do about his film? Why, when he wanted to cleanse his brain of everything, did it stubbornly put all his problems in a "to do" order front and center?

He'd been studying, planning, working. Busy with life and his own ambitions—just as his mom had taught him. She didn't want to get in his way, she'd said. Didn't want him to lose momentum.

Working was what kept his heart beating, it was what he woke up for each morning. What the fuck would he wake up to if he couldn't find a goddamn investor before it was too late? His stomach rebelled against the thought. He loved being a producer. Having the responsibility for a whole production, beginning to end, was like a drug. The more he had, the more he needed.

Finishing this movie was beyond a professional accomplishment, it was a sort of closing on the project he'd shared with his mother what seemed like so long ago. If all the work he'd been doing, all the hours that had kept him from being with those who loved him were going to be worth it, then he needed to finish this film.

And if he didn't figure out how the hell to fix this, it would be a long time before anyone would let him be in charge of putting one foot in front of the other.

Closing his eyes against it, he swung the beer bottle over the edge of the hammock and let it fly toward the stone.

Crash.

The violence of shattering glass spraying up at the hammock and out toward the yard centered his thoughts.

He swung his legs over the edge of the hammock and pulled himself up to a seated position, staring up at the sky. A thump from inside the kitchen made him snap to attention. "What the fuck." Straining to see in the darkness, he rubbed his eyes and focused again. He stood and walked quietly toward the opened French doors.

He reached his hand around the corner and flipped on the light. The kitchen was bathed in an immediate soft glow. Empty. Of course. He almost laughed, but his throat remained tight and wouldn't let the sound out.

He scanned the room. Everything seemed to be in place, all but the paper towel holder which now lay on its side. Or was it like that from earlier? Shaking his head, he rummaged through the kitchen pantry until he located the broom and dustpan. He flooded the backyard with the outdoor lights and cleaned up the glass.

Crouched down on the balls of his feet, he picked up one large shard. It had once been so smooth, part of a whole, had purpose. Now it was sharp, almost deadly—an insidious shadow of its former self.

Just like him. He was a shadow, a shard, a sharp edge of high expectations and very little tolerance. The only thing he was really good for was hard work and long hours.

And even that wasn't panning out at the moment.

"Roque." Addi's whisper bounced off her bedroom window, fogging up the glass, as Roque's taillights retreated down her driveway. Tears burned behind her lids as she leaned in against the glass, trying to see farther down the road.

She hadn't expected to see this Roque again. Vulnerable Roque. To be honest, he probably hadn't expected her to see it, either.

Breaking into a cold sweat, she stepped back from the window. With the sleeve of her robe, she wiped away the mess left on the glass, going over it twice to make sure no marks were left behind. Resting a hand over her stomach, she willed it to stop twisting and turning.

She'd caught him in a private moment. As soon as she'd seen him, she should have snuck out the front door to give him privacy, to make sure she wasn't caught. But she'd been immobilized by the pain on his face. All she wanted to do was go to him.

Addi pressed her hands into her belly as she walked back to the attic stairs and climbed up. Her head ached from the late hour, her heart ached for Roque, her conscience ached from her secrets, and her elbow, damn it. Adrenaline had camouflaged the pain when she'd lost her balance and smacked the wall of the shower, but now, oh my God. She needed ibuprofen and a long night's rest.

It wasn't until she settled on her side on her makeshift bed that she realized she'd just walked around her house and now lay in the attic—in the dark—without a flashlight. Talk about distraction. Roque personified it.

She glanced at her phone for the time. Five a.m. *Sonofabitch.* She wanted to cry. Self-pity welled in her chest. Even if the crew didn't show early, she never knew when Roque would.

No one's fault but your own, baby.

On a sigh, she pulled herself off the floor to get dressed.

Someday she'd be waking up to an alarm clock, from her bed, with writing deadlines to stick to. The wanting of it all was painful. She'd get there someday, but first, she had some growing up to do. Especially since her last boyfriend regarded her as a child instead of a woman, a partner.

She could only handle arrogant, overbearing, I-know-everything-and-you're-lucky-I'm-here-to-take-care-of-you for so long. When she'd complained one day to her mom, and her mom's answer was, "I don't particularly like him, but, honey, he has a point," Addi knew she had to make some changes. She had something to prove, to the guy, to her family, to herself.

First things first—the guy had to go.

That had felt good.

Now she had to save her home. She made her way back to the bathroom, looked around the scene of the crime from the night before, and grimaced.

The white textured walls popped clean and fresh against the Mediterranean mosaic tile of the tub and shower walls. Bamboo window blinds left open let in just enough early morning light for her to see her reflection in the mirror over the sink. She stared at herself. The night's events were written all over her face in the hollow appearance of her large eyes and dehydrated skin. *Ugh.*

Hoping her makeup would cover the worst of a night with no sleep, Addi arranged her hair down, a deep side part leaving her long bangs to obscure a good portion of one eye and part of her face.

"Tricks of the trade." What trade? Fraud? This was ridiculous.

Her temples pounded with a headache. Seeing how stressed Roque was made it very difficult to stick to her plan. Sure, the money she pocketed was barely the shoe budget of a Hollywood studio wardrobe closet, but knowing she took from the film when it was in trouble made her clever idea feel not so clever.

One thing was for sure. She needed the money, but that included her job as his assistant. The film shutting down would hurt her worse than Roque or anyone else on the crew. They could sign on with the next project, most probably already had another gig lined up, but she needed this until she heard back with something positive from her latest submissions.

If her job got cut or the film collapsed, she'd be heading back to another full-time, overtime job, and erasing years of progress toward her goal.

What she wouldn't give for hours on end spent writing again, carafes of coffee bookended with cups of herbal tea. Getting lost in her stories, her characters, the knowledge their happily-ever-after was coming in the end. Not like her current situation where any second it might end in tragedy. But to do that she needed this job, and she needed her home.

Time to put on her thinking cap. Her ideas and schemes might not have always ended up successfully, but they always ended up causing something. And at this point something was better than nothing.

By his mood last night, Roque had most likely hit the bottom of a dry well where his own resources were concerned. He wouldn't ask his dad or uncle, and the director he had was out. They needed to find a director and an investor, immediately. As soon as the time was respectable, she had a few phone calls to make.

This was Hollywood. She swore on her next book she could find both.

Chapter Fourteen

Roque walked in the front door, no longer surprised to find Addi ready to go. He threw her a brilliant smile meant to blind her from his personal hell. He exuded Hollywood elite in the fine cut of his trousers and the crisp fit of his tailored button-up. He looked refreshed, energized—happy—even though he felt like he'd played chicken with a fucking semi. And lost.

He wasn't about to put off her coffee any longer. He took a tentative sip. "Perfect way to start the morning. I could get used to this. "

He heard what he'd said as soon as he said it and, before Addi could retort in her usual feisty manner, he put his other hand around her waist and pulled her in, silencing her open mouth with his own.

The punch to the gut was immediate and stronger, bolder, than any cup of coffee—even Addi's.

Pulling back, he settled his forehead against hers. "Thanks for the coffee."

He released her, then made his way back to the kitchen.

Grabbing his laptop from the sideboard, he settled at the table. Pulling up the submission forms for the festival circuit, especially Sundance, Telluride, and Toronto, he took notes on requirements and deadlines. He'd gather the information he needed moving forward as if the film was already complete. After going through the circuit list, he pulled up his file of possible musicians to contact for three different pre-recordings they'd need for the lead actor to lip-synch to. They were using her singing as beats of her character arc throughout the film. Symbols of growth and acceptance of herself. Then he needed to work out the order of scenes for later in the week. It was easier to do a grouping of inside shots one after the other than moving the equipment back and forth.

A full morning at the computer would help him catch up and give him time to let his brain wake up. At least that had been his original thought. No such luck. Sleep was not his friend, and he felt dead on his feet.

After leaving the bungalow last night, he'd driven home, showered, shaved, and juiced up with a protein energy drink. He refused to let anyone see him lagging, especially when he didn't know how the hell he was going to pull himself out of this one. But he would. If he didn't, and soon, his film was done and the funds he'd invested would be gone.

He couldn't afford to fail.

The thought eased him a bit, and his lip pulled up at one corner.

"Why the smug smile? Don't be too cocky about that kiss. I've had better."

He glanced up to see Addi walking in, sipping from her own cup. She'd had better? Little brat. He ignored the sharp dig of possession that gouged into his gut at the thought of her being with anyone else.

Pushing back from the table, he approached her.

Eyes wide, she looked left then right as if for an escape.

Before she could make a move, he cornered her against the counter top, one hand on either side of her hips. "Is that a challenge?"

"No, nor was it an invitation." She shoved, without much determination, against his chest. "Roque," she hissed. "The crew is coming in."

"So. What."

Grabbing her hips, he set her atop the counter with ease and stepped between her thighs. His new favorite place to be—almost. The heat of her immediately demanded his body pay attention. He pulled her tight against him, then dragged his palms up the slick sides of her silk top, letting his thumbs rub up and over the swell of her breasts, dragging against her nipples until he cupped her face in his hands. "Good morning."

He nibbled at her lower lip, releasing a shuddering breath from between the pair. Taking advantage of the easy access, he attacked with persistent, tender attention, biting again at her lower lip then soothing with his tongue.

Her arms snaked up around his neck, and her legs wrapped tightly about his hips, bringing him closer. He'd give anything for their clothing to disappear so he could lose himself in her. Right here, right now. Crew be damned.

He swore into her mouth. "Fuck."

"Yes, now."

A ragged chuckle escaped him. "God, you're torturing me."

Molding a hand to her breast, he kneaded her with a slow, firm motion. Desperation, a burning urgency, filled him to painful lengths.

She groaned. "Roque."

He pulled back, easing out of the kiss, a nip, a suck. "Now. Tell me you've had better."

She peeked up at him through long lashes, a look he feared might kill him.

Running her tongue along her bottom lip, then her top, a torture all womankind had used for ages to tempt and tease, she said, "Well done, Mr. Gallagher. You keep that up, maybe a little more practice, and we'll see where you stand."

He stared at her for a beat, then narrowed his eyes with a gravelly chuckle. "You are a little brat."

"Ha." She moved him back and slid from the counter top. "There is nothing little about me." Straightening her slacks and smoothing her top, she winked at him.

She was right, there was nothing little about her. She was a big personality, had a big heart and legs that went on and on and on.

He shook his head. *Snap out of it, Gallagher.*

Addi crossed the room and opened the French doors. She paused, gazing across the space at the hammock.

He quickly glanced out to the space, checking for any signs he'd been there. Had he missed some broken glass? No, nothing.

"What."

She started and quickly shot him a look. "What?"

"You're staring."

With a scowl, she swept out a hand, palm up. "Why aren't you? Look at this place. It's just beautiful." She leaned her head against the frame of the door. "So many memories." Sadness filled her eyes.

"Do you miss her?"

She cut her eyes to his. "Yes. She believed in me."

He nodded, a heaviness filling his chest. "Yeah, I know that feeling."

Fingertips itching to feel her skin, he gave in to the urge and slid them from her shoulder down her arm, reveling in her silky warmth. As he glided his fingers over the point of her elbow, she winced and sucked in a breath.

He stilled, gently lifting her arm, investigated the area

around her elbow. "Addi, what the hell did you do?"

The flesh around her elbow was swollen and purple.

She stepped back from his touch and quickly hid the injury with her other hand. "Oh, it's nothing. I-I tripped."

"You tripped?" He couldn't help the doubt in his voice. The stricken look on her face told a different story. What, he didn't know. He pushed away his unease.

"Yeah, I tripped. Last night. I haven't unpacked everything at my place and didn't see a box in the dark."

"You need to put ice on that." He moved toward the freezer.

Shooting her hand out, she stopped him. "No, it happened last night. I'll be fine. We have more important things to do."

Stopping in the middle of the kitchen, he walked back to stand in front of her. He didn't like her being hurt, but he didn't like not knowing what she was hiding even more. "Be careful. I have a vested interest in your well-being." He followed the sentiment with a kiss to her forehead. "You look tired."

"Any headway?"

Raking his hand through his hair, he took a seat at the table. "Not yet, but I'll figure it out. I have to, it's my project."

She winked at him. "Sure, but Hollywood has barrels of money just waiting for you to spend. You just haven't found the right one yet."

He laughed. "If only this were a Hollywood production. Our saving grace is I'll work round the clock until I figure it out. One thing I'm good at is working."

Her little grin disappeared, and she stilled. Shaking her head slowly, she said, "What do you mean?"

"I don't understand what you're asking," he said.

"What do you mean it isn't a Hollywood production?" She gripped the chair, her knuckles white.

"The film's my pet project. Indie, not Hollywood. I've

busted my ass to develop the script, put a crew together, find backing, including my own hefty investment."

"No."

"Why is this so hard for you to believe?" He crossed his arms over his chest, trying to figure out what was behind her shock. Maybe it was the Gallagher name, or even the known wealth. Maybe she couldn't believe he'd put his own money behind his first film. But that was exactly the point.

She put her hands to her stomach. "That's—it's amazing, is all. Most people wouldn't take that kind of risk."

Something flashed in his chest. A risk. It was, and he fed off it. He loved the challenge, and he was determined to take this last connection with his mother to fruition. Like a dedication to all she had been to him.

He cleared his throat as he grabbed his cell. The morning had started, and he didn't want to have to sprint to catch up. Even another energy drink wouldn't help him with that. Walking toward the French doors, he waved his phone and left her with a wink.

"I'm not most people."

The panic that seized Addi's lungs as she'd hid her elbow from Roque was bad enough, but the bomb he'd dropped about the film blasted through the front of her skull. Her chin quivered, and she clenched her teeth to stop it. One lie turned into another with each conversation. She'd wanted to spill her guts no less than twenty times that morning alone, but losing her aunt's bungalow kept her lips sealed. And now he said his film wasn't a Hollywood production? A pet project, and not just anyone's, but his.

She couldn't be stealing from the man she was sleeping with. She couldn't have sunk that low.

Her stomach churned. Winding through the equipment, she forced a good morning to the crew as they set up for the next scene sequence. The star of the film was a new face to Hollywood. A young woman just out of the New York Film Academy, the same place Gage Cutler had attended.

Addi watched as the young lady read through her lines. What was her name? Stella Larkin, that's it. Vibrant and innocent. Two words that described the actress to perfection — and one of those words would never describe herself.

The cooler autumn air mixed with the salty ocean breeze did little to soothe her as she made her way to her car. If what he said meant what she thought it did, she had some errands to run.

Her car. *Oh shit.* She forgot to pull it back into the driveway this morning. She seriously needed to be more careful. Now the anxiety of discovery churned in her guts. *If I survive this, it's going to be a miracle.*

Out of breath from both exertion and stress, she ducked under the low-hanging branches alongside the road. Straightening under the brush she came face to face with a dark figure and slapped her hand over her mouth to stifle her scream.

"Fuck. Shit. Fuck. Jimmy. Oh my God, you scared me to death."

Jimmy laughed. "Calm down, girl. Deep breath. I was just checking out the surrounding acreage for shoot opportunities and came across your car." He tapped the trunk and eyed her. "Speaking of your car. Why do you have it hidden?"

Addi's words froze on the knot forming in her throat. Crap. She frantically searched her brain for a good excuse. "Oh, I was just trying to stay out of the way. With the new outdoor scenes coming up, I didn't want to slow down production." She waved off his question and opened her door, forcing her movements to be slow and casual. "Hey, I have a question."

Jimmy dipped his chin. "What's up?"

"This film. Is this really Roque's pet project? Like, it's not through a Hollywood studio?"

He snorted, with a smirk that said, "*Where the hell have you been?*" "Uh, yeah. Why do you think he's been so wrapped around the axle? The investor that pulled out contributed a large percentage, and boss man's already got a shit ton of his own wrapped up in the thing. Every penny counts at this point. And there might not be enough copper to save it."

Her stomach turned.

"Of course. Right." She slid in behind the wheel and then started her engine, watching Jimmy stare and then disappear into the foliage through her rearview mirror. Once he was out of sight, she dropped her head to the wheel and blew out a breath.

Digging out her phone, she called Sam. She'd been trying to reach her but only getting voicemail. Her sister answered on the fourth ring.

"Addi?"

"Hey, I've been wanting to talk to you."

"Yeah, sorry. It's been crazy. Hold on a second." Addi listened as Sam gave instructions to someone who sounded like a furniture deliveryman.

"I'm back. What's up?"

"I've got a problem—an opportunity—and I'm wondering if it's something Gage is interested in."

"For Gage? What kind of problem are you talking about?"

"Sorry, wrong choice of words. Like I said, an opportunity. This film I'm working with. I can tell you more later, but I think Gage will be interested. I just wanted to see if we could meet up—"

"Oh, Addi, I love that you thought of him, but we just got home, and I'd hate for him to feel pressured to take on something like that for family. He's got this next one coming up with Martin already—"

A heavy weight tightened in her chest, and a steady pounding set up camp behind her temple. Lifting her hand to her forehead, she forced out in a casual tone, "Oh, sure. No problem. Just a thought. I'll let you go."

"I love you."

"Yeah, me, too." Addi dropped her head back against the seat, staring through her front window at all the leaves and the flickering shards of sunlight peeking through. Kind of reminded her of the state of her life. Pieces. All in pieces.

Frustrated, she grabbed the steering wheel and shook it. Working on this film with Roque would be a great opportunity for Gage. She knew it. Now she just had to make sure they knew it. Her family wasn't going to take her seriously if she didn't make them.

She'd go to them once she had prepared, and they'd never have the chance to say no.

She pulled out onto the road. Between almost being caught, the news Roque was funding the film, and Jimmy finding her car, she already needed a drink. With her sister blowing her off, she might need two. She tapped her fingers against the steering wheel in time with her racing heart. Calm down, Addi. Breathe.

That was the problem, wasn't it? As soon as she thought she could, something else seized her breath. Welcome to adulthood.

If she could just make it through the next few weeks of filming she'd be scot-free, but one thing was certain. She couldn't keep living in her house.

She needed to find a cheap place she could stay until the film was over. It would put a dent into the money she'd saved, but she'd just have to have something lined up after this so she could make ends meet.

He could never find out what she'd done. He put every piece of himself in this project. There was no way he'd ever understand why she'd stolen from him. Like her family, he'd think she was too immature to handle life on her own.

She sniffed back the tears and clenched her jaw. Her to-do list was short. Get a cheap hotel room. Find an investor for Roque. Work some of her own connections. Maybe then the sour feeling in her stomach would settle.

The hotel room she could take care of in under an hour and get back to work. Sneaking her things out of the attic might prove to be a bit more difficult. She'd do it at night, but Roque paid attention to the security system time stamps like a warden. She'd figure it out.

She didn't want any more reasons to disappoint herself. She'd done enough of that in her life.

A tentative smile pulled at her lips.

The Gallaghers weren't the only ones with connections in Malibu.

Chapter Fifteen

Roque slid his phone into his front pocket with a sigh. The day had raced past him in a blur of rejections and prior commitments from everyone he'd talked to, and now the hour had reached beyond the acceptable time for calls of business. He hadn't given up, but there was little more he could do until he figured his shit out. Every minute was costing him money he didn't have. Covering the director's positon short-term was one thing, but in the end, he wanted the expertise of someone who knew exactly what he was doing. And beyond that, he couldn't afford to keep paying everyone until he secured the funds.

Addi had just returned, so it was as good a time as any. "Guys, hey."

Heads slowly turned toward him as he walked into the front room. "Hey. Stop what you're doing."

That got everyone's attention.

Addi stepped forward. "What's going on?"

Pressing his lips into a thin line, he took in each concerned face. These were his friends, his supporters; they trusted him, and he'd let them down. He wanted to punch something.

"I need to call a temporary hold on the film."

Gasps and chatter filled the room.

Putting his hands up, he called out, "Okay, calm down. It's not over. But I lost an investor, and with Kemper pulling out, I need a few days to regroup. I don't want you guys to worry. You'll be receiving phone calls from me within the week."

"But surely, you can keep filming. You'll find someone." The desperate look in Addi's face only made him feel worse. She had a lot on the line as well. He understood that. He was letting her down, too.

With a shake of his head, he said, "It needs to be done."

He watched as the crew packed up and cleared out, a cold, heavy stone dragging along the bottom of his gut.

"Hey boss, want me to stick around?"

"No, Jimmy. I'll call next week."

"I'll be ready."

The door closed for the last time, and he wandered out into the backyard, turning on his favorite jazz radio on his phone. He had so much pent-up energy, fueled by the desperate need to succeed, he thought he was going to explode.

"Are you okay?"

"No."

Pausing on the patio, he stared out across the ocean below. He smelled the honey scent of her, then felt the gentle touch of her hands, and tensed. Maybe a workout at the gym would ease the tension gripping him so tightly. It was time to call it a night.

He turned toward her. "Addi."

She looked up at him and smiled. She understood what he was going through.

That smile, delivered full force, nothing held back, and for him. He hadn't even known how much he'd been waiting for it. Ridiculous. No one waits for a smile. But then again, he was in the middle of losing his fucking mind.

He sensed a shift in her, almost as if up until now she always faced him at an angle, only exposing a fraction of herself, but now she faced him, all of her, and she was stunning.

He wanted more. More what? Shit if he knew, but more.

He pulled her close. "Tell me about why you write."

"Because I can't not."

"But—"

"Shhhh. Roque?" The sound of the crashing waves below filled his head. Her requesting tone was not to be resisted, not this night or any night. His whole body tensed in anticipation. Fuck the gym. This was what he needed.

With slow precision he ran his fingers around her back, up her sides, and over the swell of her breasts until he cupped her face. Her breath hitched.

Under the stars, in the light of the moon, it was almost as if they had their very own stage, and the anticipation gnawed at him. He forced himself to take his time and slid his lips against her until she opened for him. He more than tasted, he savored, he worshipped, with his lips and tongue and fingers. His whole body joined in—a devout congregation if there ever was one.

As he pushed boundaries he hadn't realized he'd constructed, the urge to bare her to the night air grew strong. He needed to feel the silk of her skin, the heat of her body wrapped around him, pulling him under. He'd happily drown in her, lose himself. That would be the sweetest relief from a day like this one.

Sliding his fingers under the straps of her top, he slid them down her arms until the flowing fabric pooled at her waist. With a hook of his thumbs against the fire of her skin, he shoved her shirt, slacks, and panties to the ground. She stepped out of the clothing and her heels as he let his own clothes drop to the ground, save the condom from his pocket.

The cool ocean breeze gently brushed across his skin, sending a chill along his spine to the base of his neck.

He had to look down at her now that she'd removed her shoes. She lost a few inches, standing barefoot in front of him in nothing but a lacy, shell-edged bra the color of ripe peaches. Those breasts would make the juicy fruit weep with jealousy. His mouth watered.

The change in height reminded him of how much bigger he really was. She had height, he'd place her about five feet nine inches, but even so, toe-to-toe, he towered over her. A fierce sensation of need tightened his gut, and he yanked her to him.

She tumbled into his embrace, looking from side to side like she was nervous, a smile upon her lips. Lips he wanted to taste again. Taking her mouth, he sucked and nipped, sliding his tongue along her teeth to finally wrap around the sweetness of her own. Their gasping breath met with the sound of rustling leaves, disturbed by the gentle currents coming in from the ocean. And he lost himself in the feel of her, the sound of her, and the flavor of the salty breeze on her skin.

He slid the condom down as she watched, the tip of her tongue sliding along her upper lip, all but killing him. He pulled her to him and lifted her, encouraging her legs to wrap around his waist. Nuzzling the flesh spilling from the top of her bra, he breathed her in, all of her, not just her scent, but her being. Without understanding the urgency feeding his logic, Roque lost sight of his desire to savor as the need to devour drove him to his knees. The hard stone introduced pain but only increased his pleasure.

Taking her with him, mouths still fused, he slid into her with one powerful thrust.

"I've never done this before," she gasped. "Outside, I mean."

He held her gaze. "Neither have I." And he found it was

his new favorite place, as if boundaries were optional and limitations nonexistent. No walls closing in, just the universe spread out before them.

A smile curved her lips in the moonlight.

Leveraging the weight of her at her hips, with Addi's arms in a fierce hug about his neck, he thrust in and then slowly pulled out almost to his tip, before driving home once again.

She met him thrust for thrust, groan for groan, demand for demand. Trailing a blaze of fire along his jaw to his ear, she grazed her teeth against his lobe, then the side of his neck. Another graze from her teeth followed by the firm pressure of her lips against his raging pulse sent sensations of hallelujah down his spine, tightening his balls.

Pressure built, spiraled, climbed. The sound of their gasping breath increased as their mouths fused once again, then they lowered together toward the patio.

She braced her feet on the ground, sliding up and down his length faster and deeper, again and again, making her own demands, serving her own needs.

His mind went blank to the unrelenting stone beneath his knees as Addi drove her tongue into his mouth, matching the rhythm of their flesh. Heat flared into an inferno as the pressure at the base of his cock exploded out in wave after wave.

He strained to keep his shout from echoing off the trees, instead releasing it in a growl of satisfaction.

Addi's body tensed, tightened, then bowed, her arched back driving him still deeper into her. Her cry rendered the night silent as she pressed down again and again, grinding through her pleasure. Her walls contracted around him in waves until he lowered back onto his haunches, the cool stone soothing in the midst of such heat.

Forehead to forehead, they gasped for air. His blood thundered in his ears, his muscles burned, and the relief of it all washed over him.

Addi kissed his eyes, his cheeks, finally settling her full, lush lips back to his mouth where they belonged. A swift rush of gratitude filled him, and he tightened his arms about her.

She giggled. "I can't breathe."

He gentled his grip but didn't release her.

"That was…"

"I know." He didn't want to hear what he just experienced put into words. There were no words. Just need.

Roque stared into Addi's heavy-lidded, blue gaze. She'd given him a breather from reality, a break he needed before it broke him. Now he was ready to face it again and get everyone back on set.

There was a lot more than his success riding on this film.

Addi didn't waste any time driving to Gage and Sam's house the next morning. It was amazing what a great bout of sex and a good, guilt-free—well, almost—night of sleep could do for a woman.

Sleeping on a real bed and showering with the light on had seemed like such a luxury.

Roque had been so tense, so angry, she'd wanted to soothe him. There was nothing better than skin against skin to decompress. He'd lost himself in her as she had in him. The connection when they were together was so different from anything she'd ever experienced. It must be the desperation of the situation. From the moment they'd met, she'd been in panic mode, and he'd been in production mode. That was a lot of energy between two people. And boy, was it explosive. She'd never look at the moon the same way again.

Throwing her car into park, she hopped out, walked up the steps, then lifted her hand to knock on the door. Accepting help for herself was one thing, but using her connections to help a friend was a no-brainer.

Friend.

She smiled at the realization. They'd become friends. Friends with benefits, apparently.

It swung open before she could knock.

"Addi!" Sam threw her arms around her, squeezing so hard she almost lifted Addi off her feet.

"Hey! How was the honeymoon?"

"Amazing. Come in. Check out the new place."

Addi looked around. Bare floors and stark walls couldn't obscure the beauty of the layout and the plan. "This is going to be amazing."

Sam nodded. "We love it. It'll be ready by Thanksgiving. We got the keys a few days ago, so, good timing."

"I bet you guys are exhausted."

Her sister led her into the kitchen. "Are you kidding? I could take on the world right about now. And Gage is going crazy wanting to get back to work."

Addi laughed, looking at her sister from head to toe. She was practically glowing—nothing else could express how her sister shone better than the old cliché. "You're changed."

Sam pulled her in for another hug. "I'm almost afraid to talk about it, I'm so happy."

Pulling back, Addi held her sister's gaze. "No one deserves it more than you. It's wonderful." She bit her lip and walked around the island of the big kitchen. "Speaking of Gage, I have an idea for him."

"Nothing I like better than being talked about by two beautiful women." Gage Cutler sauntered into the room in socked feet, loose jeans, and a light gray T-shirt. Addi had to blink a few times when his startling green-blue eyes met hers with a twinkle.

"Hey there, big brother."

He laughed while bringing her in for a hug. The movie star smelled of warm nights and the ocean. She'd have been happy to stay there breathing him in if Sam hadn't slid under his arm.

Addi pinched Sam's arm playfully. "Party pooper."

"Ha!"

Gage grabbed a coffee pod for the coffee maker.

Addi wrinkled her nose. "That is sacrilege."

Sam grabbed one, too. "Well, if we had you making our coffee every morning we wouldn't even think of it."

Satisfied, Addi leaned her elbows on the island. "I know you're busy, but you're looking for projects, right? Just in general. Directing opportunities?"

Gage sipped from his cup. "If they're good, always."

"I have one that I think you'd be perfect for. Hear me out before making a decision. Okay?"

Gage looked from Sam back to Addi. Sam stepped beside Gage and laughed. "Addi, come on. Your ideas tend to cause more trouble than good. They're always fun, but—"

Biting her lip against the hurt, Addi held her ground. "Thanks for the vote of confidence."

"Since when are you the sensitive one?"

Looking back to Gage, Addi waited. He kissed Sam on the temple, then moved over to a large kitchen table, the only furniture in the place so far, it seemed. Pulling out a chair, he motioned for Addi to sit down. Then he grabbed the one beside hers, swung it around, and straddled it, resting his arms across the back. "Whaddya got?"

A huge sigh of relief surged from her lungs, but she held it in check. This had to work. "Do you know Roque Gallagher?"

The corner of his mouth raised up in a smirk. "Of course I do. If memory serves, you two were having words at our wedding."

She waved away his teasing. "Yeah, yeah. Old news.

Anyway, I'm his assistant."

"You're what?" Sam almost spilled her coffee.

"I'll explain later." Looking back at Gage, she continued. "He's working on a film. His own pet project."

Gage dipped his chin. "Sure. I heard about it. Is it any good? I know he's a Gallagher, but I haven't actually seen any of his work."

Excitement urged her forward. "I'm so glad you asked. It's brilliant. He has a clear, really bold vision. It is a big risk, but with an even bigger payoff when it's successful."

Sam leaned forward, listening intently.

"Really?" He exchanged a look with Sam. "I don't know." His tone was hesitant but interested. Sam returned his gaze with an almost imperceptive dip of her chin.

Addi straightened her spine. "Look, I know stories. I've studied them, both deconstructing others' work and writing my own. I'm telling you, he is onto something that could be really amazing here. Roque Gallagher is going places with or without you, and I'd love for it to be with you."

Gage waited for her to continue.

"I'm not asking a favor, but offering you a great investment, a career opportunity. One of his investors backed out, and then the director, Kemper, jumped ship."

He narrowed his eyes while he held her gaze. She felt as if she were under assessment.

With a quick nod, he said, "What an asshole. Not surprised. That guy's so afraid of depending on the quality of his own work, he only puts his name on finished films."

"Well, Roque's in danger of losing the film altogether. Someone's been working some sort of angle spreading rumors, and with Kemper adding to the noise, Roque keeps hitting dead ends. But I know he'll make this film amazing, and the two of you together could make this film unforgettable."

That was the key. Unforgettable. It was one thing to be

amazing, but to be a film that lasted generations, that was pure magic. The two of them could make that happen.

The muscles in Gage's jaw clenched rhythmically, and his eyes deepened to a vivid green.

"Uh oh," Sam giggled.

Addi tensed. "What?"

Gage pushed up from his chair and shoved it under the table. "Set up an appointment with Roque as soon as possible. I at least want to talk to him about it."

Jumping up from her chair with a squeal, she launched herself at her brother-in-law. "Oh my God, thank you!"

He caught her with a grunt. "Hell, I need to start saying yes more often."

"This is going to be great. Sam, can you believe this?"

Her sister laughed with her but shook her head in confusion. "I don't even know what's happening."

With an excited giggle, Addi grabbed her in a tight hug. "I think I just saved my job."

Saved her job, saved the film, lightened the burden of her little secret just enough to wiggle her muscles without a pinching pain. Relief rolled off her so fast, she had put her hand on the table to steady herself.

Sam asked. "You okay?"

Addi nodded. "Yes. I think I am."

Finally, one of her ideas was a box-office hit.

If only she could say the same of her original scheme. She had to keep it a secret, though her decisions might crush her. She wouldn't be able to stand seeing the disappointment, the hurt on Roque's face, if he found out the truth.

Chapter Sixteen

Roque watched Addi walk back and forth through the front room, dusting, rearranging, picking things up only to set them down again. She wasn't fooling anyone; her nerves were strung tight. Maybe she could use a little of the medicine she'd fed him on Friday night.

His body tightened at the memory. Being with her was like losing himself in the best possible way, but not even knowing it until he was found again. There was a certain freedom to being lost. With her, he was his most basic self—no walls, no thinking, just instinct and action and heat. She threw quite a punch.

Suddenly, she clapped her hands and moved to the door, pulling it wide. "Hey there."

Gage Cutler stepped across the threshold and wrapped his arms around her in a tight hug. "Hey, yourself."

Taking his hand, she pulled him into the room. "Roque, you have an appointment."

Raising his brow, he joined them, extending his hand to shake Gage's and pulling him in for a quick bump and pat on the back. "Hey, man. How was the honeymoon?"

"Amazing. We didn't want to come back."

Roque grasped his shoulder. "I don't blame you. Want a beer?"

"I wouldn't say no."

Roque led him into the kitchen, wondering what brought the movie star to his set. His cast was full, and Gage wasn't the right fit for this film, no matter how good he was. "What's up?"

Gage took the offered beer with a smirk. Looking from Addi back to Roque he said, "Addi didn't tell you?"

"Tell me what?"

Addi bustled in, waving her hands. "I didn't want him overthinking it."

"What's going on?" Roque took a seat at the table.

Addi shifted from one foot to the other, making him antsy from her energy alone. What the hell was up? Gage took a seat across from him. "You know I just got back in town."

Roque nodded. "I heard."

"I'm interested in your project."

"What do you mean, interested?"

"Look, I'm branching out into directing. I may not have the years of experience you're looking for, but I have the passion, and I've studied under Martin."

Slowly, Roque nodded. Gage was talented beyond his acting. He'd seen the film his friend had debuted with as a director. It was spectacular. Problem was, there was still no budget to hire him on even if he wanted to. "I don't doubt your ability, man. I've seen your work. But I don't have the budget." That was why he hadn't gone to him in the first place.

Gage dipped his chin. "I want in. I want to direct, and I want to invest."

Elation and panic raced through Roque's chest. He shot

his eyes to Addi only to find her gone. He and Gage sat at the table alone. "How can you say that? You don't know the budget, the timeline. Nothing about the cast or crew."

"I did some checking into it. And I want to see what you've got. Then I'll contact my attorney to take care of the paperwork. I assume you don't want to waste any more time. The whole 'time is money' couldn't be more true than it is in this industry."

Doubt pushed Roque back in his seat, and he crossed his arms over his chest. "I don't know if it's a good idea."

"Why? You work with friends. It's impossible not to in this town. We aren't family. I have no connection to the Gallagher name besides choosing to work with all of you."

Hope flickered, but he snuffed it to a cinder. The idea that his problems were over was too much to take in at once. There was always a catch, a sacrifice. At least in this town.

But this was Gage. He was a good man.

Gage rubbed his neck. "This isn't charity. As soon as Addi told me about the project, I wanted in. So much of your footwork for investors happened when I was busy with life. Look, you and I both know Hollywood is a beast, a little less daunting when taken on as a team. And what better team than two professionals hungry to break away from who we were?"

Understatement of the century. Roque rested his arms on the table. "When are you available?"

"Now."

Nodding slowly, Roque grinned. "This is going to be fucking amazing." The film could get back on track. Production could start immediately. He had a great director. The idea he'd have the lost funds replaced was going to give him an industry-sized boner.

He pushed his chair back, the wood against wood grating in the silence. On a sigh, he cracked his neck to the left, then right.

Gage stood.

Shoving out his hand for a shake, Roque laughed. "Welcome the fuck aboard, man."

"Ha-ha, yes. Let's fucking give this town a film they can't stop talking about."

Roque slapped him on the back as they walked through the house. "Have your guys contact my guys to get the ball rolling with the budget. As soon as the papers are drawn up and we're ready to go, I'll call all my people. In the meantime, feel free to pop back and take a look at the set. I'll send you the script."

Gage stepped through the front door. "I'm looking forward to it. I'll be back tomorrow."

Roque closed the door, then leaned back against it.

What the fuck just happened?

He'd been at a loss. All of his last resources and connections drained. And now he was back in business. Just like that.

Addi.

Where the hell was she? Sneaky little brat. He checked her bedroom, the back guest room, then walked back through the kitchen. Pulling his phone from his pocket, he blew out a breath. He swiped through his text messages until he found the one he was looking for.

Addison Dekker: *Writing at Starbucks. Good luck.*

Grabbing his keys, he jumped in his car and headed toward the Country Mart. The more he thought about the partnership with Gage, the faster his heart beat in his chest. And all thanks to Addi.

He had a lot of shit, like any other thirty-something. He worked too much, played too little. None of his other relationships survived it, but Addi understood him better than all the others. After everything she'd done to help him with this film, he'd make the time for her.

With her, he actually might have a chance at a relationship. If she was interested.

Of course she'd be interested. Right? Sure, she'd acted a little distant after their night together, but that didn't mean anything.

Fuck.

Through the front doors of the coffee shop, he could see her sitting at one of the little bistro tables, lost in whatever was going on in her mind, her fingers flying across the keyboard. He'd never seen her so focused.

People walked around her, chatted, laughed, yet she never moved anything but her hands.

"Focused" didn't even begin to describe her state of mind.

She was...what? What was Addison Dekker, exactly?

She was intriguing, a challenge, a pain in the ass, a workhorse, compassionate, demanding, funny. The strangest part was he couldn't even say which attributes were negative and which were positive. They were simply Addi, and all together they made perfection.

He purchased a coffee then made his way to her table, slowing as he approached.

They'd bonded over the film and their dreams. What followed had left him shaken to his core and not a little bruised on the knees. His body tightened with the memory, demanding he grab her, right now, for another round.

Something had clicked, and he didn't just want his success for him, but he wanted to show her, too. Being with her was making him want more, dream more.

However, as far as he was concerned, it had been too long already since experiencing one of life's greatest pleasures. Not sex.

Addi.

He was in trouble. Fuck. *Where's your focus, man?*

First things first—complete the film and make sure it

was the best he'd ever done and impossible for Hollywood to ignore.

Second, figure out what the hell he was going to do with Addison Dekker.

"So, you've resorted to dropping a bomb and slipping out?"

She jumped and looked up at him with eyes that seemed to struggle to focus. Glancing from his latte back to his face, she said, "I thought I'd get a little writing in. Here..." She pushed out the chair across from her with her foot. "Sit down."

Hesitant for a second, he lowered into the chair. "I don't want to take you away from your writing—it's important you get it done. But I had to come find you."

She grinned. "Is he joining us?"

Just as he thought, she'd already taken ownership of her part in the film. He swallowed his smile. "We're on. He's stopping by tomorrow to talk over the script and see our setup. Once the papers are signed, I'll call in the crew."

She jumped up. "I'm so happy for you." Skirting the table, she dropped a hot, wet kiss on his mouth. His hands shot out to grab her but she'd already made it back to her seat, leaving him with her mocha taste on his mouth and honey in the air.

"Thank you, Addi."

Looking shy, she glanced at her lap then back to him. "You're welcome. I'm sorry I didn't think of it before."

He eyed her over the rim of the cup he'd brought to his lips. After setting the cup back on the table, he reached across for her hand. "It means a lot to me. This project...means a lot to me. Thank you."

"You're welcome. I want to see this happen for you. See your dreams come true. Seeing you work on your film is like watching a beautiful relationship bloom." She could hear the wistful tone in her cheesy words but didn't care.

"You are a romantic, aren't you?" Roque laughed.

Nodding, she sipped her coffee and closed her laptop. "To the core. It's beautiful, promising. You don't see it much these days, but I get to surround myself with it anyway through my work."

He grinned back. "I like this side of you, all soft and mushy."

She snapped straight in her chair. "I am not—"

He raised a brow.

"Fine, maybe I am. But—"

His warm hand encircled her wrist, and he caressed the sensitive underside with his thumb. "I just said I like it."

"I dated a guy once who had the mental capacity of a bolt. He always laughed when I talked about romance or my writing."

Roque's brows pulled together.

Addi chuckled. "No worries, we broke up shortly after. He never understood me."

"I want to understand you."

"I know." She shivered.

It was different with Addi. She made him better. Like his mother did for his dad. But he'd recognized years ago that he'd never have with anyone the kind of relationship his parents had been blessed with. Maybe if things were different. If he were different.

They held each other's gaze, relaxing in the silence and talking with their eyes, encircled by the comforting rhythm of indiscernible conversations humming about them.

Roque broke the silence first. "My parents were a lot like Raquel and Martin. No wonder, since two sisters married brothers."

She leaned in on her elbows, holding her cup loosely between her fingers.

"My mother and father were best friends, lovers, partners." He shook his head. "I always felt so comforted by it as a kid. I didn't have any siblings, but I always had them. And I knew I always would. Well, I used to feel that way."

She dropped one hand to his across the table. "Tell me more about her."

He stared at her, then lowered his eyes to their hands. "She was everything. Warm and vibrant, intelligent, inclusive. She brought people together. She saw me in a way no one else ever has, not even my father, and he's a wonderful man. I hope to be half the man he is someday."

Turning her hand over in his, he traced his finger along the blue-green veins running just under the surface of her skin. "I miss her nicknames; man, how I hated them as a kid." He leaned back with a self-deprecating laugh.

"What did she call you?"

He looked up at the ceiling then back to her, a look of chagrin on his wide mouth. Blowing out a breath, he continued. "Her beautiful boy." He waved away the sentiment. "My parents would have passionate conversations about raising me, the state of the economy, whether the sky was blue or azure. You name it, they had opinions. Strong opinions. But as passionate as they were about those things, they were somehow even more so about each other, about me."

He looked around the shop. "Mom was our rock. She kept us in line, loved us with such enthusiasm, guided us with such grace. Dad hasn't been the same man without her, and neither have I."

He chuckled, a low gravelly sound, then drank heavily from his cup, tipping it back and emptying it. Setting the cup down, he raised his brows. "See what happens when I talk about them? *I* turn all soft and mushy."

"I like it." Addi stood, gathered her things, and grabbed his hand. "Let's go for a walk."

He followed, and they stepped out into the cool October night. The Country Mart glowed with streetlamps and strung lights, creating a cozy ambiance perfect for an evening stroll.

"You are, you know," she said.

"I'm what?"

"The same man you were when your mom was here."

He shook his head. "Addi, you don't understand."

They'd passed through to the center courtyard, and she stepped in front of him. "But I do. There are differences, sure. No one is left unchanged after losing a part of themselves."

That caught his attention, and his eyes held hers.

"You didn't just lose your mother, you lost part of yourself, part of your soul. You feel hollow and wonder if you'll ever feel whole again."

He couldn't get any words out, beyond a slight dip of his chin.

"The boy she helped to mold into this wonderful, creative man is still there, but now he's accompanied by a tougher shadow as well, someone determined to make himself the success his mother always knew he'd be. Someone who could forge ahead in the midst of loss."

Her eyes were earnest, and he couldn't look away as she continued. "You channeled everything wonderful about what she taught you, what she saw in you, to become all you are now. You're amazing. I don't know how you did it. I can't imagine losing my mom."

"One thing at a time."

She tilted her head. "What do you mean?"

His lip quirked up at one corner. "That's how I did it. How I do most things. One thing at a time."

Addi pulled in a breath. "I'm sorry...about your mom."

Roque watched as worry creased Addi's brow. She glanced away as if she couldn't look him in the eye anymore. He wished he knew what she was hiding. He'd help her through whatever it was. She had to know that by now.

The hanging lights strung from trees and bushes cast

dancing shadows across her features.

Emotions welled in him, stretching his chest and tightening his gut, exhausted from fighting for his future the past few weeks. No one had ever understood him as well as she did, and he could see what a rare gift it was.

He hummed a comforting melody and pulled her into the gentle sway of a dance. Warmth radiated from her breasts to his chest. She had such a hold on him, and he had no idea just how deep it went or even when it had started—but he couldn't bring himself to care. The hollow ache in his gut lessened with each passing moment spent with her.

She sighed dreamily. "What song is that?"

A sharp tug of awareness silenced him. "What do you mean?"

"You hum this tune now and again; it's familiar but I can't put my finger on it."

He thought about her question. It was his mother's favorite song. It played at her wedding, in the background of his childhood memories—at her funeral. Funny it came to mind whenever Addi was around.

Instead of answering, he brushed his lips over one brow, then the other. He pulled back and smiled, gratitude releasing the tight grip of his emotions. She drew him out from behind the walls he'd constructed. He could be real with her in a way he hadn't realized he missed. "Thank you."

The blush that crept up her neck endeared her to him even more. How she could be shy after all they'd experienced together, he had no idea.

Looking up at him from beneath her lashes, she whispered, "You're welcome."

It reminded him of the first time she'd looked at him, like that first day he'd gone to her bungalow, though then it was challenge and feigned seduction fueling the look, not modesty.

People passed by, walking hand in hand, some with

children running ahead to the little playground located in the center of the courtyard. The lighthearted melody of laughter and candid conversations offered the best background music.

"You saved the film."

She shook her head. "I didn't, I..." Her brow furrowed, and she bit her lip. "Roque..."

Her modesty was sweet. "Thank you."

She pressed her lips together with a small shake of her head, then let out a breath. "You have a lot of work to do."

The fact that she understood showed him he just might be right. He hadn't been able to make a relationship work before because of his hours and his passion for his job.

But with Addi... This might be the one relationship he didn't wreck.

Chapter Seventeen

Addi followed Roque to the kitchen table, her mouth watering as the savory aromas escaping from the casserole pulled her to her seat. She admired his confident, languid stride. He walked as if he had all the time in the world, but even if he didn't, he'd get there in time. They'd spent the last couple days making phone calls to the crew and getting Gage up to speed on the project. The two men would rock the film if the way they jumped right in was any indication.

But Addi? She was in avoidance mode. After the coffee shop, Roque said he wanted to talk. But she couldn't talk. She had a feeling she knew what he wanted to say, and it terrified her. She wanted him, wanted to spend time with him, but he could never find out. He hated secrets, hated lies. They could never have a life together. She'd barely gotten started fixing her own.

But she couldn't put him off any longer without having him question why. He pulled out her chair, and she could feel his eyes on her bottom as she sat down. Heat rushed across her skin and not one degree of it from embarrassment. She pushed her concerns aside, determined to enjoy the evening. She was in paradise with a beautiful man.

"Have I told you I love that dress?"

She smoothed her hands down her sides, as if suddenly self-conscious, playing up the innocence in her tone. "This dress?"

He settled into a chair across from her, holding her gaze. "It distracts me, makes me think of you in nothing at all. I have a well-researched topography of your body in my mind. Every dip, every hollow, your taste, your sound —"

She really enjoyed this playful side. On set he was all business, so it felt like he reserved it just for her. Holding his gaze, she lowered her voice. "Two can play at that game, you know." Pulling his hand toward her, she nipped the end of his thumb then soothed it with her tongue. "And against me, you'll lose every time."

He grinned at her. "Then my plan is working. Hungry?"

"Dessert."

"Of course, I have something planned for later."

"Later? Have we met?" She snorted. "You'll get me dessert now."

Roque laughed, hard and long, the kind that made her stomach ache in the best possible way, and she smiled.

Clearing his throat, he pushed back from the table, and her eyes stuck on how the corner of his lip turned up on one side when he was amused. "Dessert, how could I even entertain the idea of no dessert? Chocolate éclairs are your staple. Besides, after everything you've done for me, you deserve it." He made a quick trip to the refrigerator, and she took advantage of his turned back to pull in a shaky breath.

She deserved something, all right. Shifting in her seat, she pasted a smile on her face. "I'm so happy everything is working out."

After setting out a molten lava cake, a plate of éclairs,

and a cheesecake, Roque took his seat across from her and stared. "You still don't understand what you've done." He leaned his elbows on the table, sending a hint of his cologne past her with the movement. "You've saved the film. Gage has brilliant insight. We see things in a similar way, which makes me excited about what we're going to do with the film."

Her heart went warm and cold at the same time. Saying she saved the film was like saying the drunk captain of a sinking ship saved the passengers. Thank God she'd already moved to the other hotel. Otherwise she feared she might be sick.

She pulled her eyes from his and looked at the desserts. "This is amazing. You covered all the important dessert groups."

"Addi."

His tone demanded she acknowledge what he was saying, but she couldn't. So instead she said, "I'm so happy for you. For Gage, too."

"Why do I get the impression you keep changing the subject?"

She shrugged, her tongue tying on any explanation she might have given.

He narrowed his eyes, then reached for one of the desserts. "Here, try this." He placed a chunk of molten lava cake on his fork, topping it with a bit of whipped cream, and held it for her, then took a bite of his own.

"Oh my God. That is divine." She'd always been a sucker for dessert, but watching him eat the chocolaty treat made her hungry for something spicy—preferably with him naked.

Addi nodded and pulled in a shaky breath. "Did you ever find out where some of the rumors have been coming from? Anyone who wouldn't want to see you succeed?"

"This is Hollywood; no one but my family and friends wants me to succeed and a few in that mix may not, either."

She pressed her lips together and narrowed her eyes. "Hollywood. Why do you even bother? From what I've seen, there's nothing but scandal and sabotage."

"Well, you're right and wrong. A world surrounded in luxury, pleasure, and glamour is all about escapism. Very few live in the center of, or benefit from, such indulgence, but everyone—anyone—can get a taste, a feel, a hint of the *good life*." He paused, then gestured toward her with his hand. "You are my reason. And people like you. Moviegoers, lovers of a good tale. For me to fill my world with the creation of stories and lives, dreams and failures, tragedies and triumphs, there's no better outlet than movies. To make something that enters homes around the world and makes people feel, really feel, even if only for a second, well then, I made a difference. I made a moment."

He reached across the table and slid his fingers under her hand, running his thumb along her sensitive skin. The sensation shot up her arm, so strong the caress almost burned.

"I want to make moments with you, Addi." The sincerity in his eyes tightened her throat. Shit! He'd distracted her with his unexpected idealism.

He reached his other hand across the table, now holding hers between his. "I care about you. I can't get you out of my head. It's not just what you did for the film, but what a friend you've become. I can't make promises. I don't do commitments. They haven't been something that's worked for me, but I can see myself with you."

She stilled, unable to move, and stared at him. He also didn't do secrets or lies. Hell, she'd already struck out before the game had begun. Panic, and then something altogether warmer, spread through her chest. Slowly the truth sank in. She was the one who was screwed, because hearing him say the words was the most beautiful music she'd ever heard. What was she going to do?

She bit her lip, restless in her seat. "I don't know what to say. I care about you, too. You have to know that." And she did. So much so the idea he'd ever find out about her original plan made her stomach hurt. She swallowed, her throat dry.

All her efforts were to try to make amends for that. Helping with the film was one way.

But this whole thing between them was something more. She recognized the rarity of it all. He saw a woman when he looked at her. A capable, sexy, woman. She gripped his hand. "I feel it, too. Whatever it is we have here."

He raised a brow. "Why do you sound so scared?"

"Because I am. There're so many things—"

Leaning forward, he whispered, "What do you have to be afraid of?"

She looked down at her plate.

They sat in silence, leaving her heart to both soar and take a nose dive at the same time. Not a comfortable feeling. She cared for him, but she couldn't do anything about it until she figured out what to do about herself. Their whole relationship was surrounded in secrets and tiny pinpoints of deceit. She'd have to find a way to fix that before she could even begin to contemplate anything else. So his inability to commit long-term worked for her. The thought actually comforted her. She couldn't do anything long-term, either. They really were in a similar place.

Now she grinned. Being with him was going to feel so good in more ways than one.

"Are you okay? You're awfully quiet."

She smiled at him and slid her hand along the top of his on the table. He turned his over, and she traced the calluses along the top of his palm. "I'm absolutely okay."

She released him and stood from the table, suddenly filled to the brim with nerves. What the hell did she have to be nervous about now? Knowing he was as into her as she was into him should ease her mind and her libido, not make it worse.

"What are you doing?" he asked.

"I need a drink."

"What?"

She walked to the corner cabinet where she kept her liquor. Grabbing a scotch and two tumblers, she spun, holding them up in front of her. He didn't have to know she was fighting a war between freaking out and jumping his bones. "This calls for a drink. A celebration. The film is underway. And so are we. So to speak."

He laughed. "It's five thirty."

"Which means it's what, eight thirty back east? The whole coast already has over two hours on us." She poured a finger of amber liquid into each glass and then held one up to him, praying it would erase her worries. "Besides, I wouldn't have pegged you as the teetotaler type."

A smile spread his mouth wide. Oh, what she'd like to do to that mouth, which was part of the problem, really. Spending time with him, sharing secrets, and getting used to seeing his beautiful face every day would be too easy. The end promised to hurt like hell. But what was a little pain for a lot of pleasure?

She already cared for him, she'd just make sure she didn't fall in love with him. Her mind left little doubt that would only make it worse. She chuckled. It was odd—she, a romance writer and a die-hard romantic, was trying to figure out how "bad" it would be to fall in love. But fiction was fiction and this was real life, her life, and she knew better.

"What are you laughing about?"

She shook her shoulders. Enough. They had a film to shoot, she had books to write, and she'd get to make love to this delicious man whenever she wanted for however long it lasted. A pretty good deal all around.

"The look on your face. Lighten up. It's only Scotch."

She held up her drink until he touched his glass to hers. "To a successful film and lots of sex."

Roque grinned playfully. "Who said anything about sex?"

She stared him down and shot back her Scotch. The burn rose in her throat like a volcano. Her eyes watered, and she blew out her breath until the Scotch settled.

Roque stared at her as if he'd encountered a crazy woman. He didn't know the half of it. She'd have to thank Chase later; their determination to handle Scotch led them to many tastings at the local bars. They always imagined a woman handling her Scotch was sexy.

By the look in his eyes, they were right.

"I'm not sure if I should be afraid or impressed."

Setting her glass on the counter, she turned and eyed him up and down. He stood in his usual attire of perfection. Navy suit pants with a light blue dress shirt and mahogany wing tips. He'd lost his jacket and tie in the car.

He sipped from his glass, eyeing her back.

Emotion filled her chest, and she pulled in a breath to ease the sensation. He'd knocked her from her secure footing enough when they had dinner at the house. He cared for her? She couldn't allow the idea to enter her mind without her insides going liquid and her knees melting.

The warmth of the Scotch rushed across her chest and fingered up the sides of her neck, leaving her feeling hot and more than a little daring. Pulling her lower lip between her teeth, she raised her arms and released her hair from its pins. She shook it out, her eyes never leaving his.

Her lip popped from between her teeth, and she ran her tongue along it.

Roque's eyes followed the movement, and he took another sip from his glass.

Thanks to copious amounts of yoga, she reached behind her back and lowered the hidden zipper. It delighted her to know she only wore a scrap of material underneath. Revealing that to Roque excited her in ways she hadn't imagined. She wanted to tease him, play with him—and then take him. Like a boss. Her grin was nothing if not devilish.

Her breath came out in little Scotch-fumed pants as she lowered one side of the dress and then the other. She hesitated with the fabric at her breasts until his eyes honed in. With his attention secured, she pulled down the dress, and her breasts sprung free over the silky material.

"Shit." He stepped forward and abandoned his drink on the counter.

She pulled the top of her dress back over herself and made a ticking sound with her tongue, teasing him. "Uh-uh, you stay right there."

"Addi."

"Roque."

With a scowl, he retreated back to the counter and grabbed his drink. Downing it, he coughed and sucked in his breath. "I still don't know how the hell you managed that."

She smiled. "A woman knows how to handle her liquor." Then she proceeded to run her tongue over her top lip.

Again, she pulled the fabric free and then pushed it down her body to pool at her feet. She toed out of her heels and stood tall in nothing but a small silky triangle the color of caramel.

"Fuuuuuuck," he whispered.

She continued to watch him watch her as she trailed her fingers up her sides and over the tips of her breasts, awakening her nipples to perky attention. They ached for his mouth, for the rough contrast of his callused hands, but she resisted the urge to step in to him and rub her body up and down the length of his.

She continued to run her fingers up and over her collarbone and into her hair, turning her head to the side and closing her eyes. With slow, purposeful movements, she traced the same path down her body and stopped above the top of her panties.

"Addi."

She lifted her head and opened her eyes, smiling. He ached, she knew it because she did, too. Their bodies worked better together than apart. She could barely wait to feel him slide into her, but refusing to rush it heightened every sensation. Every touch, every scent, the heat radiating from their bodies, the sounds of their ragged breathing when they hadn't yet touched.

She held his gaze and dipped her fingers below the edge of her panties. His eyes left her face and followed her hand. With each slide of her fingers, his fists clenched. They were the only part of him that moved. Had she broken him of his stillness? She didn't dare to think she was that powerful—but.

"Take off your clothes, Roque." She slipped a condom from her purse.

He dropped his pants and kicked off his shoes, his movements quick but sure—there was no fumbling from this man. His shirt followed.

Stepping close, she wrapped her hand around him, then holding his gaze with her own, slowly rolled the latex all the way down, finishing with a light graze of her nails against the sensitive skin of his heavy balls. Without any other words he stepped in to her and lifted her to his chest. She wrapped her legs about his waist and lowered onto him.

"Oh my God." She moaned the words as he filled her, spread her, challenged her body. She met that challenge, happily.

"Fuck. You tease."

She nipped his neck and held on tight. "Like you'd want me any other way."

He growled and pressed her against the refrigerator door.

Addi lost herself. She reached high and gripped the top of the door. The knowledge that if he let go she'd fall only heightened her pleasure, opened her vulnerabilities, and increased her excitement. The contrast of the cold steel against her back volleyed with the heated flesh along her front. She knew which she'd prefer alone, but together it was more than she'd imagined.

"Goddamn it, you feel so damn good." He pumped into her, bending forward and branding her breasts with his mouth.

They were hot and needy and greedy. Now wasn't soon enough.

Roque drove into her again, and again she met his thrust, tucking her bottom forward, opening wider with each one.

"Oh God. Yes, yes. Don't stop."

"I couldn't if I tried."

The refrigerator shook, her arms ached, her body burned with the pulsing pleasure of need. Stroke after stroke filled her, rubbing her to a point of ecstasy so sharp all she could do was scream her release. "Yes!"

He followed, burying deep, hard, faster and faster.

"Fuck, yes." His voice was low and gravelly with his own pleasure as he ground his pelvis against hers.

Bodies slick with perspiration, she lowered her arms back around his neck and held on with all her might as her body continued to pulse around him, tickling her insides in the most delicious way.

She felt him throbbing inside her, felt it slow, and then finally lowered her legs to the floor. He slid from her and pulled her tight to his body.

With his face buried deep against her neck, he mumbled, "I think I have a new thing about kitchens."

She sighed. "Me, too."

"And Scotch."

"Roque?"

He continued to hold her as their breathing slowed. "Yeah?"

"I'm hungry."

"Dinner's cold."

"What'll we do?"

He grinned. "Pizza."

Her stomach rumbled.

Roque turned with a laugh. "So loud." He shook his head. "I've never met a more insistent stomach."

"Feed it, then."

He grabbed her and pulled her in tight. "Oh, I want to feed you, but something much tastier than food."

As Addi sunk into the kiss, his taste, she agreed. He was much more flavorful than anything else she'd experienced. Dangerous, too. What just happened stole her breath. Why every time they had sex did she get pulled further in, instead of getting over him? She dropped her forehead to his chest. "You just did." Nudging him back to arm's length, she grabbed her phone and pulled in a breath. "Okay, let me order before I expire."

She called and placed the order, slapping away his hands and shushing him every few seconds as she worked double time to try and dress.

Disconnecting the call, she swung on him. "Oh my God, they are going to think I'm some sort of sex-crazed exhibitionist."

"Then maybe we won't have to wait as long for our food." He wiggled his brows and dove his hands up and under her loose-fitting blouse.

"You better make it quick then." Wrapping her arms around his neck, Addi reveled in the feel of his strong arms as he lifted her.

Roque walked through the house to her bedroom and dumped her on the bed, following closely behind. He pressed his weight into her and took her mouth. They kissed like it might be the last thing they ever did. Exploring, learning, appreciating. She didn't know how long it had been since someone put so much time and attention into a simple kiss. She marveled at how sexy she felt in his arms, how relevant. Finally, she left a loud smacking kiss on his cheek, then dodged him with a giggle when he tried to pull her back in. "You forgot our clothes."

"I didn't forget anything."

The doorbell rang.

She slapped his chest. "No time, I need food."

Roque groaned, but went in search of his pants.

Addi followed him into the hallway.

A teenage boy with more muster than muscle took in the sight of Roque's chest, then craned his neck to catch Addi peeking from around the corner. "Lucky son-of-a-bitch."

Taking the pizza, Roque nodded. "Yes I am."

He closed the door in the young man's face then didn't waste any time getting the pizza and Addi back into bed.

They leaned against her pillows, silently consuming piece after piece of cheesy, spicy heaven.

"I would willingly lick the feet of whoever first came up with this food."

Roque grimaced as he took another bite. "Not appetizing, but I get it."

"I could say worse, but I'm trying to be respectful."

"Ha! Yeah, right."

Addi continued to chew, watching him out of the corner of her eye. He really was beautiful. Golden skin, rich dark hair, and eyes the color of an icy heaven. "Why aren't you married?"

He paused and looked at her. Finishing the bite in his mouth, he wiped sauce from his lip with a napkin, leaving Addi to kick herself for not licking it away first. "I could ask you the same question."

"That's easy. I still have to grow up."

His bark of laughter made her smile.

"But I know that about me. You have already grown up."

He took another bite and chewed. Apparently he didn't feel like sharing, so she shoved the end of another piece into her mouth, savoring the tang of marinara and the savory melted cheese.

"Have I?"

It was her turn to laugh as she looked him up and down with a lascivious grin. "Very well, I might add."

His wink was straight from the devil himself. "I have the worst track record when it comes to relationships," he said with a serious tone. "But the truth is, I've missed out on a lot more than just being with someone because of work. Still, I can't pull away. Especially not now, or what would it have all been for? I end up hurting the people I love most. With the work I do, the hours, the way I lose myself in it. It just doesn't work. I've ruined a lot of relationships trying to find balance. I don't want to put myself in the position to hurt anyone again by setting expectations I can't meet."

She scooted up and offered him a bite of her pizza. After he accepted, she stole a kiss. "You just proved you can meet the expectations I've set. So we're good to go."

He snorted as he tried to swallow, his eyes going wide, and she fell back on the pillows laughing. Throwing him off-kilter was one of her favorite things to do. Life was looking up.

"I thought we'd just stay here for the night. It's already late," he said.

Addi fell back to her pillow with a smile.

"You really miss your bed, don't you?"

She grimaced. "You have no idea."

"If I remember correctly, The Huntington's beds are quite comfortable."

She grunted, then grinned wide.

"What?"

"I'm going to take a shower. A long, uninterrupted shower."

He shrugged. "Sounds good. I'll clean up dinner."

Following her toward the bathroom, he watched her set the water temperature and grab a towel. "Did I ever tell you about the night I heard something in here?"

She froze and slowly looked his way. "What do you mean?" she asked, working hard to find something to look at.

"Nothing really. I was just here late and heard a loud bang. When I came back here, there was nothing, but the room was humid like someone had been in the shower."

Addi gave a nervous laugh. "Aunt Addi always did love her hot showers."

"Aunt Addi, yeah right."

She raised a brow. "What? You don't believe in ghosts?"

"Not if it means she just watched me have sex with her great-niece."

"Oh please, Aunt Addi is up there cheering, 'Go get 'em, girl!' every time."

A look of mortification crossed his face. "Don't ever say that again."

He closed the door against her peal of laughter. Crisis averted. Turning on the water, she held her hand under the spray until it got warm. She hated the reminder of her secret. But she'd fixed it, or rather was fixing it. To start, she'd found a cheap hotel down the road, no longer sneaking around after film hours. Taking the project to Gage had felt really good, too. A smile spread her lips wide.

Her job was safe, her writing was steady, and she had days of hot sex with an intriguing man ahead of her. To top it all off, she'd get to sleep in her own bed for the night.

Things were working out well, if she did say so herself. She was taking care of her business like an adult.

And she was even beginning to feel like one.

Chapter Eighteen

Roque stepped through the door, greeted by Addi, a cup of coffee, and a kiss hot enough to burn down the west coast. She seemed to pour all the happiness she felt into the kiss.

Work on set had been going really well the past few weeks, morale was high, and attitudes even. The budget was robust, and deadlines were well on their way to being caught up. He didn't know the last time he'd felt quite so thrilled with life.

Addi released him, but he quickly reached for her with focused intent—intent on another round.

"How'd you sleep?" she asked, easing in to him.

Pulling her against his chest with his free hand, he nibbled her lower lip. "What was that for, and can we start every morning the same way?"

She pressed her lips more fully to his. The front door swung open, and she jumped back.

Roque laughed, wiggling his brows at her, and he stepped close again.

She placed a hand against his chest, keeping him in his

place.

"I think they know, Addi."

She scrunched her nose. "No. Do you think?"

Jimmy stepped up beside her and swung a beefy arm about her shoulders like a twenty-pound scarf. "Affirmative, Tink."

His new nickname for her had her rolling her eyes.

"Tink?" Roque questioned. "My thoughts exactly. I have to admit it's the first time I've ever been turned on by a Disney reference."

Jimmy laughed, and Addi slapped them both on the chest.

"I am not anything like Tinker Bell."

"Really," they said in unison.

She stared from one to the other. "This conversation is ridiculous. Don't you have some place to be, Jimmy? And you." She placed a finger on Roque's chest. "Have a movie to produce."

Jimmy glanced at the cup in Roque's hand. "Any way I can get my hands on some of that?"

Addi jabbed her thumb over her shoulder. "In the kitchen."

They watched him walk away, and Roque threw an arm around her. He slipped his fingers under the hair at the nape of her neck, tracing the sunburst birthmark. "Have I ever told you how much I love this spot right here?"

She tilted her head. "I think I need to hear it again."

"How about if I just show you." Pulling her around the corner and down the hallway, he pressed her against the wall. His chest to her back, he traced the same path of his fingers with his tongue.

"Have dinner with me tonight."

She shook her head. "We have dinner together almost every night."

"No, we eat together almost every night. I want to take

you to dinner. I just realized I haven't taken you on a real date yet. There's this place I love. Great food, great music."

She smiled. "Okay."

His grinned. "Perfect. I have to take care of a few things once we break for the evening. Be ready at eight."

She nodded.

He held her gaze for a beat, just taking her in. "Good. Let's get to work." Walking back toward the kitchen, he found Gage leaning against the counter. "Ready?"

"When you are."

"I wanted to go over the storyboards. Tighten up a few things." He pulled open his laptop, followed by Gage.

They settled into the rhythm he was coming to expect. Volleying ideas back and forth, he'd push, Gage would pull. Leaning closer, he pointed to a block. "See here? I think the whole shot would have a greater impact if the focus was on her hands. Trembling, hesitant."

Gage nodded, slowly. "I see what you mean. Really magnify that touch to her has brought nothing but pain. This is her chance to experience it in a different way, but she's terrified. Drive home her bravery in something as simple as reaching forward."

Addi walked up, studying the images over Roque's head. He could feel the heat radiating off her. Leaning forward, her breast brushed against his back and his palms heated. She pointed at one block in particular. "Her hands. I'd make them grittier. Broken nails, dirt rubbed deep in her knuckles. She's had a hard life. It will make the contrast in reaching out to something so pure really beautiful."

Roque looked at Gage. He recognized the look in the man's eye. Jackpot.

He clapped his hands together and shot up from his chair. "Let's go take a look at this through the lens."

Addi stepped back to make room for the two men. "I'll

set up lunch on the front porch to keep the backyard free and clear. You've had a few calls, but nothing that can't wait until later, and Jimmy said to tell you he'd be back by three."

Roque took in the sight of her. Her blond hair and bright blue eyes were made piercing by the deep shade of her blouse. He wanted to step in to her, to take her out back onto the hammock. Gratitude for saving his film made him grab her by the arms and leave a hard kiss on her mouth.

Once he released her, she pushed her hair out of her face with trembling hands. "Well, if that's what happens every time I give you messages, I'll do it more often."

Gage laughed. "You two have a good setup here."

Roque glanced from one to the other. His chest swelled with the rightness of it all. Everything was falling into place. He was working his ass off, and Addi stood by his side.

She understood the hours, the effort.

Nothing had ever felt so perfect.

The rest of the day raced by in a blur of brainstorming and filming. He couldn't believe the progress they were making. Taking Addi out tonight would be the perfect end to an incredible day, if he could only get out on time. But creative forces couldn't be ignored, and when he was on track with something, he had to finish. Eight p.m. quickly turned into nine, and Roque hurried to Addi's hotel.

"Fuck." He got stuck at another red light and hit the steering wheel. He hated being late. If he was already letting his work affect his other commitments, he was in real trouble. It was little things like this that could slowly bring an end to the best of relationships.

Walking up to her hotel door, he knocked, ready with an apology.

She'd moved to a less expensive hotel, wanting to save as much as possible. He understood it, he'd just been surprised. But the location was good, and she hadn't missed a beat with work on the set.

The door swung open, revealing a blond bombshell in a blue thigh-skimming dress. Her waist was cinched to impossible measurements with a wide black belt, and her heels brought her almost to eye level with him. He whistled. "You look stunning. I am so sorry I'm late. I tried calling. I got stuck in a meeting and—"

"Well, then you'll just have to make it up to me." Sucking her lip between her teeth, she looked him up and down. "And you look good enough to eat. Why don't we just stay in?"

He loved the idea but shook his head as relief washed the tension from him. "I've been wanting to share this place with you for too long." He held out his arm so she could take his elbow.

"Fine, but just so you know, this evening would be a hell of a lot easier if you didn't look so damned delicious."

He laughed. "I knew I had to do something to make up for being late. Besides, it'll just make you want me more by the time we get back. I'm sorry. My meeting ran over, and then I had a few loose ends I couldn't leave for tomorrow."

Addi simply nodded and slid onto the leather seat as he held the door open. She stretched her legs out long, lifting the edge of her dress just a bit to get his attention. As he closed the door she said, "I'm not wearing any panties."

The door fell shut with a satisfying thud, leaving him standing completely still outside. He clenched his fists, his eyes glued to the expanse of skin running long and lean from beneath the hem of her damned too-short dress. No panties. Son of a bitch. If she even bent her head to look down, her ass would show.

His fingers itched to run up along her thigh and test her statement for himself—and he just might.

Damned minx.

He made his way around the car and slid behind the

wheel. "You're going to pay for that."

She winked at him. "Good luck. You're going to need it."

He laughed and started the car. "What's your favorite kind of food?"

"Easy. Italian. How about you?"

Addi's dress hitched higher as they went, making Roque's collar all too tight and his pants impossibly snug. "What was the question?"

Her giggle made him scowl. She was doing it on purpose. Damn the woman—he loved it.

He paid the valet and led Addi into the opulent seaside dining experience. Live jazz crooned as they entered, and the airy, reflective ambience lifted him as it always did. White on white on cream was the basic palette. Lights and mirrors and sheer fabrics seemed to float the room in a bubble of ocean waves and piano keys.

Addi sucked in a breath beside him. "This is incredible."

Though the venue was packed, it was the hushed melodies of the singer that registered, softening the usual cacophony of clattering dishware and conversations.

Roque's parents introduced him to the place when he graduated college, and he made it a point to come back for any and all special occasions. This was one of them.

They were seated at a secluded table surrounded by sheers. The effect was as if they dined on a cloud. Good food and wine softened Addi's teasing agenda, and he watched her look about the space, her eyes wide and a half smile playing on her lips.

The waiter came and tempted her with a tiramisu and dessert wine. Addi bantered with him and they both laughed.

He loved how open and friendly she was. From anyone else the personal conversation with the waiter might seem odd, but from her, it was simply Addi. She stunned him with her beauty and tempted him with her grace. Yes, that was it.

It wasn't her brazen acts or flirty nature that made him yearn to feel her beneath him, but the smooth, easy way she moved and accepted people into her space.

"Let's dance while we wait for dessert."

She smiled and slid her fingers into the palm of his hand. His groin tightened at the reminder that very little separated her skin from his own.

They stepped out onto the dance floor and eased into a sultry sway. It was an intimate moving of their bodies, flowing with the swoony melody floating about the dance floor.

"This place is like a dream."

"I knew you'd love it," he said, pulling her close. His palms slid down her hips, and he played at the hemline of her dress, wanting nothing more than to slip beneath and find out if she was as hot for him as he was for her.

She stepped closer still, tempting, teasing, in the way that was all Addi.

"Thank you for bringing me here," she whispered.

"Thank you for coming."

She stared at him with all he'd never known he'd needed to see shining from her eyes, but then she looked away with a slight shake of her head.

"What?" He rested his forehead to hers as he moved them around the floor in slow glides with the music.

Pulling in a shaky breath, she said, "There's something I need to tell you."

The last thing he wanted the evening to turn into was too serious or too intense, and her tone sounded serious. He pulled back just far enough to reach into his jacket and then offered her a small, thin package.

She looked at the brown paper wrapped in twine. "What's this?" Her eyes wavered. "Roque, I—"

"Open it and find out."

She hesitated, then accepted the gift, turning it over in her hand. "You didn't need to get me anything."

"It's nothing big."

They stood in the middle of the dance floor, couples entwined and moving to the music all around them. He watched her eyes widen in wonder.

"Remember asking what song I always seem to hum when I'm with you?"

She nodded, holding his gaze, hers naked and vulnerable.

"It was my mom's favorite. She and my dad almost separated once. She thought it would break her, but it didn't—I don't think anything could—and they made it through. She always said this song epitomized the way she loved better than any other song did."

Addi opened the package, her lips parting in a soft inhale. "All of Me." She glanced at him from beneath her lashes like she was wont to do, her eyes welling with unshed tears. "Billie Holiday." In her surprise, the paper fluttered to the floor, and she turned the CD over in her hand. "Why do you hum it when you're with me?"

He held her gaze. "I don't know."

And he didn't.

He thought of everything that had happened since they started working together.

And what he did know was the more time he spent with her like this, and the more understanding Addi was about his passion for his work, the more he didn't want to let her down. History tended to repeat itself, and few ever really learned from it.

He hoped he'd learned from his past. Because he was determined Addi would be the exception for him.

Chapter Nineteen

Addi marveled over the excitement of the film as she drove toward her sister's for Thanksgiving dinner. The film had made consistent gains on set, and she had carved out space to get her writing in every day. And whether Roque worked by her side on the business of the film or took off for meetings over drinks, her writing time was uninterrupted and consistent. He got it.

They'd discovered so much in common—their obsessive love of peanut butter, a propensity to listen to jazz while they worked—but she also loved their odd little differences. She usually ended up wearing what she was eating and he always looked like he'd just stepped off the cover of a magazine, but somehow even those little things just bonded them more strongly.

Steeling herself against the end, she decided to revel in the now since there was no way they'd have forever. She thought about the night at the restaurant. The dancing and the CD had touched her in ways she couldn't explain. Roque had shared a piece of his mother with her, and it was a painful subject for him.

After dinner, they drove toward home, but when she slid his hand up her thigh Roque pulled the car over. They only made it home after he'd shown her the stars from the back seat of his convertible. She'd decided then and there to study astronomy.

"What are you grinning about?"

Addi looked up to see her sister, Sam, walking toward her. She'd lost herself in daydreams and had yet to make it out of the car. She opened her door and grabbed her keys. "Who's grinning?" Throwing her arms around her sister's neck, she squeezed tight.

Sam hugged her back, meeting her intensity. "You. Like a fool."

Addi laughed. "I've been writing."

"Sure. Writing. And it has nothing to do with a certain sexy producer?"

Ignoring Sam's comment, she slid her arm around her sister's waist and asked, "Is Gage home?" She wiggled her brows, going for her lewdest look possible.

Sam laughed and bumped her with a hip. "Shut up. God, I remember the first time you two met. I wanted to kill you."

Addi skipped ahead and turned to face her sister, walking backward. "Hey, I said I'd take sloppy seconds; I was doing you a favor, if you ask me."

"Nobody's asking you. You're so gross."

Addi laughed. "Thank you."

Sam opened the huge double doors into the house and let Addi through. Stepping inside, Addi's first impression was how airy and light the space still was now that it was furnished. Large open rooms, lots of natural light. The home exuded the perfect combination of earth and water, suiting Sam and Gage perfectly.

"Come on, everyone's in the kitchen."

Thank goodness the place was huge, because the whole Dekker clan— their mom, dad, and brother Luca, as well as the Cutler clan, Gage, his dad, and his sister Bel—filled the space.

Gage's father, D.C., was at the island with Addi's mother, Dee, and Bel, preparing sauces—like a good man. Gage, Luca, and her dad weren't being slackers, either, as they bantered at the large, bistro-height table, peeling potatoes.

As they entered the room, Gage looked up and smiled. "My favorite Dekker sibling." He walked around the table, arms wide for a hug.

She squeezed him back. "My favorite Hollywood movie star."

"Hey, hey, hey, keep your hands to yourself, Cutler."

Addi froze at the sound of the familiar voice. A voice that slid up her spine with the promise of midnight delights, and boy did he keep his promises. What in the hell was Roque doing here? It was both the best and worst surprise. Her family could read her like a book.

Gage pulled her to his side, taunting his buddy. "But my hands *like* where they are, old man."

Addi bit her lip as Roque narrowed his eyes. Saying it was a thrill to be the focus of such banter didn't even cut it, juvenile or not. "I didn't know you'd be here."

He smiled as he strode up and then slid his hand around her neck, pulling her to him and away from Gage. As he pressed a kiss to her mouth, she reeled with both the desire to lean in to him and the urgency to run.

No, no, no. Her family would never let her get away with this unscathed.

He pulled back. "I didn't, either. Aunt Raquel informed me on the way over."

Terrified of what she'd find, Addi peeked over his shoulder. It was worse than she imagined. Raquel looked on with the smug smile of the cat who ate the canary, and her mother's mouth hung open. She could only imagine what was going on in that head of hers. *Crap.*

Luca and her dad could care less, but Bel and Sam both had a hand over their mouths, staring in wide-eyed delight. *Crap.*

Nothing could make it worse, or so Addi thought, until Mr. Gallagher, Roque's father, walked up and pulled her into a bear hug.

He smelled of Old Spice and ocean breezes, warm and comforting. Addi liked him immediately and couldn't stop herself from hugging him back. "Nice to meet you, Mr. Gallagher. Officially, I mean."

Roque grinned at his dad.

"Call me Mac." He pulled back to look at her. "And very nice to meet *you*. I see my son has excellent taste."

"Oh but—"

"Of course I do, I got it from Mom." Roque looked down his nose at his father, humor lighting his eyes.

Macklan Gallagher laughed and slapped his son on the back. Leaving his hand on Roque's shoulder, he said, "I've missed you."

Something passed between the two men. Feeling as though she were eavesdropping, she looked away. "Hey, Daddy." She made her way to the table and hugged her father, dropping a kiss to the top of his head. There was no mistaking whose father he was. In looks she was all Frank Dekker, even though her personality was very much like her mother's.

"It's good to see you, kitten. What, I'm not important anymore? You too busy to visit your old man?"

She chuckled and nudged him. "Very busy, but not too busy. I figured you and Mom had enough on your hands with Sam and Gage getting home."

Sam piped up. "Don't even try to blame me."

"Why not, when it's true?" Addi replied. She walked to the island and ladled gravy into a serving dish. Roque stared at the two women, and Addi could only imagine what was running through that brain of his.

"Roque, what are you staring at?" The question came from Sam along with a playful shake of a wooden spoon.

Addi snorted. "He probably hasn't seen anyone so short before."

Sam's eyes snapped wide. "Brat, you've only got me by an inch. More likely he's missed seeing boobs." She swirled her fingers right in front of her chest. "Because someone else in this room doesn't have any."

Addi's jaw dropped open, and Roque swallowed a laugh.

"I do, too…you…yours…" Addi sputtered, then picked up the wooden spoon, dipped it in the mashed potatoes and flicked it at Sam.

Sam shrieked. "You didn't."

Addi laughed so hard tears poured down her cheeks as a white glob slipped from Sam's forehead to her cheek.

Dee moved quickly between the two. "Now girls—"

And got a face splattered with gravy from Sam's spoon.

Addi gasped, and a look of horror replaced the vengeful grin on Sam's face.

The rest of the room fell to immediate silence.

"Mom, I'm so—"

Dee raised her hand. "Don't. Say it."

"But—"

Addi stepped next to her sister and swiped some gravy from her mother's cheek, then sucked it from her finger. "Well, gravy's good. Let's eat."

With that the room snapped to attention and in short order the table was covered in food and everyone had taken their seats. Well, almost everyone. A few minutes later, Dee entered from the kitchen, an apologetic Sam at her heels. "If you hadn't stepped between us…"

Dee slowly turned toward her daughter.

Sam put up her hands and backed away. "Never mind."

Gage pulled a seat out from the table for her. "Come on over here, Sam. You should be safe."

She glanced to the seat at the opposite end from her mother and grinned. "You're probably right."

Addi shook her head. The whole thing was ridiculous. Roque must be certain they were all crazy by now.

Mac asked, "How's the film going?"

"Amazing now, thanks to Addi," Roque said.

Addi's heart warmed. "It really is, you should see him and Gage together—"

Her mother beamed at Roque. "Thank you for taking such good care of our girl."

Addi froze mid-sentence and turned her head toward her mother. Disappointment and then resignation washed over her, and it must've shown on her face, because Roque slid his fingers under her palm.

"Take care of Addi? As if she'd let me. She's a force on the set. I've never seen anyone earn a following as quickly as she has. She has every one of my crew wrapped around her finger and willing to jump at the slightest word from her. She's been the first on set and the last to leave every day. And she brought us Gage. If anyone gets credit for taking care of someone else, it's the other way around."

Dee shot her daughter a look of surprise, then smiled at her husband.

Addi slowly turned to look at Roque and could tell he meant every word. She leaned in to him and whispered, "Thank you." Then she pressed a kiss to his lips. Pulling back, she studied his face, but it was a myriad of unreadable emotions. Luca asked her a question and the moment was gone as she turned back to her brother. "What was that?"

"You and Sam never listen," said Luca, shaking his head.

"And you are such a buzzkill."

"Am I?" His warning look didn't worry her one bit. "Hey, Addi...how's the house?" But it should have.

Crap.

The glint in his eye told her he knew something about the foreclosure. But how? Damn him. She shouldn't be surprised; Luca always did have a way of finding things out. Hell, how many times had she and Sam been caught sneaking out of the house or hanging out places they weren't supposed to because of Luca and his bloodhound nose? Too many to count, that was for sure. He either told on them or blackmailed them—he was a lawyer at birth.

A nervous chuckle escaped her lips, and she cleared her throat in an attempt to squelch it. Swallowing down a familiar sensation, she made a face at him. "Quite well, actually."

Her mother spoke up. "What's wrong with Aunt Addi's house?"

Addi narrowed her eyes. "You mean my house."

Roque's phone rang. "Sorry. I need to take this."

Mac followed close on his heels without saying a word. She didn't blame him. Family drama was about as comfortable as a sleeping bag made of ants. She watched them leave the kitchen, and then shot a look at Luca. She'd deal with him later.

On one hand she was glad her audience had thinned, but she still couldn't help the pinching sensation at the base of her neck. The one time she could really use his support, he had to take a call.

Of course.

Dee frowned. "Addi. What are you thinking, dating your boss?" Waving her hand from Addi to Sam she said, "What is it with my two girls and all this drama?"

"Mom." Addi said, pressure building in her temples.

Dee threw her hands up. "What? Tell me it isn't true. You have to think about these things."

"I am thinking about it. You all keep telling me I needed to get work, or rather that I should never have left my old job in the first place."

With a regretful tone her mother replied, "Well, you shouldn't have, honey. I tried to tell you. And now you're sleeping with your boss? Even you know what a mess that can make."

Mortification shot up her spine, and she set her jaw. She was done playing this game.

Her mother stood and, opening her arms, she beckoned Addi to her. "Oh honey, come here. I don't mean to be hard on you, it's just—"

"Enough." Addi kept her tone soft but firm as she stood. "This is my life. I am not in high school anymore, I'm not a child, and I'll do what I think is best for my life. Roque is a good man, and he means a lot to me, he is not just some random guy. I know what I'm doing. And you know what? I believe in myself, even if you don't." And she did. A feeling of power washed over her, and she softened her tone even more. "Someday, I hope you'll see it and believe in me, too."

Roque hesitated at the doorway, then walked into the room. He slid his arm around her, pulling her into his side and whispered, "Thank you." It felt like the right place for her to be as he squeezed her in reassurance.

"Hey, who's calling on Thanksgiving?" she asked.

With a shrug, he answered, "Not everyone has family. Work calls. I've got to answer." He held her gaze. "I'm sorry."

She stared at the casual expression on his face. "I kind of needed you." She whispered, hating how desperate her words sounded as soon as they fell from her mouth. He'd warned her that his hours working never really found a pause. She just hadn't realized that meant holidays, too.

He squeezed again. "I'm here now."

She nodded, but wanted to shake her head "no." Sure. He was here now, but she'd needed him earlier. Was this what a relationship with Roque would be like? Pulling in a breath, she gently shook her hands. She couldn't let her mother see any signs of indecision. Because regardless of what she thought, Addi had her life under control. Maybe for the first time, but it had finally happened.

Mostly.

Thanksgiving had come and gone, leaving Roque with new memories and a full belly that lasted for days. Watching Addi with her family had been funny as hell, once the tension eased after her conversation with her mother. He'd been so proud of her, standing up for herself like that and defending him. It wasn't easy to tell the people you love to back off. But sometimes it had to be done.

After everyone had gotten over the shock of Addi putting her foot down, Dee cracked jokes, Frank acted like he didn't hear or see anything, and Luca shook his head in mock horror. Sam and Addi gave Luca a hard time every chance they got, and he seemed to hate it, but Roque suspected deep down their brother would miss the banter if they stopped.

He laughed at the memory as he sped down the road. Thinking of Addi, he used his hands-free to put in a call. Voicemail gave him the enjoyment of her voice, but the frustration of missing her—again.

He was already a few hours behind his original schedule but he needed to swing by his aunt and uncle's place. His mother always encouraged him, as an only child, to remain close with his three cousins.

Pulling into the drive, he parked, then jogged up to the

front door. His aunt invited him in with a hug. "Oh, darling. So good to see you. Thanksgiving was fun, wasn't it?"

The self-satisfied look on her face mystified him, but he agreed. "Where are the boys?"

His aunt's eyes lit up. "You know how those boys are. Always off and about. Martin Jr. is on location for his most recent project."

Roque nodded. Martin Jr. was a director like their dads. The industry ran in the blood, and he'd grabbed on with both hands. "That's right, he told me he was taking off last week at the gym."

Raquel winked and then continued, talking with her hands, abalone shell bangles flashing at her wrists. "Kyle took Liam to Europe for a backpacking trip. You know how that one goes. I swear he's a nomad. I'm not sure if he'll ever settle down." A look entered her eyes that always made him want to run. She loved a challenge. If Kyle wasn't careful, his mother would have him married off by the weekend, even if he was on a different continent.

"I needed to grab a script from Uncle Martin. He said he'd come across something I might be interested in."

"It's right here." She picked up a package off the counter in the kitchen. "Anything to drink?"

He winced. "Sorry, I gotta go. I'm already running behind today." Goddamn it. If it wasn't an issue directly related to the film, it was something else. Always more. Any hold he'd had on balance was slipping away faster and faster each day.

"How's Addi?" Her act of feigned interest did not slip by him; she was dying to know. He wished he had a better answer. It felt like months since he'd last held her. Time was both endless and instant when it came to Addi.

"She's great. But I haven't been able to see her much the past few days. And now today is getting further and further behind."

She walked him to the door. "I understand, but honey, there's always time for those in your life you care about. It's all about making the time."

He kissed her cheek and jogged to his car. That was exactly what he was afraid of, trying to make time. Hearing Addi say she cared about him to her family meant a lot, but the nagging feeling that he'd screw it all up tightened down on the muscles in his neck.

In record time he arrived at the bungalow to find Gage and the crew working out a scene. After watching a few minutes, he joined them. "I like what you're doing, but have you considered shooting this with the ocean in the background? A simple change in perspective will give a little underlying meaning to the scene. Magnify it."

Gage and the cameraman made some adjustments and studied the layout of the shot, but they just couldn't get it right. Roque scrubbed his hands back through his hair. What the fuck were they missing? After making a few adjustments, they tried again. He marked the time on his watch. He'd promised to meet Addi at the Country Mart for a quick bite before the night shot they wanted to get. He had a few hours yet to get a dozen hours of work done. The tension in his neck tightened a bit more.

Gage called action. They filmed the sequence, made changes, tweaked the lighting, and filmed it again. Gage threw ideas at Roque, and he tossed them back. Sometimes they were in sync, other times it was as if they worked on two different films. Kind of like trying to balance work and life. They were two different worlds.

"I think we got it with that last one," Gage said. "Great suggestion. Come take a look."

Through the small screen they watched the layout. Excitement rushed through Roque like a drug. It was a hit he'd take over and over again. His phone rang, startling him.

Glancing at the screen, he winced and answered it. "I'm sorry. We ran over, and I lost track of time."

Addi spoke from the other end of the line. "Oh. I wish I would have known. We could have just rescheduled."

Fuck. "I know, I'm so sorry. I'd planned on being there and then just—"

"Forgot."

"I didn't forget, I lost track of time."

Silence came across the line. "A call only takes a few seconds. I know it's been crazy getting Gage completely spun up on the plan, and with the holidays, and the schedule is tight again. I just—"

"I warned you about my hours, Addi." Of course the night had to turn into this. They finally made headway on the scene, but he'd taken two steps back with Addi. Fucking great.

"Yes, you did. But that doesn't mean you can simply check out altogether. All I'm asking for is a phone call. A little courtesy. If you remember, I have a lot going on, too. A lot I could have been doing instead of planning for a night that I think you knew wouldn't happen from the beginning."

Guilt pushed at him, and he didn't like it one bit. He shouldn't have to explain every little thing. He'd been upfront since the beginning. "You could have called, too." As soon as the words were out of his mouth, he regretted them.

Silence. Fuck. "Look, Addi—"

She cleared her throat. "I have to go."

He loved that she was the kind of woman who would stand up for herself, but in this instance it was both a salve and a burr. No matter how well she understood the business, he was so afraid of hurting her and ruining what they had.

His habit of losing sight of everything but what he saw through the camera lens had already cost him dearly.

And now it seemed it would again.

Chapter Twenty

The following day, it was past midnight and well into the morning before the crew finally left. Addi followed Roque into the kitchen and watched him wash his hands and scrub water over his face.

He stretched from side to side. "It was a good day."

"It was. The sequence today was brilliant."

Staring at her, he approached in that lazy stride of his and wrapped his arms around her waist. "I'm really sorry for missing our date. For being an ass."

She bit her lip, peeking up at him from beneath her lashes. "I know how you can make it up to me."

"And how's that?"

She slid her fingers against his nape and gave a gentle tug. "I've missed you. I just want to feel you. Wrap around you. Is that too much to ask?"

He grinned, pulling her back to her bedroom. Walking her backward toward the bed, he slid his mouth over hers. As quick as he tasted, he released and pushed away, and she missed his heat.

But she couldn't fault his motive. He rid her of her top and bottoms and yanked off his own as well.

She lowered to the bed and lay waiting for him, legs bent, arms open wide.

He stared. "God, you're the most beautiful fucking woman I've ever seen."

Flattery would get him everywhere.

He lowered back to her, and she wrapped her legs about his waist, bringing the long, hard length of him to her.

He pressed the broad head of himself into her, and her walls clenched rhythmically, trying to pull him in farther. She'd been ready for days.

Achingly slow, he pulled back out.

Addi had had enough. She wanted him, hard, and now. They were too busy to go slow, too busy to take their time.

Pressing her heels into his ass, she lifted her pelvis and took all of him in one fast, long slide. "Oh, shit. Yes."

"Addi." Her name was a course groan from low in his throat.

She lowered, only to push back up. Grabbing his face between her hands, she poured every ounce of her being into a kiss meant to ignite.

It worked. Thank God. She didn't want slow. She didn't want tender. She wanted raw heat, slick skin—she wanted *now*.

Bracing himself with his hands on either side of her head, Roque gave her what she needed.

Thrusting into her with long, full, fluid movements, he moved his mouth to one breast and slid a hand between their bodies, working her sensitive flesh with gentle precision.

Her core tightened and spiraled, opened again and again. Sensations flared, built, gained speed and intensity.

She dug her fingers into his back, pushing down to meet his every thrust and grinding down for a split second before he moved again.

Slick skin slid effortlessly, the beautiful, almost frictionless caress adding to her already blazing center. Her heart raced in her chest with every stroke of his large, work-worn hands. He pulled back, and she tried to keep him pressed against her, running her teeth along the edge of his neck, grabbing his lower lip. He pressed a kiss onto her mouth, then pushed back and stood.

His body radiated tension, his muscles bulged, his jaw clenched, hands fisted at his side. In any other situation, the man would illicit fear, but like this, oh, like this, excitement shot down her spine and built pressure between her legs in a ball of heat.

"Where are you going?" She heard the breathless quality of her voice and didn't care as long as he came back to her.

He turned on a light. "I want to see you." Kneeling at her feet, he grabbed her ankles and pulled. She shrieked as she slid across her blanket.

Roque dropped between her legs, his weight on his forearms along either side of her body, and dove back in for a kiss. He didn't ask, he took. He didn't finesse, he plundered, and he thrilled her body with every bold brush of his hand and determined stroke of his tongue.

The heat of his body set her afire, his chest against her breasts and his erection rubbing a delicious path between her folds as his tongue did the same to her mouth.

Pressure built to a white heat, and she wrapped her legs around his waist, desperate for him to fill her again and fulfill the promise his body made.

Lifting off her, he grabbed himself and rubbed against her, then dipped inside just enough to make her beg. Again and again, teasing. She writhed under him, demanded, whimpered, begged. "Roque."

He trailed a hot tongue along her jaw and down to her

breast. He sucked and twirled his tongue around her nipple until her body arched.

"Roque." She yelled this time. Too crazed to care, her body wound so tight she feared she'd break.

Rolling onto his back, he lifted her over him until she straddled his hips. He stared at her through lust-hazed eyes, the blue glowing from between the rows of his midnight ink lashes.

She didn't want to wait, wouldn't wait and, wrapping her hand around his hard flesh, lifted her hips until she could sink onto him in one drop. She cried out as his body filled her, stretched her, challenged her to take in more.

Dropping her hands to his well-muscled chest, she lowered her lips to his as she slid forward, then back. Again and again, while tasting the dark spice of his mouth. She grabbed his hands and wrapped them around either side of her hips, encouraging him to press lightly with his thumbs just above her groin, into the soft lower area of her belly. Waves of rolling pleasure shot to her core, wrapping it in pulsing contractions, and she shot up, pressing down harder, faster.

He continued to massage the area with his thumbs in a circular motion, creating a sensation so sweet, so intense, so blindingly hot, she repeated his name over and over, begging him not to stop. "Like this?"

"Oh God, yes. Just like that." He fulfilled her demands, pressing into the soft skin as she pushed her body beyond reason—his thumbs increasing the white hot pulsing of her core until she shattered with a cry.

Roque lifted his hips, thrusting up into her body, so high her knees left the bed. She held on tight, riding out the last waves as he filled his hands with her breasts.

His groan echoed off the walls in the darkening room.

They were one, and Addi couldn't tell where she ended and he began.

Roque slowly lowered his hips to the bed and her knees to the mattress. She melted onto him, keeping him inside her, a part of her, as she dropped her forehead gently to his, their panting breath the only sound, and he laughed. She joined him, accommodating his mass as he slid to her side.

Muted by shock, she pulled in a few breaths to regain some composure. Every time he touched her, she learned something new. Her body was capable of feeling things with him she'd never known possible. She was open to him, felt safe with him. It completely changed the experience. It scared her and made her float in a drunken state of euphoria all at the same time. She chose to focus on the euphoria.

She grinned. "That totally makes up for forgetting about me."

"If this is what I get, I may forget about you even more often."

Pinching his side, she squealed when he retaliated in kind.

With a groan, she pushed up from the bed. "Come on, let's go. I have to get back to the hotel and shower. You have meetings in the morning."

"That is why you are perfect for me. You get how crazy it all is." He groaned, too, as he stood. They quickly dressed and kissed at the front door.

Before taking off in their separate cars, Roque stopped her. "Thank you for spending some time with me. I know the hours are crazy, but you're helping me make this dream happen. I can't believe how close I was to losing it all."

She took in the sincerity in his eyes and passion in his voice. The knowledge of the part she'd played in his financial situation at the start of the film chased away the warmth of his gratitude, turning it cold. She hated having this secret from him, she hated hearing his praise, knowing the whole time she'd deceived him from the beginning.

After everything they'd been through, she was falling for

him hard. As an adult, she had to face her mistakes, face the consequences. She couldn't keep up the facade of perfection. It ate at her.

Saying good-bye, she drove to The Huntington to find Chase.

"I'm happy to see you, but why do I get the feeling something's up?" Chase said as she let her in.

Addi moved to the couch and grabbed a pillow, clutching it to her chest. "I need to tell Roque the truth. I feel terrible. Chase, I'm scared."

Chase pressed her lips together with a brow raised. "Love, I know you're scared, but this is what I was worried about. I think you were so focused in the beginning about your own end that how anyone else felt in this whole scheme was nothing more than collateral damage."

Pain and shamed dropped in Addi's stomach. "Ouch. I guess I deserved that. But you know me, Chase. I love people. This scheme was about taking advantage of Hollywood's squandering." She bit her lip and sighed. "That was before I found out about Roque's investment. And now it keeps eating at me."

Chase smiled, then brushed past Addi and dropped to the sofa.

Addi hung her head and slowly lowered to the couch herself. She hated lying to Roque. Had it only affected Hollywood, she'd be fine, but feeling the way she did about Roque turned her harmless plan ugly and sour.

"I love him, Chase. He's going to hate me. He's broken it off with other women for less. But I have to tell him. I hope what we have is different, that he cares for me enough to listen. There's no way I can move forward with this shadow over me."

Saying the words out loud released a wash of fear and excitement through her chest. She loved him, and what bad timing that was. She was in no place to love someone, to have expectations, make plans. But there it was, settling on her like the warmth from the sun.

A gentle hand brushed back her hair. "I thought you did. I was just wondering how long it would take for you to admit it," Chase said, with a soft laugh.

Addi rolled onto her back and peered at her friend through strands of hair that had fallen across her forehead. Her emotions had her on a roller coaster. She sighed. "I can't do anything about it. My little farce will not sit well with him, besides…" She pointed at herself. "Look at me, I'm a mess. I've got too much to work on before I bring somebody else into my crazy."

Chase grabbed her hand. "Oh, love, you're wrong. You're not a mess, you're courageous. Fearless. Which was part of my problem with this. I'm scared for you. You know I don't do well breaking the rules." Her self-deprecating laugh carried around the otherwise silent apartment.

Chase pushed Addi's bangs off her face and tucked them behind her ear. Chase nurtured, worried. Her comfort zone was in rules, structure, regulations—control.

And Addi's was chaos.

Chase smiled. "Don't push away your chance at love, but don't sabotage the chance before it starts, either. I can't believe I'm saying this, but are you sure you want to tell him? It's done and over and really nothing came of it."

Addi yawned, gratitude for such understanding warming her. "You're a good friend, Chase. Too good. But it's about time I grew up, and facing what I did is part of that. And about the love thing?" Her heart squeezed. "There's nothing to sabotage beyond my own heart's silly interest. Roque is a Gallagher, a producer too busy for commitment. He's Hollywood, and I'm a wannabe writer whose home was in foreclosure."

Chase opened her mouth to argue, but Addi put up a hand.

"It's true. I'm fine with it. I'll make my way someday, but first I've got to finish this film and keep my home on stable ground. As for Roque and I, we get along really well together." Thinking of him warmed her. She pictured his face, and a smile kicked up the corners of her mouth. "I will eke out every second I can, but I have to tell him. If he goes his way, I'll take every wonderful sensation and emotion and feeling and memory that is Roque Gallagher and write an epic love story to remember him by." She laughed at her own melodrama.

Chase crossed her arms over her chest. "Why does that sound so sad?"

Addi stared at her friend with determination. "Because it is. But it must be done. I'm going to give him back the money from when I was still in the house and tell him what I did. Then I'm going to hope like hell he'll focus on the fact I didn't want there to be any secrets instead of the secret itself."

"If you're sure."

She nodded. "I am. Now go. You have an early flight. I'm going to crash on your couch."

Chase disappeared into her room, and Addi watched until the door closed. Dropping her head onto the back of the couch, she thought of Roque's laugh, his crooked smile when he found something amusing, and how the scent of him always seemed to envelop her like an embrace.

She grabbed her purse and rummaged through it to find her phone and checkbook. After a few quick calculations, she wrote a huge check. This meant she'd have to find some other way, a job after this, to keep her home stable, but it would be worth it. Her heart clung to the hope he would see her honesty now as something worthy of forgiveness. It was time to tell him. She'd wanted to the night he'd given her the CD, but his gift had interrupted her confession.

It was too late to call him now, but first thing tomorrow, she'd set it up. A date night at home would be best. Then she'd have the time and privacy to explain everything.

For the first time in her life, she felt truly in love with a man she was proud to call a friend. She hadn't planned on it, but it happened. Now all her mother's admonishments echoed through her head, mocking her declarations of independence.

Her stomach squeezed into a tight ball.

This was why no one liked growing up.

Roque watched the sequence Gage directed from his chair off to the side. The sun was already setting on the horizon, making him frustrated about the too-few hours in the day. The night before, their filming had been delayed by rain, and now this one was going to have to wait until tomorrow if they didn't get it done before the light from a perfect golden hour faded.

The juggling of events and time was actually one of the things he loved about producing. He gained satisfaction in puzzling it all together and making it work. But it was different when he was seeing someone. Making her fit into the puzzle was challenging at times, and he so often screwed up. One too many pieces to fit.

The scent of honey hit him, then he felt the light touch of Addi's hand. She whispered, "Hey, how's it going?"

He stretched up and pressed a kiss to her mouth. The punch to his gut was immediate, and his hands itched to pull her onto his lap. Would the urgent need for more ever end? And what the hell would he do when he screwed it up?

She smiled down at him. "Catering will be here in an hour. I'll set it up out front. Jimmy is back with the paperwork for the offsite filming. He's found a great place down on the Malibu Lagoon for you—last minute inspiration," she teased. "Wait until you see his photographs. He's a genius."

"Great. We've got a few more takes here, then we'll break for dinner."

She squeezed his shoulder, a look of worry furrowing her brow. "Don't forget we're doing dessert at your place tonight."

He nodded. But it would be a miracle if he could carve out the time. They already had lost hours to make up somewhere or fall further behind. "I'll try. If not, we'll reschedule—"

"It's important." Her phone buzzed, and she quickly grabbed it from her slacks to silence it, with a furtive glance at Gage. Looking at the number, she said, "I've got to take this. Then I'm going to finish up a few things and get some writing in." She kissed his cheek. "See you tonight."

Before he could answer, she was slipping back through the French doors leading into the kitchen. Fuck. He sighed. She was simply going to have to understand. Their night in could wait. Shooting the scene he needed for the film couldn't, with the weather this week and more rain predicted.

Gage waved him over, and they watched the scene play out on the screen. "Good, right?"

Roque watched the shadows move alongside the actors as if they were part of the cast. The concept of the contrast of light and dark was older than he was, but it worked. "Brilliant."

Gage slapped his shoulder. "Agreed. Good. We'll go to the sound studio tonight once the sun sets and the glow is gone. It's gonna be a late night."

Roque hated disappointing Addi and worried it wouldn't be the last time, but excitement over the film pushed at him just as hard. "I'm in. Let's eat."

They called for a break and the cast made their way to find food. Roque watched them eat, remembering back to many meals that he'd shared with his mom while his dad had been on location or stuck at the studio or whatever film set he'd worked on all hours of the day and night. They'd missed his dad, sure, but when he was with them, he was all in. Present. No distractions or trails of unkept promises. It made the time they did have together some of his favorite memories.

He'd turned out to be a workaholic just like his dad, but he'd yet to master the ability to turn it off and set it aside when necessary. Maybe if he figured it out, he might just be able to make it work with Addi.

But first they had to get caught up on their filming schedule.

He shoved some food down his throat then headed to the sound studio to meet Gage.

Walking into the studio, he couldn't quite marry the modernized renovations with the scent of stale smoke left over from the 1970's. So much history echoed from every corner.

He stepped into the sound room and almost lost his head to the boom of a shotgun mic. Ducking, he continued on his way until he found Gage. "Hey, have you seen Addi?"

Gage grunted. "Saw her take off earlier when we were eating." Adjusting the sound mixer/recorder to the standard 48 kHz, he looked up.

"Shit."

"Trouble in paradise already? I thought you two had it easy." Gage laughed.

"Anything would seem easy to you after what you guys went through. No, it's fine. I just have to cancel our plans tonight. She was set on meeting at my place, but it'll be close to morning by the time we get out of here."

Gage dipped his chin. "At least." He waved his hand. "Ah, she's a good girl, she'll get it."

Roque wasn't so sure.

He'd call her in two minutes, as soon as he finished this.

He made his way back to the control room and took a seat behind the audio mixing console. He could already feel things slipping through his fingers. They got to work, putting their actors through the paces, and sound bite after sound bite disappeared into hours.

Raising his head from the console, he cracked his neck. His muscles were sore, his body fatigued. Even his brain hurt. Gage called for a break, pulling Roque from his fog. He checked his phone. It was almost midnight. Fuck. He'd never even called her, and he and Gage needed to get back to the cottage and ready the set for tomorrow.

Gage finished setting up a few props in the backyard to be used first thing, and Roque stepped back to get a better look.

He punched in Addi's number as he studied the pieces. "Hey."

"I'm just walking in the front door." She disconnected.

Roque called to Gage. "I'll be back out in a few."

"Everything okay?" he asked.

"Sure. Addi just stopped by."

His buddy winced and waved him off.

Pulling open the French doors, he made his way through the stillness of the kitchen. Addi was in the front room, sitting in the corner of a couch they'd moved in at the beginning of filming. It must feel odd to Addi to sit in her own home surrounded by someone else's belongings.

"I'm sorry. I lost track of time."

She scooted to the edge of the couch, folding her hands in her lap. "I went back to your condo after writing and baked cupcakes, wanting to surprise you. Ice cream filled cupcakes. My specialty. I set everything up and then waited."

"I meant to let you know after dinner I'd have to cancel, but you'd already left, and then we started filming."

Pushing up from the couch, she crossed her arms over her

chest and shrugged. "Roque, I know you're going to be busy, I know this industry means long hours and short visits, but I really need to talk to you, and you could have called. I'm at least worth that amount of time."

He stepped in front of her. She smelled of baked goods, but instead of making him hungry, it weighed heavy in his stomach. "Look, I should have called, but I got caught up. You know how it is when you get lost in your own head. And we're not anywhere close to being done. I'm sorry, but they're waiting for me out back. You can go home, sleep. We'll reschedule a date. I'll take you out and make it up to you."

Her brows furrowed. "I don't need you to make anything up to me. I need to talk to you. This isn't easy, Roque."

Why couldn't she understand? No choice he could have made would have handled everything he had to take care of. He hated it, but sometimes other things had to wait. "Addi. Come on. Life isn't easy, but this isn't that big of a deal." He waved his hand indicating the situation between the two of them. "What do you want me to do? I'm the producer. The film is on shaky ground, and I need to be involved in every part of it. How does it look if I leave for a date when everyone else is missing their family time and vacations and weekends? Gage is giving up evenings with Sam, and *they* just got married. I can't expect that from him and not do it myself."

She reeled back. Her face was white, making her eyes a vivid blue in stark contrast. He wanted to pull her in and kiss the look off her face, but irritation about why she was blowing this up into such a big deal kept him immobile.

"Don't talk to me like I'm a child. And it's good to know what's between us isn't a big deal."

"That is not what I meant, and you know it. I'm talking about cancelling our plans. We'll do it another time."

"I know you're busy. I know this project is important to you. It's important to me, too. I've been needing to talk to you and you can't even call? Who needs to grow up now?" She grabbed her keys. "Have fun with the preparations."

He watched her walk to the door. "Addi, come on."

She stepped through, quietly closing it behind her. The silence their heated words left behind roared in his head.

He let out a breath. That hadn't been his finest hour, but he couldn't wrap his head around why she was that upset. So they'd reschedule for later in the week, or even tomorrow. Big fucking deal.

But for some reason it must have been.

It was already starting. His inability to hold on to a relationship. He'd really thought if he could do it with anyone, it would be Addi.

What the hell was he missing?

Chapter Twenty-One

"Rise and shine, beautiful." The husky whisper of Roque's voice against her ear woke Addi from a fitful sleep. She rolled over and yawned with her hand over her face. "What time is it?"

Roque opened the blinds. "It's a little past ten. I have a surprise for you."

His words brought her ugly reality crashing down on her head. Their fight, and her stupid confession she hadn't delivered yet. After she'd left the bungalow, the rest of the night had disappeared in a blur. She'd planned to tell him as soon as he stepped through the door, assuming he'd come to her hotel. Tell him the truth, rip it off like the proverbial Band-Aid, but in this case, it would hurt. Bad.

But he hadn't come. Then they were back at work, trying to pretend they hadn't fought. It had been miserable. She was not proud of how she'd handled their conversation or her disappointment when he hadn't shown up. It had all been wrapped in her fear of having to tell him the truth. The way she was acting, he'd leave before she even had the chance to tell him.

Rolling onto her back, she peeked at him through puffy lids. Crying was not her friend. "We need to talk."

He smiled. "Sounds great, but it has to wait. We have plans. And I promised to make up the other night to you." With the energy of a child, he clapped his hands together and then grabbed her thigh and gave her a shake. "Get up, get dressed. Something nice, but not formal."

Addi grimaced. She had to do it now. "Roque, I can't, we really need to—"

"Hey, it's not every day you turn thirty—let's go."

Without waiting for an answer, he swept out of the room, calling over his shoulder, "You have thirty minutes. I put coffee on the bathroom counter for you."

She had no idea how he'd slipped into her room with coffee without waking her up. It was a testament to just how exhausted she was.

Dragging herself from the bed, she padded into the bathroom. She could have wept and kissed Roque's feet at the sight of the steaming cup of coffee on the counter as promised. She took a large sip as her eyes rested on her reflection in the mirror. Her birthday, and thirty at that, stared her in the face. Well, it was memorable all right, it would be the birthday she ruined the rest of her life.

She gasped and then choked on the hot liquid, spraying coffee all over the glass. Her eyes watered, and her chest burned.

"Hey, are you okay in there?"

"Swallowed wrong," she rasped out. As her breathing slowly returned to normal, she coughed a few more times and then finally pulled in a normal breath.

She tentatively looked back in the mirror. Well, that's no better. She'd spent most of the night in a fitful sleep full of nightmares, not finding any rest until the sun rose.

The crying from the night before, along with the stress and horrible sleep, left the skin under her eyes dehydrated like a raisin, with bags, smudged mascara, and blotchy skin. Her hair stuck out like the snakes of Medusa.

The door opened followed by a horrified gasp.

Addi found an elegant, and alarmed, Raquel at the door. The woman's arched brows rose high and her mouth fell open in shock.

"Addi, my dear, what happened to you?"

The dramatic tone in Raquel's tone made her want to laugh while her reality made her want to cry. Neither would do her any good at the moment.

"Fell asleep with my makeup on."

Raquel shook her head and narrowed her gaze. "Darling, that"—she twirled a well-manicured pointer finger in front of Addi's face—"is not from leaving your makeup on. You look like you got in a fight with a raccoon and lost." She leaned in and whispered, "Talk to me, darling. What's going on?"

There was never getting anything past the Mother of Malibu. Addi blinked back tears and shook her head. "No, nothing. Just a rough few days."

Raquel raised a brow.

"Really, I'm fine," Addi assured her before returning her attention to the sorry state of her reflection in the mirror. Turning on the faucet, she waited for the water to warm up and glanced at Raquel. "What are you doing here this morning?"

The refined woman studied her but kept to herself whatever thoughts were on her mind. A small sigh escaped her lips. "Okay, I'll let it go." She clasped her hands together. "It isn't every day a young woman turns thirty. We have plans."

Addi shook her head. "You guys didn't have to do anything, really."

Raquel waved her hand with a laugh. "Please, any excuse to throw a party. You know me. Now, wash your face and put on your makeup. I left a surprise for you on your bed."

Addi scrubbed the dirt from her face, wishing she could do the same with the guilt turning in her gut. Raquel wouldn't be feeling so generous once she found out about Addi's scheme. Chase had been right all along; she should have listened.

Doing her best to hide the stress taking up residence on her face, Addi made her way back to her bedroom. There, in the middle of the bed, lay a simple silk sheath in ice-blue. She slid her fingers over the fine material and sighed. Roque and Raquel had already slipped out of her hotel room, leaving her to dress. She'd give anything to go back and start over, not be so damned arrogant the day Roque showed up.

Careful not to stretch the material, Addi stepped into it, knotting it over one shoulder. The sheath skimmed her curves with perfection, showing off her toned muscles like a frame around a piece of fine art. Slipping into a pair of silver one-strap heels, she pulled open her door. The least she could do at this point was not make them wait for her any longer. Besides, there was nothing else to be done with the ravages of bad decisions and insomnia on her face. Firming her resolve, she went in search of Roque and Raquel to see what they had planned.

Addi was shocked as she glanced around the backyard paradise belonging to Martin and Raquel. Raquel had strung ice-blue and white sheers across the top of their large outdoor pergola. Lights hung from the palm trees and from fern to fern. A champagne fountain served partygoers elegantly in front of the outdoor waterfall feature along the stucco wall. Overwhelmed couldn't begin to describe the myriad of emotions drowning Addi at the moment.

The skies were a brilliant blue, a bit warmer than expected

for the first of December, but perfect for an outdoor lunch. Only a few clouds dotted the sky.

Buffet tables laden with a light seafood fare bordered two sides under the pergola, and in the very center a large tower of chocolate éclairs, with "Happy 30th birthday, Addison" written in white cream on a chocolate fondant plaque set squarely in the front.

She giggled at the sight, touched at the attention to detail, the thoughtfulness. Thoughtfulness she didn't deserve.

Pulling in a breath to steady her run-amok emotions, she turned as her mother approached. She hugged her and held on tight. "Hi, Mom."

Her mother pulled back and looked at her closely. "Happy birthday, my beautiful girl."

Addi smiled.

"Are you okay?"

Addi forced her lips to spread wide. "Of course. Look at this. I can't believe you all did this for me."

Her mother looked around and then back to Addi with a satisfied grin. "It was all Roque's idea. Raquel and I just helped out with the decorations and catering, but that éclair cake was his genius. Perfect, isn't it?"

She placed her hand on Addi's upper arm and squeezed. "He's a good man, and he really knows you."

Addi pulled in a breath. "He is, and he does."

Raquel floated up to them on a cloud of white chiffon, her dress twirling about her ankles as she came to a stop. "Hello, darlings."

Addi embraced her and kissed one cheek, then the other. "Everything is just amazing. I can't thank you enough."

Raquel waved her words away. "You're family."

The two women looked her over, then Dee spoke to Raquel. "She's hiding something."

"Oh, I know. She'll have to tell us eventually."

Addi rolled her eyes. "Oh my God, the two of you together should come with a warning."

"Exactly what I've been saying." Sam walked up.

"Sam, save me."

Sam looked from one woman to the next. "Hell, no. Better you than me, sister."

Dee wrinkled her nose at her two daughters. "Manners."

Addi laughed and Sam joined in, wrapping her arm around Addi's waist. It felt good, being with family. She was so lucky to have all of them, to be part of this family. A warmth spread through her heart.

"Can I get in on this?" Gage asked, stepping up to wrap his beefy arms around the two women. "I think I've dreamed of something like this."

Sam elbowed him in the gut.

"Oomph. I deserved that. But still." He flashed them all a devilish grin.

Addi laughed as Sam warned, "You better quit while you're ahead, buddy."

Gage released Addi and put both arms around Sam. He stole a kiss, then settled her tight against his side.

Addi loved watching them. Their love and closeness showed her everything she was missing. Everything she could have had with Roque if she hadn't messed it all up.

As if conjured from her mind, Roque walked up and winked at Gage. "I'm jealous. Sisters."

Sam laughed, and it was Addi's turn to shake her head. "Men—you're all alike."

Roque's grin spread wide across his face. He stuck out his hand to shake hers. "I'm Roque."

She raised a brow and shook his hand. "Addi?"

"So, you know your name or are you asking?"

She laughed. "I'm wondering what you're doing."

He watched Raquel and Dee melt into the background,

and Sam and Gage stroll off hand in hand, then looked back at her. "I've heard all about the infamous Dekker sibling."

She shook her head with a grin. Where was he going with this silliness? He'd said the same thing when they first met at Sam's wedding. *Ohhhhhh.* "And?"

He narrowed his eyes at her. He knew she knew. "And, I was wondering if you'd like to go out with me this weekend."

She stepped back and looked him up and down. "Not no, but *hell no*." She loved the expression of shock that crossed his face before he could hide it behind his veneer of control.

Without warning, he shot out his hand and grabbed her wrist, pulling her toward him. He'd surprised her enough that she fell forward with a step right into his arms. Exactly where she preferred to be. "I'm sorry for canceling our plans and being such a shit."

"You say shit a lot."

"Only when you're around."

She pressed her lips to his, and he immediately tightened his grip, pulling her closer into him, moving his lips against hers.

She broke the kiss with smaller ones placed at the corners of his mouth, his brow, and the end of his nose. The warmth from all the love she felt mixed with the anxiety of having to be honest with him. But he deserved it.

He smirked. "What was that?"

"Thank you," she whispered. Tears filled her eyes. She tried to blink them away but only produced more. She pulled in a breath. "Thank you for this lovely party, for bringing all my family together." She glanced around.

Everyone was there. His dad, and aunt and uncle, of course. Gage, Bel, and their dad, D.C. Her mom, dad, brother, and sister. Chase and a bunch of the crew working on the film. What a thoughtful, wonderful thing to do, especially when the film was only a couple of weeks from wrapping up, a particularly busy time.

With his hands resting on her lower back, he looked down at her with heat and something stronger in his eyes. "It's my pleasure." He released her. "I have something for you."

Before she could protest, he stepped away and walked over to the table holding the éclairs. He reached beneath the table skirt and then came out with a package in his hand.

"Roque, please, no more gifts. You've given me too much already."

"You were meant to have this. I knew it the moment I saw it."

Addi hesitated and then took the package. Wrapped in silver paper with a fountain of ice-blue ribbon cascading off the top, the package looked more like a cake than her birthday éclair tower.

He smiled as she looked from him to the package. "I know you need to make your way, and I have to make mine. Our work is challenging and it will be difficult. There will be times I have to cancel plans or miss out on events, but I will still always be there. I'll be present. I won't hold you back or hold you down. You don't have to be scared of what might happen. We won't be perfect 100 percent of the time, but I will be by your side. Every day. I want to see where we can take this, Addi."

She opened the package with trembling fingers, his words burning through her heart. She slipped off the ribbon first, then peeled back the tape one piece at a time to reveal a black velvet case about the size of her hand with her fingers splayed out.

She looked up to find Roque watching her with an intensity so strong she could feel it.

"You're making me nervous."

He only gave one nod of his head in response. "Open it."

Lifting the lid, she breathed in, then forgot how to breathe out. Silence followed. She didn't know what to say, what to do. She could never accept a gift so generous.

She shot her gaze to his, both shock and awe in her voice as she said, "The black abalone necklace from Raquel's party."

His smile said it all. How much he loved her, how much he wanted her to have the gift, but she couldn't. There was no way.

She shook her head. "Roque, I can't take this. It's too much."

Stepping up to her, he slipped the fan of abalone from the box and stepped behind her. He leaned close and lowered the necklace over her head, attaching the clever clasp in the shape of a shell at the base of her neck.

Her fingers fluttered against the gift that lay cool against her skin. "Really, I can't—"

"Shhhhh…stop. This is my gift to you. I saw it in your eyes the night of the gala. Raquel was right. It was made for you." He stepped around to face her. "You're stunning."

The shells lay cool against her skin, but his eyes branded her with such heat she needed a fan, even with the comfortable December breeze. "Roque."

"Thank you."

Her brows pulled together in confusion. "What?"

"You're supposed to say 'thank you.'"

She stared into his eyes. Every time she wore the piece she'd think of him, the intense blue of his gaze mirrored in the rainbow of abalone, the cool catch of his certainty in the feel of the shell against her skin, and his steadfast nature in the security of the clasp embracing her neck.

She ran her fingers over the smooth shell just above her breasts and whispered, "Thank you."

He tilted his head. "You're welcome." Then he leaned in to kiss her, tilting her world.

Floating in the feel of his lips against hers, his taste

melding with her taste, she wondered how she'd ever be able to let him go.

You have no choice.

Roque rounded on Addi, pushing her back against the wall beside the fountain. He overwhelmed her with his presence, his strength, his integrity, his passion for everything he did.

She stared up into his warm gaze. Everything he had done for her poured into her heart in a great crescendo: the opportunity to save her home, his respect for her writing, sharing his mother's favorite song, and her party. She'd explode if she didn't tell him.

"Roque."

He smoothed an errant hair from her face. "Addi." He smiled down at her and pressed a smooth kiss to her mouth.

She licked her lips to savor his taste. Her heart broke in half, two sides falling away from each other, no way in sight to ever mend. "I love you." Her whisper trembled from her lips.

He stilled but for a rhythmic flexing in his jaw, and the focus in his eyes intensified. Warm fingers cupped her chin, and he lowered his mouth to hers once more.

The warm glide of his tongue teased of éclairs and champagne.

Pulling back, he looked into her eyes. "You have no idea how much your words mean to me. I never thought I'd trust anyone enough to love them or let them love me, but you, I trust you, Addi. I love you, too."

Panic crawled up the back of her throat. "I need to explain something to you. It isn't easy."

Every thread of the life she hoped to weave into a future was right here, but reality yanked at the tapestry, unraveling it before her eyes.

Raising a finger, he said, "One second." He turned slightly to pull his aunt into his embrace as she walked up. "Thank you for helping me pull this off."

His aunt glowed under his praise. "Why, of course."

Martin cleared his throat and slapped a hand to Roque's back. "If I can tear you away, my boy, I need to discuss something with you. It won't take but long."

Roque's hand fell from Addi's waist. "Of course."

She grabbed his hand. "But I need to talk to you."

His smile promised much more than talking. "And we will. I'll find you in a bit. Enjoy your friends."

Addi watched him walk off with Martin as she felt the weight of the check she'd written in her clutch, dread pooling in her heart.

"What's going on, darling? And don't insult me by saying 'nothing.'"

Addi's shoulders fell. "I've screwed everything up, Raquel."

Raquel studied her and then took her hand and pulled her to a corner table. "Sit, tell me. I can help."

Sorrow grabbed Addi with a solid grip, and she had to fight back tears.

"Come now. No tears at your birthday party."

"I've kept something from Roque."

Raquel smiled. "Is that all?"

"It isn't a little something."

With a wave of her hand, Raquel leaned back into her seat. "I never condone keeping secrets." She smiled and leaned in. "Unless they're mine, of course. But in relationships it's bound to happen once or twice; the goal is to live so you never have to."

Addi shook her head. "You don't understand."

"It's called perspective, and you need a little. When Martin and I started out, he took our whole savings and put it in a project that failed. He lied to me, and I was horribly angry at first. But what followed put it all into perspective. Lying can be overcome; just try not to do it again."

A faraway look entered Raquel's eyes, sadness pulling the corners of her painted lips down. Addi remember hearing stories about how Martin had attempted suicide so long ago. She couldn't imagine.

Placing her hand on Raquel's, she squeezed. "You're right. It'll be fine. Perspective. That's what I need." She wasn't so sure, but she sure as hell didn't want to see that look come over her friend's face again.

Addi glanced at the crowd. So many people who loved her. Love. Roque loved her. Love could move mountains, or so she wrote in her stories.

Strength and awareness raced through her. He loved her. He threw this party for her. He wouldn't walk away for one mistake.

She sat straighter in her chair and smiled at Raquel. "You're right. Everything will be okay."

"You love him, don't you?"

Addi's insides liquefied, warmth surging into her chest. "I really do."

"I knew you would."

Addi raised a brow.

Raquel shrugged. "Well, who wouldn't? Just one look at the two of you tells the whole story. A very romantic story at that. You should write a book."

Addi laughed. "Yes, I should. And sell it, too."

"I've never seen him so happy. It's been so long since he's laughed or lived like this. The pain of losing his mother the way he did was just too much."

"He's told me a bit about her. She seemed like an amazing woman."

Her friend's eyes flashed. "We were sisters and best friends. I miss her every day."

Addi reached across the table and laid her hand on top

of Raquel's.

Roque joined them. "Care to dance?"

It was now or never, and she couldn't move forward until everything was on the table. She slid her hand into his. "I'd love to."

They moved onto the dance floor, swaying to the sultry beat. "I really need to tell you something, and I don't want you to interrupt."

"Sounds serious."

A nervous giggle escaped her lips. "I'm hoping you'll see how funny it all really is. But I need to be completely honest with you."

He slowed a bit, and pulled back to look into her eyes. She immediately longed to hide her face in his neck while she confessed, but that wouldn't be the mature thing to do. Of course. All of a sudden she longed for the days of being a child, when people expected mistakes because of your age.

"What is it?" he asked.

"You know how the bungalow was in foreclosure, and I had to save extra for next year's taxes and—"

"Addi." His muscles under her hands tightened to granite.

She quit moving with him to the music and opened her clutch. Pulling out the check, she handed it over to him. It was only a few thousand dollars. A drop in the bucket really, but it meant something to her to pay it back. "I owe you this."

He glanced at the check with eyes clouded by confusion. His mouth pulled up at the corner. "What's going on?"

With her heart slamming in her chest, she put her hand out to him, and he took it. "When I signed on to work for you, I pretended to stay at the Huntington, but instead slept up in the attic and banked the hotel money to make sure I could pay my taxes next year."

He dropped her hand, a small laugh escaping his lips. "What? That was close to twenty grand."

"I know it was wrong. I—"

"You stole from me?" He stepped back.

"It's not like that. Really, I..." Her words trailed off as she watched him close down and pull away. All the happiness she'd felt, all the love, and the visions she'd had of tomorrow washed away.

She'd been honest, and she'd given him the money she owed.

And now it was time to pay.

Chapter Twenty-Two

The music kept playing, but family and friends one by one noticed the change in the atmosphere.

The conversations around them stopped. He would not make a scene.

He shook his head. Nothing changed the facts. Stepping backward, he turned to the house. He had to get out of there. Talk about being a failure in relationships. His own girlfriend had been stealing from him. That was how worthless he was.

She followed behind him. "Wait, Roque. Please."

Her fingers wrapped around his upper arm, and he pulled from her grasp as he stepped inside. "Don't."

She stopped just inside the door and closed it. "I've been trying to—"

"You've been trying to what?" He tried to temper his voice, but the pain in his chest shook any control from his grasp. "Trying? You should have told me. No exception."

"Okay, you're right." She reached out to him, her lips trembling. He wanted to pull her to him to ease both their pain and push her away all at the same time.

She tried again. "Please let me explain." Pulling in a breath, she wrung her hands in front of her waist, the abalone necklace reflecting the light, mocking him with its place over her heart. She paced and then stopped a few feet from him, but not touching. Smart girl.

"I should have told you no matter what. I kept trying to, but we kept getting interrupted."

God dammit, he didn't have the time or the energy for this conversation. "I can't do this right now." He shook his head. "You were stealing from me."

"Yes…no." She shot her hand out, but he yanked away from her. "Roque, I know Hollywood spends money with no thought, I didn't know it was yours. I'd never—"

His past suddenly collided with his future, and all the emotions he'd shoved down, controlled, for so long ripped loose. "You stole from *me*," he shouted, shoving a finger into his chest. "From me, Addi. My money, my savings and dreams and…" He swung around, unable to process the words that had come out of her mouth. "Son of a bitch." The woman he cared about, could see himself staying with, had lied to him, not just once, but day after day. "You did this even knowing about the connection with my mother."

He was numb. Raquel closed the French doors and then ushered the guests away from watching his humiliation. Honestly, he didn't give a fuck, he didn't give a fuck about anything anymore.

Addi's sobs fell on deaf ears—he didn't care, couldn't feel. He'd been better off in his shell, closed off from emotion. He wished he'd never met her.

Her horrified expression was well played. Like she didn't know. How could she not have known? How many times had they talked about their projects, sharing everything?

She reached out to him again, a look of shock on her face. "I had no idea. I would never—"

His brows shot high. "Never? You'd never what? Steal? Lie? Use me for your own gain?" The echo of his harsh laugh bounced around the room. "Apparently you'd do just about anything to get what you want, Addi. This is beyond irresponsible—it's childish. Mature adults work for a living, and they earn their paycheck. They don't hide in attics and pocket other people's cash."

The whole evening had gone from horrible to unbearable. Tears stung his lids, but he refused to cry for this woman. She didn't deserve it. He was losing nothing.

Then why did this feel like a death?

He turned toward the door.

"I'm sorry, I'm so sorry."

He ignored her words and stepped outside. "Maybe one of these days you should try working for *your* dream a little. Then if something goes horribly wrong, you might understand how I feel."

"You said you'd always be by my side." Her words were spoken through the thickness of tears.

Slowly turning, unaccountable agony tore through him and he shouted, "You didn't stand by mine, Addi. This whole thing was about a *house*."

Martin stepped through the French doors with his hand out. "Roque."

Roque grabbed the front door and slammed it. The image of Addi's tear-streaked face, her arms wrapped around her waist, would stay with him. He wanted to turn around and slam the door again and again and again.

He was done.

He should have known.

Because he knew Malibu. And the place was full of backstabbing. Why he thought Addi would be different, he'd never know. It was a hard lesson, but one he'd never forget.

"Oh my God, oh my God, oh my God. What have I done?" Addi bit on her knuckle, trying to hold back her tears.

Her father pulled her into his arms and held her.

That broke the dam, and she cried for all the mistakes she'd made, for the people she'd hurt, for the pain she caused Roque. Not with one lie, but several. Had she known, she'd have never gone forward with her plan.

Her stomach turned, and she lurched toward the kitchen sink, leaving her father holding thin air. She threw herself over the side of the sink and retched.

Her mother stepped behind her and pulled her hair back from her face. "Oh, baby."

Addi closed her eyes. How many times had she heard those words? That tone? The you-need-someone-to-take-care-of-you-why-wasn't-I-a-better-mother tone.

Raquel walked up with a cool washcloth and laid it on the back of Addi's neck. "There now, darling. I sent everyone home. The party was wrapping up anyway."

"Talk about entering thirty with a bang," Martin said in a gruff whisper.

"Martin," Raquel admonished.

"What? Frank?" Martin asked.

Addi's father shook his head. "You're on your own with that one." He put his arms out to Addi.

Grabbing the towel next to the sink, she covered her mouth and walked into his arms. "I made a big mistake, Daddy."

"We all make them, baby. We all make them."

Chase stepped up. "Come back to my place, hon. That way you don't have to go to the bungalow." Turning to Sam, Chase asked, "Do you want to come with us?"

"Of course. I'll text Gage and tell him I'll be home tomorrow."

Addi shook her head. "No, go home, Sam. Don't be silly."

Sam walked up and wrapped her arms around Addi. "Who's being silly? Of course I'm coming, you're my baby sister."

Addi sniffed and new tears streamed down her face. She was a fool, an idiot, and worse, if someone called her baby one more time, she'd scream. The tightness in her chest wouldn't let up, and she doubted it ever would.

Chase grabbed her bag. "Come on girls. Raquel, if you wait until tomorrow I'd be happy to come over and help clean up."

Raquel laughed. It sounded odd to Addi's ears, as if her brain couldn't process the concept. "Don't be silly, darling. That's what Martin's for."

Addi looked over at Martin's stricken face. She'd normally have giggled but couldn't muster the strength or appropriate emotion.

Her dad spoke softly. "Go. Rest. Tomorrow is a new day."

Tomorrow.

If only.

But she'd seen the look in Roque's eyes.

If only she could go back to the first time she'd opened her front door to him and start over.

Chapter Twenty-Three

Roque pushed out another rep. His muscles screamed. Eventually his body would be so tired he wouldn't be able to think, and maybe then he'd finally have some peace.

"Dude, take it easy." Martin Jr. lifted the bar to put it back on its perch.

Roque tightened his grip. "No. Five more."

"You're going to tear something. Don't be an ass."

"Fuck you." He pushed out another chest press.

Martin Jr. flicked him on the forehead, the sting shocking him, but not as much as the action did. Was he fucking kidding? *Did he just flick me?* Motherfucker.

Releasing the bar into his buddy's hands—and at this point the word "buddy" was loosely defined—Roque sat up. "What the fuck?"

He caught the towel thrown toward his face, glaring over the offending object at his friend.

Martin waved his look away. "Either go see her, or call me when you're over it. Working out with you like this is stupid and dangerous."

Roque slung the towel around his neck. "What's the real problem, Gallagher? Can't keep up?"

Martin Jr. snorted. "With Roque Gallagher? Any day of the week. But I haven't seen him in almost two weeks. The jackass sitting in front of me acts like he's a teenage asshole with a small ego and smaller di—"

Roque shot his hand up. His cousin was right, but the past couple of weeks exhausted him with the constant fight to stay away from Addi. As much as his mind said no, his heart—ugh, he wanted to retch—pulled at him to check on her, make sure she was okay. So he did what he did best. He worked. All day and all night. Hell, he had the time. No one waiting for him at home, no one counting on him for anything.

Might as well stick to what he was good at.

Besides, it served its purpose—keeping him away from Addison Dekker.

They'd finished the main filming at the bungalow and got the hell out of Dodge. Now they had a few offsite location scenes to film, and then it was time for post-production edits. He'd bury himself in that, too.

Martin Jr.'s eyes narrowed. "She really fucked you up, didn't she?"

Roque blew out a breath. "I should have known something was up. She'd get nervous and vague. I had a feeling but couldn't put my finger on it. I missed little clues." He shook his head. He knew she was afraid of the dark, but he bought the whole "walking in the dark elbow injury" hook, line, and sinker. He'd been too distracted with the film, with her. Snapping the towel from around his neck, he stood. "Well, not anymore."

"Dude, my mom said she was desperate. Going to lose her house."

Roque stilled. Was his friend really defending her lies? Her secrets? Her stealing from him?

Martin Jr. put up his hands. "Okay, I recognize that look. Never mind. What the hell does my mom know?"

For the first time in days, Roque cracked a smile. If Raquel ever heard her son utter those words, she'd kill him. If anyone *knew* anything, it was Aunt Raquel—at least according to her. "I dare you to tell her that."

"Fuck you, too."

Now Roque did laugh. It came out awkward and rusty.

The two men walked toward the locker room and Roque flexed his pecs. His chest ached already, but then again he couldn't tell if it was his muscles or his fucking heart. Damn pansy-ass organ.

"You need to talk to her, hear what she has to say."

Roque stopped before stepping into the locker room. "Why the fuck would I do that?"

Martin Jr. raised a brow. "Because she's putting the house up for sale."

Shock stripped him of words for a beat. Addi was selling the bungalow? Why the hell would she do that, after everything she put him through? There was no way she was selling that house. After what she did, he'd make sure she kept it, lived in it, a constant reminder of what she'd chosen.

"The hell she is."

Addi walked through the empty front room of the bungalow, heart heavy but eyes stone dry. She'd done all the crying physically possible over the last two weeks and hadn't a molecule left.

The crew had cleared out the day before, taking every scrap of evidence that proved they'd even been there. She'd received a call from Jimmy informing her she could move back in and that he wished her well and Roque was an ass, of course. But Addi knew better. She appreciated Jimmy's kindness, but they all knew who the ass really was.

The movers would bring the remainder of her things back the next day. In the meantime her room and the kitchen were both intact, minus the odds and ends, equipment, and the crew. It felt like yesterday she'd been wishing she had her house all to herself, and now she'd give anything to go back to that day. All the people, the chaos, Roque, and the chance to be honest without being forced into it.

Her stomach rumbled, but the idea of eating made her want to retch. Besides, it wasn't so much the feeling of being empty of food. Losing Roque left her hollow.

She scanned her labors. The cupboards were spotless. Her back ached, her muscles ached—her heart ached—but her kitchen sparkled.

A weary sigh escaped her lips, and she blew at a strand of hair that had escaped her ponytail to tickle her cheek. Rubbing the back of her hand across her brow, she took stock of what still needed to be done in order to get the house in selling condition.

The thought pulled at her heart and filled her with self-disappointment and regret. Aunt Addi would have never let anything happen to her home. She'd been a spitfire, full of liquor and spice. A little of her warmed and energized, a lot would knock a person on their ass. Addi could picture her dressed in all her wild colors, flowing skirts and scarves, and sometimes a turban just because she could, and the hell with what anyone else thought. She taught Addi not to apologize for who she was, but in this case, Addi needed to. "I'm so sorry, Aunt Addi." Her whispered apology floated about the lemon-scented kitchen, and she sat listening to its ghostly echo.

The doorbell shrieked, catching Addi so off guard she screamed in return. Slapping her hand to her chest, she cursed. "Why the hell did I turn that monster back on?"

Swinging her cleaning rag over her shoulder, she made her way through the open and airy front room. The contrast to the chaotic mess of the film crew almost gave her pause, but she wrenched open the door before her visitor could consider ringing the damn thing again.

All of her breath left her lungs in one full exhalation. "Roque." Her voice so low, she barely heard herself over the pounding of her heart. Hope flared and then snuffed out with finality at the look on his face, leaving her hollower than before. The crash always hurt worse after the high.

He stared at her, his hands fisted at his sides.

She soaked in the sight of him. He looked bigger somehow, more handsome than ever, but his eyes lacked the passion and joy she'd always attributed to the intensity of his gaze, and it was her fault. The pressure in her chest suffocated, silencing her from asking his forgiveness. She deserved his contempt. Pulling her shoulders back, she met his slicing gaze.

He looked past her into the house.

"Do you want to come in?"

"Are you seriously selling this house?"

She stepped back at the vehemence in his voice. He followed, then slammed the door behind him.

He pointed his finger at her. "After all the work you did to keep your secrets, why am I not surprised?" He ended with his voice low, saying the words in a staccato tone.

She gripped her hands at her chest. Desperation for him to understand thickened her voice. "I have to. I don't see any other way."

"Too bad you didn't come to that conclusion earlier, like an adult."

She deserved that, but it didn't make it hurt any less. His words stabbed like tiny insistent daggers, sharp, relentless, making her bleed. "I gave it all back, all that I had, anyway. When I saw you never cashed the check I wrote you, I sent one to your accountant. He took it from me a few days ago. I'll pay you back the rest as soon as I figure out exactly what I need to do with the house. My main option is selling."

Something flickered in his eyes, but they quickly shuttered with cynicism. "I'm touched. I suppose you want a 'thank you' for your sacrifice?"

Tears burned behind her eyelids, tightening her throat and threatening to choke her. She pulled in a breath to steady her chaotic emotions. "I'm trying to figure this out because it's the right thing to do."

"*Now* you're worried about doing the right thing? Where the hell was your conscience two months ago?" he said. "You put on quite a show with your dreams and your need to stand on your own two feet. What you needed was my money."

What she needed was for him to go; her heart couldn't take it. The Roque standing in front of her was nothing like the man she knew. He lashed out because she'd hurt him. But seeing him this way, hating her, deserved or not, was too painful. She'd made a huge mistake, and she was paying for it, but she couldn't stand here and take his anger any longer. She had to draw the line somewhere, and before she fell apart right in front of him. Not that it really mattered, since she had no dignity left.

He didn't think she was responsible enough for him, and right now she couldn't blame him, but she was changing. She was owning her mistakes and moving forward. It looked like the end for her and Roque, but it wasn't the end for Addison Dekker. She was finally beginning.

Still, the pain in her chest threatened to knock her legs from under her.

Walking over to the door, she opened it and spoke softly. "I can see this is the last place you want to be." She needed him to go before she made a fool of herself and begged him to stay, to forgive her, to give her a second chance. But that time was past. This was not the man who loved her a couple of weeks ago, and she wasn't the same woman. She was stronger now, smarter. She'd made a mistake and now was working hard to make it right. The truth of that helped her stand tall, helped calm her heart and pull in a breath.

He stepped in front of her, blocking the sun. "I loved you, I opened my heart to you, and all you did was look after yourself. I thought we were partners. But I was wrong."

The pain in his voice broke her will to be strong. Tears ran freely down her cheeks. "I loved you too—I do love you. I didn't know the money was yours. You have to believe me."

He clenched his jaw, the muscles leaving hard lines across his cheeks. "We're over. I don't have to believe anything you say, ever again." Stepping through the door, he turned back. "You knew things about me I never shared with anyone, and you used them, very effectively, I might add."

Shock silenced her for a moment. She couldn't truly believe what he was saying. She shook her head. "No, I never—"

"But you did." He slashed his hand to halt her words. "I didn't come to hear any more of your stories. I just wanted to return your check. If living in this house is so important that you'd steal, then you might as well keep the money."

He stepped off the porch into the sunlight, and his eyes held hers for what she feared would be the last time. "I hope you're happy."

She reached out to him, hating herself for putting such pain in his eyes and agony in his voice. "Please."

He shook his head, the emotion gone, cold stone in its place. "Good luck with your writing. Fiction suits you."

And with that, he turned and didn't look back.

Addi watched him go, regret and anger combined into a thick wedge in her heart.

He was really gone.

She closed the door and sunk into her couch, looking around the room, remembering the first day he'd stopped by and the first night he'd stayed with her.

The truth might be the responsible thing, the right thing, but it was also the painful thing. She turned his check over in her hand and stared at it.

She'd take fiction any day.

She couldn't stand to be alone in her home for one more second. She wanted her family.

"Mom, please. I have to do this myself." Addi leaned back against the counter in the kitchen. Sam and Luca sat at the table peeling potatoes, and their dad prepared the steak with his secret herbs. If they tried to peek, a hip-shoving contest never failed to ensue. "Not until you're married," he'd always say.

Attempting to distract her mother, she eyed the rub. "Sam, you have Dad's recipe now, don't you?"

Sam continued to peel potatoes, whistling a tune of innocence and refusing to look up.

Addi pushed away from the counter. "I can't believe you're keeping his secret."

Sam looked up this time and wriggled her brow. "The power feels awesome."

Gage looked down at his phone, a smug look on his face. "Got to take this." He disappeared through the sliding glass door onto the back porch before Addi could try and get the recipe out of him.

"Coward," she said.

"Or very, very smart," Sam returned.

"Sam, quit distracting your sister. Seriously, Addi. Let us help you."

Damn. Distractions usually worked. She sighed. "Mom."
She walked up and rubbed her mother's shoulder. "I told you,
I need to do this one on my own. Please don't ask me again."

"But my dear dead aunt's home?" Her emotional plea
fell upon deaf ears.

Addi shook her head as she walked over to snatch a red
pepper strip from the platter her father worked from. He
slapped at her hand, but she snagged a few more and ate them
with a smile.

She wasn't budging. Standing up to her mother wasn't
easy, but it was time. "Nice try, Mom. You've been harping
on me to sell that house and move back home since the day
I moved into it. You have no more emotional attachment to
that home than I do to your pleas."

Dee widened her eyes and then threw her hands up with an
air of drama they'd all come to love and adore and—who was
she kidding—barely tolerate. "Sam, do you hear your sister?"

Sam shared a look with Luca. "Don't try to pull me into
this. I get what she's saying."

"Oh please, why'd I even ask you?"

"Why indeed?" Sam chuckled.

Dee turned to Luca. "Honey, isn't there something you
could do? Some sort of legal mumbo jumbo to get your sister
out of this without her losing her home?"

Luca pushed back from the table and carried the potato
peels over to the trash can. "Who wants wine?" He pulled
down a Cabernet from the wine shelf and focused his energies
on opening it. "I'm going to put my 'mumbo jumbo' talents to
work."

Addi put her hand over her mouth to smother a giggle,
delighted hc'd actually made a joke, since he was usually so
serious. She was surprised she had the giggle in her.

Her poor mother received no help from the Dekker
clan, and she hadn't even bothered asking their father. Frank

Dekker would simply kiss her and tell her to let it go. Addi imagined mothers had a much more difficult time doing such a thing. Kind of like asking a writer not to write or a singer not to sing. A mom had to mother. It was in their blood.

Addi loved Sunday dinners at her parents' house. They always had great food, great conversation, and many, many laughs. Usually at Sam's expense—she was more fun to tease—but apparently not tonight. And Addi could use a good laugh. On her way over to dinner she'd vowed to keep it light, good-hearted, and focus on everyone else. Her mother made that task near impossible with her constant demands for Addi to let them help her save the house. Well, she'd already made up her mind. She would figure out the mess she'd made all on her own—only this time, she'd start out the way she meant to continue.

A sigh demanded to be released, but Addi sucked it back. The last thing she wanted was question after question about Roque. She thought about him enough on her own without having her family bring him up at every turn.

So far they'd been keeping all the conversations pointed toward Aunt Addi's house. She could handle that.

As her mother prepared the sweet potato salad and her father grilled the steaks, Addi wandered over to the back patio area. Gage had finished his conversation and stepped through the sliding doors as she slid out.

Sam met her at the door with two glasses of wine. She tilted her head and studied Addi. "You look like hell, sis."

"Ouch." Addi took the wine. "Is it that bad?" she asked as the two settled into lounge chairs nestled in one corner of the little backyard oasis.

"It is to me, but I'm your sister. You're putting on a good show, though."

Addi leaned back. "Good, I can't handle twenty questions right now."

"Have you spoken with him yet?"

"And question number one. Yeah. He stopped by yesterday and returned the money I sent to his accountant. He told me—"

Sam straightened in her seat. Addi couldn't believe how hopeful she looked. There was a time when Sam had held the title for most pessimistic. Now happily married, she was all rainbows and butterflies.

Addi pressed her lips together and swallowed past the lump in her throat. Her heart heavy and her throat tight, she continued. "Good luck with my writing."

Sam smiled.

"And that fiction suited me."

Sam frowned. "Oh wow. That sucks."

Addi's eyes welled. Jumping up from her seat, Sam sunk in next to Addi, pulling her close. "I'm so sorry. I know this hurts, but you two will work it out."

"I don't think so. He said we're over. There's nothing I can do. I thought selling the house would prove how sorry I am, but he doesn't care. I'm looking for other options, but I'm afraid it may be my only one."

Sam sipped from her glass, and Addi polished off hers.

"Then why sell it? You love it more than any of us ever did. And he gave you back the money. You could figure it out." Sam waved her hand at Addi. "Makes sense; you're so much like her."

Addi leaned over her sister and set her glass on the table. "I have to sell it, Sam. I'm not keeping the money. It's about time I grow up and act like an adult. Settling my debts is the beginning of doing just that. Whether Roque agrees or not, paying him back every penny is necessary, for me and for him. Selling the house is the only way. It's not like I'm signing a writing contract any time soon." She settled in next to her sister, remembering all the times they'd lain just like this when they were children, calling out shapes made of clouds and talking about being president one day. It all seemed so simple back then. "Besides, I think, deep down, losing the house is the right consequence for playing so loosely with someone else's money. Hollywood or not, my scheme was wrong."

"But oh, so clever. I'd have loved to think of something like that when I was dealing with all that crap after Ethan died."

Addi nodded. "Unfortunately, I used your experience to justify it all to myself." She shook her head. "You won't believe some of the trouble I got myself into."

"I can imagine. You're my sister, remember?"

"What am I going to do, Sam?" Addi whispered, her heart in a painful squeeze. She couldn't breathe.

Her sister smiled at her and tapped the tip of Addi's nose with a finger. "What you always do."

Addi kept staring.

"You're going to find a way to get your way. Some things might have changed, Addi, but not everything."

Addi snorted, though it missed her usual energy. She appreciated her sister's confidence but was a bit insulted, too. She didn't *always* get her way. Not always. She could think of a time or two where she didn't get what she wanted. Her writing was one, and there was…

She thought hard. Well, fine, she usually got her way, but as much as she wanted it to be true, this wasn't one of those times. Roque made it crystal clear he wanted nothing more to do with her. Addi could only handle his rejection so much. It hurt worse than anything she could remember, as she'd known it would.

The hard things hurt, and everyone had to deal with them. She couldn't go through life afraid of those things anymore.

She'd give anything, even Aunt Addi's home, to get her way just one more time. If only she'd known two months ago what she knew now.

Her home was with Roque. No more and no less.

Chapter Twenty-Four

Roque scrubbed his hand through his hair again, immediately cooled in the shadow left by the cloud blocking the sun. They'd been filming at Topanga Beach trying to get the shot right all morning, but every time the lighting changed, the whole scene fell apart. He put up his hand, calling a stop to the action. "Gage, this just isn't working."

His director considered him with crossed arms over his chest. "It would be going great if we could actually get through a whole ten minutes before you yell 'cut'. That's my job."

Roque studied the playback on the screen. "No, it's not right. The lighting keeps fucking up the mood."

"No, you keep fucking up the mood. The lighting is offering a hint of reality to the scene."

Roque shot his hand toward the sky. "The weather isn't working. It's—

Gage shot up from his chair and walked toward the tent. "Cut! Let's break."

Following him to the tent, Roque grabbed a water from the cooler and twisted off the cap. "Look, we discussed this scene beginning to end and back again."

"Exactly. So let me shoot it," Gage said. He leaned back against one of the tables. "Have you called her?"

Roque scowled. "Don't go there. Now's not the time."

"It is when it's affecting the film."

"She is not the reason we can't get the shot." Roque tossed his empty plastic bottle into the recycling bag.

"You're right. You are." Gage looked out over the pounding surf, then back to Roque. "Let me do my job."

"Listen—" He glanced at the empty tables and then at his watch. Panic filled his chest and he grabbed his phone. "God dammit. I forgot to order lunch."

Pushing away from the table, Gage, too, checked the time. "Shit, there's no way you'll get anything catered on time at this point. I'll treat the crew to lunch. What are you in the mood for? Sushi or a burger?"

"Fuck. It's my problem. I'll treat." He released a breath, trying to relieve the tight squeeze in his chest. Addi had taken care of the meals. Scheduling the catering never made it onto his to-do list, with the slew of other items he'd needed to take back onto his plate. Sliding two fingers between his lips, he let loose a loud, impatient whistle. "We've another hour to work, then we'll load up and go to lunch."

His announcement was received with nods and smiles as the crew took their places. Gage spoke to the cinematographer, pointing and nodding with intermittent grunts of approval. Roque looked back at the sky with its fickle clouds, and scowled. He was in a mood. He felt it, and so did everyone else.

They ate lunch and muddled through the rest of the afternoon. He was disappointed with every shot they took, and Gage loved every one.

"Man, you're crazy. These are brilliant."

"They're mediocre at best. We're missing something."

Gage clenched his jaw as he helped pack up the equipment and load it into the trailer they'd backed to the edge of the parking lot. "Look, sleep on it. Let's study it again tomorrow with fresh eyes."

Something caught his eye over Roque's shoulder, and he jerked his chin in that direction. "Maybe you can talk some sense into him."

Roque turned to find Martin Gallagher approaching, hands in his houndstooth slacks pockets, looking every bit an academic scholar. Martin grinned. "Talk sense into Roque? We both know the answer to that."

"Cute."

Gage helped the cameraman close the back doors of the trailer and then slapped the side. Brushing sand from his hands, he leaned over to grab his bag. Speaking to Martin, he said, "It's been a day. I'm off." With a salute to both men, he followed the rest of the crew into the parking lot. Roque watched as they all slid into their cars. They weren't worried. Their names were ones of many on the film, not the main one. Must be nice to be so free of stress or ownership. Even as he thought it, he knew he was being unfair, but fuck if he couldn't shake the cloud hanging over his perspective all day.

Martin stepped in beside him, and they walked a bit along the boardwalk.

Finally, Martin broke the silence. "What's going on?"

With the barest shake of his head, Roque sighed. "It didn't work today. Nothing worked today."

Martin grunted. "Sounds like a typical day on the set to me."

"Gage seemed to think it all turned out…'Brilliantly' is the word he used, I think. It worries me that our visions aren't aligned."

Martin laughed and clapped him on the back. "Nothing is

going to look good to you right now. Have you talked to her?"

"Don't."

"Boy, the fact you think you can just lose yourself in your work as if nothing has happened is ridiculous. You don't have time to dwell, but you'll have to manage how missing Addi is affecting your work."

"I don't miss Addi, and not having her here has nothing to do with today. The fucking weather and my lack of planning is what screwed today up."

"Sure," Martin said. "You and Addi made a great team."

Roque stopped walking. "I worked just fine before ever meeting Addi, I'll be just fine without her."

"But you're better with her."

He did not need Addi to complete this film, and he didn't need his family and friends treating him as if he didn't know what the hell he was doing. He was making a name for himself before she ever entered his life, and his film would be a success without her. "I don't want to talk about it anymore."

"Roque."

"Enough." He started walking, and Martin fell into place alongside him again.

"Why don't you come over for dinner? Your aunt would love to see you."

Roque stretched his neck from side to side. "I can't. I have work."

"Son, you always have work."

Roque swung around. "You're right. I do. So, if you'll excuse me." Leaving his uncle on the boardwalk, he made his way to his car. He didn't need anyone reminding him that he put his work before anything else, that his work kept him from being with those he loved, or seeing the signs when those who said they loved him really hadn't. He didn't need any of it.

Between Martin and Martin Jr., it seemed they were all more worried about how Addi was getting on than how he was. Well, that was fine. The next thing he'd hear was that he was the one who needed to apologize. Hell, it seemed as far as they were concerned he didn't deserve her in the first place.

Well, at this point they could all go to hell as one big happy family.

Making his way home, he lugged his stuff to his condo and set up to study the film shot that day. He viewed different shots over and over again until he forgot what the hell he was supposed to be looking for.

His phone buzzed, and he glanced distractedly at it to find Addi's number highlighted. Visions of her grief-stricken face when he left her house surfaced. He'd been cruel, but no crueler than her. Ignoring the phone, he leaned in to view a few frames again. He tried to focus, but the knot in his gut wouldn't be ignored.

He missed the scent of honey in the air when she was around.

With a curse he shot from his chair.

And with one forceful sweep of his hand, he sent all of his notes and notebooks flying off the table and crashing to the floor.

Addi made her way to the bare kitchen and went through the motions of making coffee. That would be the last thing she'd put into storage. Every image of Roque sipping from his cup was her punishment for the things she'd done wrong. If only she'd listened to Chase, if only she'd found work before getting herself into this mess. If only.

With her cup in hand, she stepped through the back door to the yard and walked over to the hammock. It was just under seventy degrees, and the December sky was a brilliant blue with the sun shining, almost as if it were laughing. She sank into the hammock and lay back, shielding her eyes. The world mocked her with its bright glowing days and winter songbirds. She needed to move somewhere where the outside matched her desolation inside. Addi rolled her eyes. What she really needed was a good kick in the ass to stop feeling sorry for herself.

Too restless to lie down for long, she swung her legs over the edge and scooched forward. A glint of light caught her eye, and she slid from the hammock to investigate. Rummaging through the grass with care, she found a shard of glass and stared at it.

The memory of Roque's pain the night he'd come to the house and thought he was alone, along with her own actions, sliced at her. Just one more example of her deceit, she'd lurked and watched, uninvited—trespassing. He'd been hurting. It never occurred to her at the time that she'd hurt him, too. Keeping her secrets to herself was supposed to be harmless, a means to an end.

She turned the piece of glass over and over in her hand. It was both beautiful and menacing, a symbol of the pain Roque experienced with his mother. The pain existed because of incredible beauty that had touched his life, but the loss of that beauty sliced with a sharp, clean cut.

She turned the piece over one more time, and the edge cut through the skin at the tip of her finger. She winced and sucked on the injured part. When would she learn? Don't lie, don't keep secrets, and don't pick up broken glass.

She inspected her wound and found it wasn't deep, just insulting.

"What are you doing back here? I rang the bell but you didn't hear it, and God only knows how that's possible."

Addi snapped her head up as Sam walked through the French doors from the kitchen. "You rang the bell?" Her voice sounded flat to her ears.

"That thing shrieks like a berserker."

Addi pulled up the corners of her lips at the joke, but the movement lacked the usual lightness of emotion that accompanied it.

Sam stepped forward and wrapped her fingers around Addi's wrist, yanking her up from the hammock. "What happened? Oh, my God, Addi. Come on, I'll —"

Addi pulled back against her sister's insistent tug. "No, stop. Sam. Stop."

Yanking her hand away, she turned to sit back down.

"You need to clean it out, you don't —"

Once again, the people in her life found her incapable of the simplest things. Anxiety burned and seized in her chest. Her breaths came hard and fast. She was a grown woman. Damn it.

"I can take care of myself." Addi shouted in succinct beats.

Sam stepped back, a look of shock morphing quickly into pain. Addi brushed past her sister. She hadn't meant to hurt her, but she didn't have the energy to be careful of someone else's feelings.

Sam followed her into the kitchen. "I was only trying to help."

Addi spun with her arms spread wide. "I know. I can't do anything. Poor, poor Addi has to have someone take care of her, has to have someone do everything for her." Tears streamed down her face as she yelled between sobs. Apparently her tears weren't all gone, after all.

Sam put up her hands, her eyes wide and concerned. "Whoa, wait a second. That's not fair. How often have we all had to come running to your side? What do expect us to do?"

"Mom is always 'baby this' and 'baby that'. Daddy, too, hell, you even called me that the other night."

"The other night? Addi, you *are* my baby sister. When you're hurting I want to make it better because I love you, not because I don't think you can handle it."

Addi shook her head. "No, my whole life—"

Sam's expression hardened. "Your whole life we've loved you, we've taken care of you, because you were the youngest. You never complained about it before, now I get attacked?"

Addi returned her sister's hard stare. "I am not a baby."

"Then quit acting like one," Sam yelled.

Walking over to the kitchen sink, Addi rummaged in the cupboard and found peroxide and Band-Aids.

"Old habits die hard. When you're hurting I go into big sister mode." Sam put her hands up in surrender. "You've shown us you can do anything you put your mind to. Hell, who else is brave enough to leave a stable job to pursue a dream before actually making it?"

"You mean, stupid enough."

Sam shook her head. "No. I don't. You've always amazed me at your verve, your passion. You were the fearless one, the feisty one." Taking the peroxide from Addi's hand, Sam opened the cap and, holding Addi's finger over the sink, poured a small amount over the cut. As the wound bubbled, Sam blew on it to ease the sting.

Addi smiled at the top of her sister's head and pulled in a shaky breath. "Really? You think I'm brave?"

Sam looked up from her task. "Incredibly. It was the beginning to this change I've been seeing in you. With time, Mom and Dad will see it, too." Leaning her hip against the counter, she handed Addi a Band-Aid. "Remember when I went through all that trash with Gage? I almost lost him because I was so scared. You aren't afraid of anything."

Pain throbbed with each heartbeat behind Addi's eyes. "This is different," she whispered.

Sam pressed her lips together and shook her head. "It's not."

"Sam, you've been doing things on your own, depending

on no one but yourself, forever. Marrying Gage didn't change that. I've never stood on my own two feet. You or Luca or Mom and Dad always did everything for me." Addi removed the adhesive covers and wrapped the bandage around her finger. She glanced up and held her sister's gaze. "The bungalow went into foreclosure. I had to save it. Just me. On my own. I couldn't bear to lose this house." She sent her hand in a wide arc to encompass the home she so adored. "I couldn't bear to let you guys down…again."

"Oh, Addi." Sam wrapped her arms around Addi's waist. "You'll figure this out, too."

Addi sniffed. "Mom didn't think I should quit my job."

"What else was she supposed to think? You may not want to hear it, but you leaned on them even when you worked full-time. The writing industry isn't exactly kind. She worries about you. We all do."

Tears welled over and streamed down Addi's cheeks. "Well, you don't have to anymore. I'm done filling the role of baby sister." She sniffed. "My mind is made up. It's time for me to grow up, Sam. Aunt Addi left this place to me and, as much as my heart aches to sell it, I might have to. I loved Aunt Addi, we all did, but this is something I have to do. I have to have a consequence in order to learn, apparently. Losing Aunt Addi's bungalow will do the trick." She dropped her head into her hands.

"Don't you think you've been punished enough?"

Turning her head from one side to the other, she whispered, "He won't talk to me." Her heart ached for the scent of him, the warmth of his skin when he held her, the timbre of his voice when he whispered in her ear. She'd had every dream she hadn't realized was hers in her hands, but couldn't quite get a grip soon enough to make them real. Her chances with Roque were gone, so the best she could do was go after the positive direction her writing was finally going.

But even the prospect of writing success seemed hollow without the man who had stolen her heart.

"He's hurt and hiding. Men do that, believe me." Sam ran her hand over Addi's hair. "He'll come around."

"I wish you were right. But not this time. This is one romance I can't write a happy ending for."

"You'll find a way." Sam grabbed her bag. "Listen, I gotta run. Gage and I are meeting the landscapers to go over the design for the backyard." She walked to the front door. "Call me. Okay?"

Addi nodded.

Sam hesitated another beat, making Addi laugh. Pointing toward the door, Addi demanded with a smile, "Go. I'll be fine."

The house fell into silence once again, and Addi walked into the kitchen, then hopped up on the counter. She wanted an éclair—four, really—but she hadn't dared to bring anything messy into the house. It was hard enough for her to stay tidy even without the delicious pastry.

With a lazy sigh, she turned her laptop to face her and clicked on her email.

Spam. Advertisement. Spam. *Omigod.*

Staring at the "from" name, she pulled in a shaky breath. Her dream agent.

Her fingers shook as she clicked the cursor to open the email.

Dear Addison Dekker,

She read through the correspondence as well as she could with tears blurring her vision and disbelief tightening her throat.

Your writing shows great promise.

Pressing her hands to her chest, she tried to swallow past the lump that had formed.

Please send me another sample, then I'd like to speak over the phone.

The completely overwhelming feeling of relief coupled with ecstatic hope was too much on top of her sadness over Roque, her disappointment with herself, and the possible loss of her home. Her emotions bubbled up, and tears flowed freely down her cheeks.

A lightness eased into place, nudging the heavy weight of shame from her back. The agent she wanted to partner with saw promise in her writing.

In *her*.

A small giggle escaped her lips, and she tasted the salt of her tears. Tipping her head back just a bit, she pulled in her elbows and opened her chest as her instructor always suggested in yoga class.

She was making progress, after all.

But she needed to do it in a sustainable way. If she sold the bungalow and paid back Roque, she'd be able to afford a small studio apartment and maybe a part-time job that would allow some flexibility for her writing. She didn't need to live large, but she did need to live her dream.

And that was reasonable.

She'd learned a lot the past few months. She'd fallen in love. Not only with Roque—and that wasn't changing anytime soon—but with herself, too. With her possibilities, with the potential of her future.

She couldn't have Roque.

But she did have hope.

Chapter Twenty-Five

Roque came to, welcomed by an incessant pounding in his head. His stomach rolled from the stench of stale beer in the air, and he looked around for the offenders. He grabbed the empty beer bottle from his lap and the two from beside him on the couch and threw them in the trash, wincing as they clattered together at the bottom.

Gingerly dropping his feet from the coffee table to the floor, he held his head in his hands and took in the mess around him. Notes about the film were strewn all over his couch, alongside his tie and jacket. His laptop sat on the table open to the same screen for the past two hours. No progress.

His phone rang.

He wanted to ignore it, but saw it was Gage. "What."

"Where the hell are you? We've been waiting almost thirty minutes."

"What time is it?" Roque raked fingers through his hair, biting back the angry retort from the tip of his tongue. Slowly, Gage's words sunk in. "Shit!" They'd had an interview with the press about the movie at six, then he'd agreed to have dinner with his dad at eight.

"Exactly. You know, this project only works with both of our heads in the game. Come on, man. They're here and ready to go. There's no way in hell they'll wait any longer."

"Can you answer a few questions and tell them I had an emergency?"

An aggravated sigh came across the line loud and clear, followed by Gage's voice. "This better not happen again. I can't believe you forgot. This is not the time to start falling apart."

"It won't. I've been working through the film edits and lost track...fuck."

"I get it. Listen, I'll whip something up about two featured interviews. I'll throw in some sort of promo incentive and have them reschedule your half. Don't mess it up next time."

Roque disconnected the call, then tossed his phone onto the cushion.

God dammit.

The silence of the house roared in his head. Pushing up from the couch, he went to his room in search of a movie. *Roman Holiday* seemed to gravitate to his hand without any will of his own. Wasn't that perfect? A love story filled with secrets that had no chance of ending well. He made his way back to the couch after sliding in the DVD.

The opening music immediately relieved some of the tension gathering at the base of his skull. He never had trouble working in silence before, and he couldn't figure out what the fuck his problem was now.

Dropping to the cushions, he pulled his notebook onto his lap and stared at his chicken scratch. Post-production editing was underway but moving slow. He and Gage couldn't agree on the opening shot, stopping them before they started. He shoved the pad of paper aside. With a sigh, he leaned back, his hands behind his head, and watched the film. Gregory Peck found Aubrey Hepburn asleep on a public bench. Now that was a man with class and presence. The only thing Roque had lately was a fucking headache.

He remembered back to when he introduced the movie to Addi. His chest tightened.

She'd loved it, like he did.

The movie had always been a favorite, introduced to him by his mom and dad. They loved it, having spent their honeymoon in Rome. Roque loved it for the impossibility of finding such love and then having to let it go. He also found the simplicity of the cinematography refreshing in a time when production seemed so complicated that the actual story was often forgotten.

It was amazing how different the movie felt when he watched it with Addi compared to now. He shook his head, securely grounded in his new reality. Warm beer, an empty house, and work he couldn't focus on.

And Addi was gone.

He flipped over his phone. No texts or calls, no unannounced visitors on his doorstep. He was more alone than he'd ever been. His dad knew not to push, and his friends knew he'd only be an ass. Everything irritated the shit out of him these days. The sun was too fucking bright and his friends too fucking loud. The only thing that gave him any peace was sleep.

But even that was in short supply lately. He'd lie there night after night, eyes wide open, sleep further away than an Oscar. It was wearing on him.

Yawning, he pulled his laptop onto his thighs, placing his feet on the table with his ankles crossed. He again watched the options he and Gage were considering for the opening shots, but halfway through realized he quit paying attention. "Fucking great." If he wasn't interested in his own film, no one else would be, either.

He couldn't believe he'd missed the meeting with the press. That would look great if Gage decided to walk, too. And the delays in the editing were costing both time and money. If he couldn't get his head out of his ass and focus on the film, he'd lose that, too.

But what the fuck did it matter anyway? His film could be a huge success, he could be surrounded by his friends and family, but when he imagined it all, the pride he felt was because of the smile on Addi's face as she stood next to him. By his side. But she wasn't by his side. She was further away than anyone ever could be.

Addi was gone.

And he'd lost everything that ever really mattered to him. She'd poisoned his passion with her verve and spunk. Without her there, his work seemed cold and empty.

Now, even if he was a success, it would be tainted and hollow.

Checking the time on his phone, he figured he could keep at least one of his appointments. Besides, he needed to get away from his condo—it reminded him of what a mess his life had become. He found a clean shirt, then hunted down his keys.

He was a workaholic, which had robbed him of both his mother's last days and his ability to be worth a damn in a relationship. But he'd been trying. Apparently, trying wasn't enough. Because Addi was just the most recent in a line of women he either failed so completely they left him, or else simply used him until he couldn't take it anymore.

Being used hurt the worst.

Roque shook his head as he sunk into his favorite spot in the corner of the couch in his parents' library. "Don't even try it, Dad. I'm not in the mood."

Mac scoffed and forged on as he set the jukebox to play. "Don't tell me what to do, boy. I can talk about whoever I want. And I want to talk about Addi."

Roque had made a mistake accepting the dinner invitation from his dad. Dinner had gone fine, but he'd known this was coming. There was a reason he'd been avoiding everyone. He ran his hands through his hair, then down over the stubble of his chin. He needed a shave and a shower. What the hell had he been doing the past week?

Sulking. Fucking baby. "I need a drink."

Mac poured a finger of Scotch into two tumblers and walked back to his seat, passing Roque his drink along the way. "Salute."

Roque lifted his glass to his father's, remembering how a certain someone was able to throw one back, and then let a hot mouthful burn down his throat. He blew out a breath, enjoying the heat spreading across his chest. Fucking hell, he was tired.

"I missed a meeting with the press." Maybe he needed some time off work to clear his head.

"I heard. Your uncle told me."

"Of course he did." Roque shook his head. His aunt's and uncle's ability to keep a constant pulse on Malibu never ceased to amaze him. It was true, the saying that mothers and fathers had eyes in the back of their heads.

"Well?"

"Well what?" Roque raised a brow, anger digging into his chest with the question. Addi's face rose in his mind, tearing at his heart, filling his gut with dead weight. He was sick of the pain. Anger helped numb it, or at least that's what he told himself.

"What are you going to do about her?"

Roque tossed back his drink and then coughed as the

burn seized his lungs. "Shit."

His dad laughed. "Well, what the hell'd you expect? This ain't your first Scotch, boy."

Roque ignored his father, trying to find his breath. Trying to find reason behind the intensity of his feelings, his anger, his pain. Why? Why hadn't he been enough? Addi's actions felt like a betrayal of incomprehensible levels. He'd been a good time and a means to an end for her, but not much else.

When his mother told him about her cancer, giving him very little time to say good-bye, he'd have sworn it was the most painful experience in his life. This challenged that, though, and he'd never thought anything could be more painful than losing his mom. Nothing except the realization that she hadn't told him about her cancer, because she knew he'd drop his work for her, and she knew how much he loved his work. So she'd chosen for him.

And now Addi. She'd found her way under his skin and into his heart. Fucking shit. She'd been alive and well and his. Dreams of their future had teased him, excited him, had him making plans.

Now he faced his future alone.

"Have you thought about why you were so upset about your mom's decision?" His father's voice broke through the haze and numbness, leaving him confused with the change of subject.

"Seems clear to me."

"Is it?"

"Dad, why the hell are you asking me this now?" Roque rubbed his chest.

"Because I didn't realize I needed to before."

Roque set down his glass and clenched his fist. His father was ridiculous, the conversation was ridiculous. He needed to go home. He stood.

"Sit down."

"Seriously, I need to go."

"Sit. Down."

Dropping to the couch, he glared at his father. "You shut down after Mom died."

His father never blinked, just studied him with a calm and resigned look. "I was afraid that's what was going on here."

"Do you deny it?"

"No, I don't."

Macklan Gallagher stood, poured another two fingers of Scotch in Roque's glass and then paced the billiard room, his hands in his pockets, a faraway look on his weathered face. "God, I loved that woman."

Roque's throat burned with the threat of tears. The last thing his dad needed was him crying on about his mother, while the man had lost the love of his life.

"She got me in a way no one ever had, ever could." He looked up at the ceiling and blinked a few times before going on. "She was more than my wife, she was my life. No, not my life so much as the air that gave me life, energy, love. I lived, really lived, because of your mother. And you."

Mac stopped in front of Roque and studied him. "I'd go through losing her again and again just for the experience of her love even once."

Denial soured the liquor in Roque's gut. "That's crazy, that's—"

"Love."

Roque fell back against the cushions of the couch.

His dad poured another drink, then dropped to the couch next to him. Both men leaned back with their eyes closed, a comfortable silence only those who were really close could enjoy.

"I miss her," Roque whispered.

"Miss who?"

He rolled his head to the side, scanning his father's strong profile. "Mom stole from me, too. Stole time."

She'd stolen time, but also choice, and options, and knowledge. Roque had shut himself down after that. He'd chosen to be independent, to make sure no one could hurt him again.

Mac opened his eyes and sipped from his glass. "She never intended you to feel that way, but she knew you'd quit what you were doing and run to her side. She didn't want to hold you back, in fact, she felt it was her sole purpose for living to hold you up, push you forward. Watching you go after your dreams was her dream come true."

Roque pulled in a breath, blinking to hold back the tears burning behind his lids. *God damn it.* "But I missed so much time."

"In her mind, she was making sure you were taking full advantage of the time you had. Son, she mothered you up to her very last breath."

"That's not true." Roque pushed up and leaned his elbows against his knees. "She never stopped. Every decision I make I think of what she'd say. No, she's never stopped mothering me."

His dad gave a rusty laugh. "If anyone could find a way to control things from the other side it would be your mother."

He glanced at his dad and then looked away. "I feel her around me all the time."

His dad nodded. "Me, too."

Roque stood and returned his glass to the sideboard. "You'd really go through it all over again?"

"No question. The pain doesn't matter. It never really goes away anyway, just becomes more manageable. The question is, why are *you* so bent on being in pain when you don't have to be? The love of your life is still here." His dad paused and rubbed a hand over his chin. "It's hard to watch you throw it away."

Roque couldn't process worth a shit. Everything his dad admitted spun in his head. He nodded at his father and turned to leave.

"Roque?"

Hearing his name spoken in such a soft tone had him turning quicker than if his father had shouted.

Mac's brows furrowed. "I'm sorry if you needed me, and I wasn't there."

"Fuck." Roque walked back to his dad who'd stood from the couch. He wrapped his arms around the strong man and squeezed with a gruff cough. "You were always there for me, Dad. Always."

Mac nodded. "And now?"

Roque cleared his throat, and the two men released their holds on each other. He knew what his dad asked, but he didn't know how to answer.

"All of Me" floated out low from his dad's stereo. Both men froze and looked from each other to the old jukebox in the corner of the library.

His dad chuckled. "Always in our business, that one."

Roque cleared his throat. He swallowed and then a grin spread his lips wide. His mom had always been there for him, for them. He'd been so angry she'd made the choice she had—angry she'd taken the choice from him. For so long he agonized over her thinking his work was more important to him than she was, but now he could see he'd been wrong.

It had been because she knew it was so important, period. She knew how much he loved his work, and she knew he'd have walked away from it all in a heartbeat if he'd found out she was sick.

It hadn't been because he was a workaholic or because he put his work before those he loved in his life.

He hadn't failed her.

She'd simply loved him.

A few hours later, Roque opened his eyes to a dark room and a heavy throw flung over him. Before driving home, he'd needed to sleep off the rest of the Scotch he'd drunk while he and his dad had been talking. Now the house was quiet and still. He strained to hear anything from the direction of his dad's room, but nothing stirred save for his heartbeat in his own ears.

With a small groan, he stood from the leather sofa, taking a moment to find his balance. He felt around the end table for his keys and knocked into the tumbler he'd used earlier. The sound seemed to echo through the room and he froze, holding his breath. When it was quiet once again, he finally found his keys and made his way through the house.

He stepped outside and tilted his head back to take in the night sky. Pulling in as much air as his lungs could hold, he then let it out in a rush. The air was salty and cool. It reminded him of the night he'd gone out on the beach with Addi and he'd first told her about his mother. He'd never shared that with anyone before.

Instead of getting in his car, he turned and took the pathway around his dad's house to the beach. Thoughts of his mom, Addi, his dad, and the film swirled through his mind as he stepped off the walk and onto the sand. His mom would be proud. He and Gage still had a bit to go, but they'd finish, and in a way no one would ever be able to forget.

He went over the conversation he'd had with his dad. Holding on to the pain of missing out on time to say good-bye to his mother seemed like a good excuse to avoid dealing with it. He'd been crushed to lose her, then he'd blamed himself and choked on his anger, until nothing was left but fear.

He feared he couldn't be enough in a relationship, that he wouldn't be able to prioritize and make those in his life feel like they were important. The ending of every relationship he entered had played out in his mind before the first date. He set himself up to fail right from the beginning, letting his past drive his future. And the way he'd treated Addi—God. It had all been because he was letting fear make his choices.

He'd lost control, but in losing it, he was able to find his way, because he was no longer afraid.

And if he wasn't afraid of what would happen, if he could have a say in what his future was, then he could go after Addi. Couldn't he?

Her actions, too, were out of fear. He could finally see that. Fear of losing her home, of failing in her family's eyes and in her own eyes. She'd been so afraid, she dreamed up her ridiculous scheme and hid in the attic of her own house—even though she was afraid of the dark. His lip quirked as he imagined her swearing while she tripped through the house.

Fear could have such a deep, dark hold on people, and it had been so hard to see on his own. But he was getting rid of that weight.

The idea made him feel lighter than he'd felt in weeks.

But he'd treated her, their time together, as if his work was most important. He hadn't followed in his father's footsteps, making her feel like a priority but instead like an option that he could put off—shove aside. All to make sure his mistaken view of his mother's actions wouldn't have been for nothing.

Addi had never made him feel worthless. He'd done that to himself.

If he could make those mistakes while loving her, it was only fair to allow her mistakes while loving him. And people were full of them, would keep making them, no matter how hard they tried not to. It wasn't about the what, but the why. The intent behind the action. If he'd been brave enough to really look at Addi's intentions, he'd have seen a very frightened woman trying to make her way imperfectly through an equally imperfect world.

He'd been just as guilty, so how could he blame her? So much lost because of fear.

Well, not anymore. There was no longer any reason. He'd been wrong. What he wanted now was right in front of him for the taking.

If he could only get her to see him the same way he saw her, and forgive him for how short he'd fallen.

R oque walked beside Martin Jr. as they made their way down the sidewalk of the Malibu Pier to their lunch meeting. He should be elated, but the heaviness in his chest kept him stuck on solid ground, and he scowled.

"Dude, you're the only jackass on the planet who could be unhappy holding an accolade like that." Martin Jr. slapped at the article in Roque's hand. "That's a fucking honor—every producer dreams of getting that kind of review."

Roque ducked the hand flying at his arm and tucked the magazine in his bag, pulling the strap higher to anchor it. He shot Martin Jr. a look. "Quit hitting me, man."

His friend slapped his other arm and then laughed as he walked ahead through the door of the restaurant where they were to meet a few other industry professionals.

It wasn't common for an independent film to get such buzz so early on, but damn if it hadn't just happened. The fact he was Macklan Gallagher's son was part of the hum, but more because he didn't use the association than because he did. His film, his project, was all him and his team.

But the good feeling of his award didn't last long with Addi's face a memory instead of seeing her beside him in person. He'd figured out what a mess he'd made of things, but figuring out how to fix things had taken time. While his accountant helped research that particular problem, the post-production of the movie had to be finished. He and Gage worked nonstop until they both agreed they'd hit gold.

And they had.

He blew out a breath. "Looks like we're the first ones here." With a nod, he slid into the chair pulled out by the waiter.

Martin Jr. slid in across from him. "Good, I've been waiting to hear your plan."

Roque stilled. "My plan?"

"Yeah, the one where you figure out how to get Addi back. I'm not into the whole commitment thing, but the two of you are pretty damn perfect for each other. I figured now that things were moving right along with the film, you'd get back to the important things."

Roque studied his friend. "The important things."

Martin signaled for the waiter. "Water, please." Turning his attention back to Roque he said, "So out with it."

Leaning back in his seat, Roque pulled his arms against the resisting fabric of his suit. "I said some fucked up shit. She's not going to want to listen to me."

Martin leaned forward. "That's it? We say dumb shit all the time."

"You've got a point. I've had to figure out something she can't refuse, something that makes it look like she's helping me instead of me helping her."

His buddy laughed. "Good luck with that, nothing scarier than a helpful woman."

"I dare you to say that to your mother."

Martin slowly slid his middle finger up the bridge of his nose.

"I don't know. What if it's too late?"

Martin sighed and glared at Roque with a look of annoyance. "Seriously, dude. Did you just say that?"

Roque ran a hand over his trimmed scruff. "Fuck, man, I

can't wait to see you all wrapped around yourself over some chick. I'll remember how helpful you were."

"That's where you and I differ. I ain't doing it. Nothing a night out on the town can't fix, and I don't have to deal with anyone getting in the way come morning."

Addi never got in the way. On the contrary, morning was the best time to see her, all warm skin and sweet honey. He could practically hear her sleep-thickened murmur of appreciation as he pulled her close.

Martin snapped his fingers in front of Roque's face. "Dude."

Roque blinked and shifted in his seat. God damn it.

He needed Addi. He wanted Addi. What the hell would he do if he couldn't get her back?

He needed to figure out what he was going to do to fix the shitstorm he'd created. In the back of his mind he could hear his mother say, "You can do anything you set your mind to, my beautiful boy."

And if he learned anything from his mother, he learned he damn well could.

He needed to prove to Addi that he could forgive her fear and that he was no longer reacting, no longer making choices out of fear himself.

Roque blew out a breath, a weight falling from him, the first rays of pride floating free as he slapped the magazine back on the table. He flexed his muscles in his suit, the movement stiff but good. He knew what he was going to do, and his movie was heading toward box office success out of the gate.

He rubbed his hands together as two gentlemen joined them at their table.

Time to negotiate. But Hollywood was child's play compared to what he would face tomorrow.

Chapter Twenty-Six

Addi paced her front room for the tenth time, cursing as she smoothed the fabric of her skirt for the fifteenth time. Who the hell needed a walk-through on Christmas Eve? They couldn't wait until the day after the biggest holiday of the year, for Pete's sake? The buyers had already put their offer through. It was a no-brainer, since they hadn't even tried to negotiate the asking price. So here she was. Her realtor had already worked miracles, and there was no way she'd ask him to work on the holiday.

She moved a stone pitcher, stood back to look at it, and then returned it to its place. Nerves skittered up her neck, and she stretched it in one direction, then the other, trying to chase them away. She had no choice but to let the morons come by. The sooner she sold her home, the sooner she could start over. And man was she ready to get on with her life, get on from her pain. As if that were remotely possible.

Her heart was broken in half. She pressed the heels of her hands against her lids to keep from crying, careful not to mess up her makeup—she wanted to sell her home, not send the people running. If only she could go back.

She would have never known the kind of love she'd found with Roque was possible. It wasn't the kind in fairy tales, but better, the kind that came from caring, from choosing one person every day, the kind that grew richer through mistakes and deeper through forgiveness—at least that's what she'd thought. Now she wondered if it would have been better not to know such a thing existed, wondered if it would have hurt a lot less.

Addi pulled in a breath. Her heart hurt and her future looked bleak, except for her writing. What good was being a romance author if she couldn't escape into her own fantasies? She anticipated a lot of writing in the next few months, so she'd better figure it out.

Walking around the room one last time, she rubbed at nonexistent dust, fluffed the already puffy pillows, and smoothed the sheers that hung straight and sure. Chase had offered to come over, but Addi refused. Christmas was one of the very few holidays the Huntingtons actually found the time to be together, and she wasn't about to keep them apart.

Her own family was hanging out at Sam and Gage's, waiting for her. She imagined the house decked out in lights, wreaths hung and wafting the scent of holiday pine, ornaments and lights like glittering jewels glowing from every nook and cranny. And her favorite, the Christmas tree. Sam and Gage had a huge one already overflowing with presents underneath. She'd bet, at that very moment, they were all singing carols around the fireplace. Okay, that might be a stretch, but whoever the jerkface was who so adamantly wanted to see the house right away didn't know that. And it was before ten in the morning. Really? She'd barely downed her second cup of coffee.

Aunt Addi's doorbell shrieked, yanking Addi out of her grumblings with a jump and a hand slapped to her chest.

She smiled. Now the damn thing was a challenge — could she survive longer than it did?

With a shake of her head, she walked over to the door, glancing in the mirror for a quick check. She smoothed her brows and reminded herself to be nice.

Pasting on a smile, Addi pulled open the front door. She gasped and stepped back at the sight of her guest. "You."

Roque Gallagher's eyes flickered wide for a beat, his only reaction to her shock. He yanked a sheet of paper from his portfolio and looked from it to the address numbers nailed above her door.

Her heart slammed in her chest and a warm rush swept through her body, but her stomach twisted in apprehension. She didn't want to hurt today. "Why are you here?"

His lips stretched into a tentative grin. "No, you're supposed to threaten me with calling the police."

She wanted to smile at his attempt to recreate the first time he'd come to her house, but his harsh words from their last meeting kept her frozen in place. She ignored the curious flutter in her heart.

"Addison." He dropped his bag to the porch and stepped forward, intent and much more in his gaze. He stepped toward her.

Addi put out her hand. "No, no. I, ah, I have a buyer coming to look at the house. You need to leave. Please." She could smell his cologne, and the heady scent clouded her head with lustful images and warm memories, breaking her heart further. She couldn't let him touch her or she'd break for sure, and now was the time she needed to stand on her own two feet. "I'm sorry, but you really have to go. Happy holidays to your family."

"Happy holidays?"

"Roque, I told you, I have a—"

He held her gaze, shifting from one foot to the other. He

looked over her head to the front room and nodded. "Yes, this is exactly what I expected."

She looked behind her into the front room, then back to his confirming nod. Confusion left her mute, and she couldn't take her eyes off him. His beautiful face, the strong line of his silhouette, the tapping of his thick fingers against his thigh. Something was different, an energy she hadn't sensed before.

He bent and grabbed his bag, making her jump, and then stepped past her into her house. Suddenly the space seemed small, and all the air had gone missing.

She pulled in a calming breath, trying to wrap her head around what he was doing.

Setting his bag on one of the living room chairs, he turned to her. "Give me the tour one more time, please."

She stepped forward and then froze. "A tour?"

Roque closed the distance between the two of them, and Addi shot her hand out to stop him. His chest pressed into her fingers.

She couldn't breathe, couldn't think, her heart struggled to beat and her lungs forgot how to pull in air. "Roque, I…"

"I hurt you, cheap shots tossed at you out of anger and pain. I understand why you did what you did. I understand the fear, because I've been letting it rule my decisions, too. I forgive you, and hope that you can find a way to forgive me, too." His gaze didn't move from her face, and her hand rushed to her chest.

"I couldn't comprehend the idea you would sell a house that was such a home to just anybody. A house that wasn't just your home but *our* home. At least until we have a horde of children, then we'll need something bigger, or better yet, we'll add a second level." He held her gaze, his Adam's apple dipping with a hard swallow. "I made a choice. Not out of fear, but out of love."

Her eyes filled with tears, and shock left her fingers numb

and cold. She took a step back. She didn't understand, tried to force her brain to catch up with reality. *Our home? Hordes of children?* She was terrified of reading him wrong, of hoping, of misunderstanding his words, because her heart wanted them to be true more than she'd ever wanted anything in her whole life.

The smile on his face diminished, and he reached out a hand. "You wanted to do the right thing by selling the house and returning the money, and you can still do that. Sell the house to me. I'm homesick, and the only remedy is buying this house and letting it live up to its full potential. Besides, I'm selling my condo. I don't have anywhere else to go."

"You're selling your place?" She shook her head, because he couldn't be serious. She needed to do right by him, and how could she do that by selling him the house?

"You can give me back the money still owed. I understand your need to settle your debt, but there's a catch, Addi. You can only pay me back if you live here. With me."

Addi couldn't wrap her brain around the plan Roque described. All her dreams, her passions, her heart, all wrapped around this man. And he was offering them to her.

He rushed on and stepped toward her. "We both win. You can do what you think is right, you can keep your house, and I, I get to keep you. I was afraid of loving you too much, of not being enough, but not being with you only made it worse. My dad said he'd lose my mom all over again just to experience her love the one time. He was right."

Roque dropped to one knee and held Addi lightly by the fingers of her left hand. "Addison Dekker, I love you. I want to wake up to your coffee every day."

She giggled, placing a hand over her mouth to stifle the sound and hold back the sob that threatened to strangle her.

Reaching out, he slipped his hand into hers, lowering it from her face. "I want to marry you, but if you aren't ready,

I understand. We don't have to rush it. Just know I want you with me." With a tilt to his head, he gave her a crooked grin. "And I want to go to sleep every night to your smile. You work harder than anyone I know—though you don't realize it yourself—and you are caring and kind and funny as hell. We'll never be perfect, but we'll be perfect for each other. Will you do me the honor of moving into my new house with me?"

It took her a moment to find words. "You really forgive me?"

"Yes." His gaze steady.

"And you realize you were an ass?"

"I was a huge ass, Addi. But I don't want my past to be my future. I want a lifetime of us forgiving each other and learning how to be the best versions of ourselves. And I think we can only do that together."

Addi dropped to her knees in front of him and hugged him, burying her face in his neck. "I'm so sorry about everything, I'll never lie to you again. I—"

"I know. And I'll make sure you feel like a priority, not an afterthought of my work." He rubbed her back, splaying his hand wide and pulling her close to his body. His hard abs and firm chest were so welcoming she wanted to burrow in and never come out. "You didn't answer my question. Will you move in with me? Let's build a life together, Addi, and show Hollywood how it's done."

Addi couldn't stop the rush of emotion that tightened her throat. He trusted her, forgave her, and wanted to make her his. But she shook her head through her blinding tears. "No."

Roque stilled. "No?"

She kissed each cheek. "I won't move in with you, but you can move in with me. And—"

His shoulders sagged with apparent relief, and he growled. "Woman. You're terrifying."

She giggled. "One more thing. Yes, I'll marry you. You

may regret it, but I'll marry you."

Roque stood, pulling her along with a laugh. He lifted her off her feet and swung her around and then crushed his mouth to hers. Her heart swelled so much in her chest, she felt like there was no room left for air.

He pulled back, cupping her face in his hands. "Goddamn, you're beautiful."

She sighed with a wink. "You're coming on to me."

He pulled back slightly, his teeth flashing white against his tanned cheek. He teased against her lips. "I told you when I came on to you, you wouldn't have to ask."

Epilogue

Roque and Addi walked through Sam's front door and into the warm embrace of family at Christmas, and there was nothing better. Everyone was there, including Roque's dad and Jimmy.

Addi spotted him first and made a beeline for him. Roque stopped her, pulling her back to his chest. "Where are you going?"

She pressed a kiss to his mouth, no embarrassment, no hiding, and she loved it. "When I promised you forever, I assumed there was at least a ten foot radius of allowable separation."

He laughed, the glint in his eye teasing. "Only five, but I forgive you for forgetting."

Pressing her lips together, she batted her lashes at him. "As *you* promised to." She took his hand, the feeling of his warmth rushing straight to her heart. "I want to go see Jimmy, make sure he's comfortable in this crazy gang all alone."

Roque laughed. "You're worried about Jimmy? He'll love that."

She wiggled her brows. "It's what I do."

"Go. But come back."

She lost herself in the intense blue of his gaze. She didn't know how she got so lucky, but she'd work hard every day to show how thankful she was. "Always."

Turning, she winked at him and got a slap on her ass. She jumped. "Roque."

Shaking her head, she wove through her family, leaving hugs and grabbing squeezes along the way.

Jimmy sat off to the side near the bar by a large stone fireplace, watching the crowd with interest on his face. He tipped a glass of eggnog at her as she approached.

She kissed his cheek with a grin. "I never pinned you as an eggnog man."

He smacked his lips. "Delicious."

She nodded toward the pitcher sitting close to his arm on the bar top. "That why you're keeping it so close?"

"Let's just say I like to take stock of what I like and keep it close." He winked at her. "How's Roque?"

Addi scooted next to him and leaned against the bar, looking out over her family. Frank and Mac laughed at their own hilarity at the big round kitchen table, and Martin stood with Sam at the piano while Gage played "Jingle Bells." Luca worked feverishly on his cell off in the corner of the living room's large leather couch. Addi shook her head. Her brother needed to relax.

Dee and Raquel walked up with Gage's sister, Bel, in tow. Raquel led the way with her hand limp and her knuckles out in a demure greeting to Jimmy. "And who do we have here? I don't believe I've been introduced."

Addi didn't buy it for a minute, because Raquel knew who everyone was in Malibu—but she'd play along. "Raquel, this is Jimmy. He works with Roque, and he's an up-and-coming photographer, I believe."

Jimmy eyed her and then turned to Raquel. He dipped his chin and, with his fingertips barely under Raquel's, brushed his lips over her knuckles. She expelled a small breath, her eyes bright.

Addi gave a slow mental clap of approval. *Nicely done, Jimmy.*

On a nod, Raquel turned to Bel. "Darling, have you met Jimmy?"

"Callahan, Irish father, Italian mother." He nodded at Bel. Addi felt him tense at her side and looked at his face, curious. He didn't just watch Bel, he studied her, his expression so intent, he almost seemed angry.

Bel resisted the push forward from Raquel but ended up right in front of Jimmy nevertheless. Addi almost laughed outright at the look of shock and awe on Bel's face.

Bel looked at Jimmy and then quickly at Addi. "Any eggnog left?"

Jimmy jumped into action, grabbing a tumbler and pouring a smidge into the glass. Turning, he held it out to Bel with a serious face, the corners of his mouth upturned into what Addi imagined he believed was a smile. She'd have to tell him to work on that.

Bel looked at the miniscule amount of eggnog in the glass and raised a brow.

Poor Jimmy was slow at catching on, and Addi had to smother a giggle. "More? I figured you wouldn't want too much. By the looks of you, you're not one for eating."

As soon as the words were out, Addi's jaw dropped open. She blinked at how quickly the man went from class to ass— even if he had no idea what he'd just done. Of all the things to say to Bel, that was one of the worst.

Bel narrowed her eyes, then with a smile to Addi said, "Nice to see you, Addison." Shoving the glass back into Jimmy's hands, she grabbed the pitcher and with a defiant stare chugged straight from it. She came up for air, wiped her mouth with the back of her hand, and then stomped away with the pitcher in hand.

Jimmy whistled, Raquel grinned like the Cheshire cat, and Dee laughed. Addi joined her mother. Only in her family. She slapped Jimmy on the shoulder. She felt like she'd been doing that since they'd met. "What the hell?"

He shrugged. "I didn't know, I—"

Roque walked up and slid next to Addi, pulling her close to his side. "Your partner in crime here needs some classes in manners," Addi said.

Roque looked to Jimmy, his brows raised in question.

"Don't ask."

Raquel clapped her hands together. "I think it's delightful."

Addi grinned at the excitement practically pouring from the Mother of Malibu. "What is?"

Raquel slid her arm through Dee's and turned, but added, "Love is in the air, Addison. Love is in the air." She blew a kiss to her and Roque. "Just as I knew it would be with the two of you."

Roque shook his head. "Aunt Raquel."

She paused to put up a well-jeweled hand. "There's a reason Addi's bungalow was the only available rental."

Addi's jaw dropped.

They watched as the two women made their way across the room.

Jimmy stood from the stool next to Addi. "What the hell is that woman talking about?"

Roque and Addi exchanged glances, and then Roque said, "I don't know exactly, but I think you're about to find out."

Jimmy's eyes widened in a look of panic Addi never thought she'd see. He downed his eggnog, and then grabbed for the pitcher to pour another glass. His hand met an empty space. "God damned woman."

Addi laughed, and Roque pulled her to him, wrapping his arms about her waist. "Do you think she was serious about the bungalow?"

Addi looked up at him. She kissed his nose, his chin, and then his mouth. If Raquel did have something to do with it, she'd have to be sure to thank her. Every dream Addi never knew she yearned for was right in front of her. "I don't know, the woman's full of Malibu's secrets."

Roque kissed her back. "I have a secret, too."

She raised a brow. "Oh you do, do you?"

"Yep." He looked so pleased with himself. "You make me happy, did you know that?"

She turned her head from side to side. "I think you've kept that secret too well. You'll need to show me."

He tightened his hands about her. "Do I make you happy?"

"I'm an open book, Gallagher, for as long as you're interested in reading me." She grinned.

He pulled her in to his chest. "Oh, I'm interested. I know for a fact you're a master at happy endings. And like you said, I really do need to show you."

She giggled and grabbed his hand. With the family entertaining one another and dinner at least an hour away, no one would miss them.

He followed her up the stairs. "Where are we going?"

Addi winked. "I'm going to show you just how good at happy endings I really am."

His eyes widened, and she turned back to the stairs, taking them two at a time.

Roque was right at her heels, and she pulled him into Sam's guest room and closed the door.

She found she really liked his kind of secret, because this kind, they'd get to keep happily ever after.

Acknowledgments

To my children and husband, otherwise known as my hearts and soul, thank you for believing in me and always knowing I could do this even when I didn't. Brian, I'll never get used to how supportive you are. I'm in awe.

To my big brothers, Tommy, Todd, and Billy—as goofy as I am, you've always held me up. Tommy, you've always known I could do it. Todd, you put your support into action. Thank you for reading my first book. Billy, you're the best cheerleader a girl could have. To Paula, my sister of the heart, I'm forever in awe of you. And to my mom, who's continued to mother me from the other side, I hope I have a fraction of your grace. Thank you.

To Kathy and Jim Krans, you've always loved and supported our little family. You have a special place in our hearts.

Thank you to my editor, Kate Brauning, who somehow knows exactly how to lift me up and push me forward without letting me fall. To Naomi Hughes, for your extra set of eyes. To Entangled Publishing, thank you for giving this writer a home. You've all made my dreams come true.

Thank you to the marketing team—you hold a special place in my heart—to the production team and everyone in between. You're my very own superheroes.

Thank you to my generous friend, Marina Adair. Your kindness and support have been exceptional, as are your words gracing my cover.

Thank you to Jessica Snyder and Kameron Claire for your efforts in helping me make this book better. Your critiques and edits helped to push me to be a better writer. And thank you Taylor Reynolds for your continued and tireless support through all my crazy rantings. You are a saint.

Thank you to my street team, MK & CO for your friendship and for believing in me. I love everyone in this family, from the very first to the still to come.

One more exuberant thank-you to the readers of this book. Experiencing life with you in this way is magical. I hope that at least one scene, one line, or simply one word resonates with each of you. And to my sisters and brothers in the fight against breast and all types of cancer. I know both sides, having lost my mom to breast cancer at a young age, and surviving myself. I got hit during the last edits of my first book, worked through a mastectomy during the edits of my second book, and finally received my cancer-free call and reconstruction during the edits of this book. My writing is one of the things that carries me through. I have many more books to write.

To my Facebook family, you held me up with such overwhelming love I'll never be able to express what it meant to me to have so many people sending out healing light, praying, pushing positive thoughts, and checking in to make sure I'd win in both my health and publishing. Many of you I've never met in person. I'm still spinning from it all.

Thank you.

Hugs and loves and peanut butter, MK

About the Author

MK Meredith writes contemporary romance promising an emotional ride on heated sheets. She believes the best route to success is to never stop learning. Her lifelong love affair with peanut butter continues, and only two things come close in the battle for her affections: gorgeous heels and maybe Gerard Butler…or was it David Gandy? Who is she kidding? Her true loves are her husband and two children who have survived her SEAs (spontaneous explosions of affection) and lived to tell the tale. The Merediths live in the DC area with their two large fur babies…until the next adventure calls.

Discover the **Malibu Sights** *series...*

MALIBU BETRAYALS

Hollywood screenwriter Samantha Dekker spent the last year picking up the pieces from her husband's suicide and her subsequently ruined career. Now she has the rarest of Hollywood opportunities: a second chance. But it means working with the one man she swore never to see again. Hunktastic A-lister Gage Cutler knows that Sam blames him for her husband's death. All he wants is a second chance of his own—to prove he's not the player she remembers. And Malibu is the perfect backdrop to make a girl swoon...

Also by MK Meredith

SEDUCING SEVEN

Made in the USA
Middletown, DE
10 September 2016